Never Back Down

Ever Chace Chronicles
Book 5

SUSAN HARRIS

NEVER BACK DOWN
Copyright ©2018 Susan Harris
All rights reserved.
Crimson Tree Publishing

SUMMARY: Never. Back. Down. Since the day that she was abandoned on the shores of Valhalla, and fought her way to be the fiercest Valkyrie, Erika has lived by those three words. There has never been a challenge Erika has backed down from; apart from Loki. But when Erika embeds herself in a supernatural fight club in the hopes that she can weed out Odin's location, Erika will be put to the test.

ISBN: 978-1-63422-427-7 (paperback)
ISBN: 978-1-63422-325-6 (e-book)
COVER DESIGN BY: Marya Heidel
TYPOGRAPHY BY: Courtney Knight
EDITING BY: Kelly Risser

This book is dedicated to Gizmo,

The best dog I could have ever wished for.

You are loved and you are missed

xxx

S hadowed by the trees, he watched her move around the apartment. She was completely unaware that he watched her as if she were prey, studying her movements. She followed the same routine, checked her windows and doors, and then curled up on what must be a chair by the window, the glint of her knife reflecting against the moon's light. She hardly slept, tossing and turning in a fitful sleep for the last three nights, sometimes waking to screams.

He longed to scale the shop front and slip in the window she kept open, simply to hear anything that might have tracked her down. He wanted nothing more than to wrap his arms around his mate and affirm that she was safe, she was loved, and she was needed at home.

The rain began to hail down, thunder rumbling even as lightning streaked through the obsidian sky. It drew her to the window, her golden hair tumbling down to her shoulders, a stern look on her face. Her eyes moved in the general direction of where he watched her, yet they simply passed over him, even as the wolf held his breath, sure that his mate would sense him lurking in the shadows.

Stepping out of the light, Ever backed away from the window, and Derek shook the wet from his hair. Erika had been right when she told him to follow the lightning, for the town of Wigan in Greater-Manchester had seen the worst storms in their history, with freak lightning storms and the continuous rumble of thunder, roaring in the skies. Some thought the end of the world was coming, and perhaps it was.

The phone in his pocket vibrated. Derek slipped it out and ignored all the missed calls from Ricky, from Sarge, and just about every goddamn person in Cork, apart from the one person who had never called him to chastise, Melanie.

Derek heard the sadness in her voice as the littlest vampire spoke. "Derek, I know you have things going on, but Ricky needs your help.

If you get this message... I don't know, Derek. I think we're losing him."

He didn't need Melanie's truth-seeking abilities to hear the words ring through in his ear. Werewolves could smell a lie, hear it in a racing pulse, and notice the small tells that gave a person away. Just what the hell had happened in the days since he was gone?

Clearing everything from his phone, he punched in a number, aware that it was time to end Ever's foolish quest to run away and save them all by throwing herself upon Odin's sword. The phone rang twice before it was answered, but Derek had to wait until the thunder stopped rumbling to speak.

"I found her. She's safe. I'll be home soon."

"Derek? Where the hell are you?"

The rumble in his boss's voice resembled the thunder as he questioned Derek, but Derek simply pressed disconnect. Wolf in his eyes, he allowed his lips to curl up into a snarl, but bit down on the urge to howl at the moon who was his master.

Ever was depleted and could not ride the lightning for at least another week. Now was his chance to sneak up on her. He'd rip away that stupid bracelet and talk some sense into her.

It did not matter to man or wolf whether she was human or Valkyrie; Ever was his and his alone. Odin could not have her.

In the myths and legends, it was the great wolf Fenrir that brought about Odin's end. Derek might not be the monstrous wolf; however, he was a monster, and he would enjoy ripping Odin apart for what he had done to the woman who held his heart.

Tomorrow, he would pounce.

CHAPTER
ONE

Erika

Erika had never seen such a wondrous sight, the sandy beaches of Valhalla even more breath-taking than the pictures she had seen, the crystal-clear water lapping against the shore as sand as soft as cotton teased her bare toes. Her hand held tight in her mother's hand, Erika peered up at the woman who had given Erika her eyes. The dark tresses flowed down her mother's back, twisting at the nape by a golden rope. Dressed in a long, flowing gown knotted over one shoulder, leaving the other bare, her skin was almost golden, the same colour as the sand that kissed Erika's feet.

Her mother was one of the most beautiful women in the Vanir, though she was not magical at all. When she smiled, it was as if the heavens opened up and sighed down upon them, for there had never been a more beautiful smile in all of Asgard.

A warrior woman stepped out of the trees, dressed in battle armour, the glint of the silver gauntlets catching Erika's attention. The warrior wore a simple leather skirt and a cropped-sleeve vest top with the emblem of the Valkyrie etched just above the heart. The muscles on her stomach were pronounced, proof that Freya was more than an armpiece of the gods, but a force to be reckoned with. Freya looked at Erika as if she were an insect, and Erika felt fear course through her entire body. This woman's features held none of her mother's softness; Freya was battle hardened and stern. Erika felt a *whimper creep up her throat, but her mother squeezed her hand tighter in reassurance.*

Though she was stern, there was no denying the woman was beautiful, but beautiful in a different way to Mother. Freya, the goddess of war and death stood before Erika, assessing her. She inched closer to her mother, ignoring the intensity of Freya's eyes on her.

"You've brought her later than expected."

"I wanted a few years with her before I had to say goodbye. Her father approved it."

Erika's ears listened intently, because her mother rarely ever spoke of her father, and even five-year-old Erika had never heard his name uttered before. Freya walked around Erika, and Erika wanted to cry and beg her mother to take her home.

"She is small for a Valkyrie."

"What she lacks in height, sister Freya, Erika makes up for in heart. Her father's blood runs in her veins more so than mine ever will. She will be safe here from those that would hurt her. You will train her to be a warrior and her destiny will be more than you or I could have predicted."

"How has she been trained thus far? I do not have time to delay the training of the others while she catches up."

Erika did not like the tone in the warrior's voice as she spoke to her mother, and the coiled temper that simmered below the surface of the child now bubbling over. Erika slipped her hand out of her mother's grasp, flashed to Freya's side, and within a matter of seconds, had the dagger Freya had sheathed at her ankle pressing against the goddess's femoral artery with a snarl.

She may be small, but people disregarded those whose appearance tended to deceive.

Freya smiled down at her, causing Erika to dig in the blade a little harder. Freya growled at her, yet Erika simply looked up and held the gaze of the woman who would train her to kill and become a soul sucker. To make her Valkyrie.

"She will do."

Relief sagged in her mother's shoulders as Erika dropped the dagger in the sand and flashed back to her mother. "Momma, I want to go home."

Her mother dropped to her knees in the sand, her arms encircling Erika into a fierce hug. "You must be strong, my little warrior. For the destiny that you have awaiting you is bigger than my selfish need to have you with me. I will love you until the stars fail to sparkle, and the sun fails to rise. Remember, my sweet baby girl, that it is not the size of the girl in the fight, but the size of fight in the girl."

Her mother pressed her lips to Erika's forehead, stepping back with a final nod to Freya, before she vanished into the night, tears evident in her eyes.

"Momma! Momma! Come back! I'm sorry. I promise to be better, I promise to be good. Momma, please come back."

Erika's screams broke through the silence of the night as she sobbed her heart out and screamed until Freya fisted fingers into her hair and dragged her across the sand. Erika kicked and lashed out, so Freya dropped her to stand on her own two feet. The young girl launched herself at Freya, feral in her attack. Freya blocked the strikes easily, for when her temper awoke, Erika was nothing more than a ball of fury.

Exhausted, Erika sank down into the sand and allowed the tears to silently fall from her eyes onto the sand. Her momma had left her. She was alone, would always be alone.

"Come, little warrior, and meet your sisters."

It was then Erika looked up and saw the curious eyes peeking out from behind the foliage at her. Erika didn't want sisters; she only wanted her mother to realize she had made a mistake and come take her away from these people.

When Erika held Freya's gaze once more, jutting out her chin in defiance, shock coursed through her when Freya laughed, a harsh sound like it had not happened in a long time. "We may just make a warrior out of you yet, little girl. There is more of your father in you then I expected. Now stop your wallowing and get up. Your training begins now."

Freya beckoned a tall, muscular child with hair as white as ice out of the bushes, tossed a blade at Erika, and said. "The first to draw blood is the winner. No rules, only not to the death. Go."

The blond charged at Erika, who froze for a moment before grabbing the dagger and dodging the blow that had been intended for her. Erika kicked up sand, sliding across it so that she dodged the blow as the girl slammed down what looked like a mallet into the ground. Erika used her speed to dodge the blows, reeling when the side of the mallet caught her in the stomach.

Dropping her dagger, Erika stumbled back as fire laced her belly. The next knock came to the side of her head, drawing blood that dripped down, pooling in the sand. The towering girl stood over Erika as tears threatened to overflow.

The icy haired child grinned down at Erika and said. "Welcome to the Valkyries, Systir."

Erika looked up and into the horrified blue eyes of a young girl with hair the colour of sunshine, a hand clasped over her mouth. Her opponent smashed her foot down on Erika's face, and she tumbled into darkness.

Erika slowly opened her eyes, grinding her teeth when the unwanted memory interrupted her meditation. Eminem's "Lose Yourself" pounded from the speakers. Centuries old, Erika had long forgotten her mother's name and still had no clue as to who had been the sperm donor who was her father. But the memory triggered a recollection that Freya had known all along who Erika's father was. Maybe, just maybe, when this was all over and she was not dead, Erika would have a word with the woman who had raised her and created a bloodthirsty warrior who enjoyed revelling in blood and war.

A knock sounded at the door as Erika jumped to her feet, striding over to open it. A young girl dressed in barely there shorts and top gave her a small smile.

"You're up next, Miss Sands."

"Cheers, Vicki."

The girl raced away. They were afraid of her. And so they should be.

Erika grabbed the tape on the battered dresser and proceeded to wrap her bare feet, then moved onto her hands, yanking it off with her teeth to tie it up. Bouncing back and forth on her feet, Erika rolled her neck, aware that she was not alone in the room. He'd been there for every single fight, yet the trickster god who was a major pain in her ass hadn't so much as shown himself.

But she knew he was watching, waiting.

Yanking off her t-shirt, Erika stood in just her sports bra and shorts. The air turned hot, almost suffocating, as an invisible hand caressed her arm, then moved over the plains of her stomach. Erika remained perfectly still as another knock sounded at her door.

"Remove your hand or I will rip off your arm and beat you to death with it."

Erika felt his breath on her neck, and the air was breathable again. Turning off the stereo, Erika could hear the cheers and jeers from the crowds in the arena below, and her pulse quickened in anticipation. Striding to the door, she gathered her hair off her face and dragged it into an untidy ponytail. A lot of her sisters kept their hair shortened. It lessened the chance an enemy could use it against them in a fight. The last person who had come near teenage Erika with a cutting shears was lucky that she had not cut off the offender's hand for trying to take her hair from her.

Pulling the door open, Erika grinned as she strode out of the room, the sound of the crowds making her itch to draw blood. It was as if all the troubles of the last few months vanished when she was in the octagon. Erika took her frustrations out on her opponents. It mattered not if they were seven feet tall, had horns that would rip through flesh, or claws that would render her blind; she would defeat them all.

Freya had sent her on this mission, to find a Berserker, one who might lead them to Odin's sleeping place. While it had to be Ever that took his life to break the curse, Erika could have fun cutting him up, just for fun.

Erika perched on the balcony overlooking what was affectionately called the arena, which was essentially a mixed martial arts octagon-shaped cage that pitted supernaturals against each other. The abandoned mansion used to be a house, and the entire downstairs had been gutted and opened up until the arena was born. The balcony where she stood held the richest of the rich within the supernatural community, and champagne flowed even as bets were taken. There were creatures in three-piece suits, designer dresses, and far too much gold.

Down below in the dungeon, the riff raff and degenerates heckled the fighters, baying for blood and death. Erika closed her eyes and breathed in the scent of it, only opening her eyes when the Master of Ceremonies began to speak, the din around the arena going deathly quiet.

"Ladies and Gentlemen, you are welcome to tonight's main event, and I guarantee it will be a treat for every single one of you."

The crowd gave an enthusiastic roar, silencing once more when the flamboyant man held up a hand. He had hair of royal blue and pointed ears, which told Erika that he probably had some Fae in him. His suit was as blue as his hair. No matter how elegant his appearance, Erika knew exactly what he was, a chaos demon, and one who relished in the chaos others created.

As if he knew she watched him, the Master of Ceremonies, Felix Grande–which totally seemed like a made-up name to Erika–glanced in her direction and gave her a grin that made the hair on the back of her neck stand to attention. Felix gave a nod of his head, and then continued on with his little speech.

"Tonight, we have two of the fiercest warriors on earth pitted against each other. There are no rules, and death is all the reward the losing competitor will receive. So, shall we begin?"

The roar almost deafened her as the music began and Limp Bizkit's "Break Stuff" played over the speakers. Erika grinned, approving of her opponent's choice of music. The fury came out from the tunnel, bouncing on her feet as she punched out and back, causing Erika to roll her eyes. Furies were vicious sons of bitches, but they lacked the discipline Erika had.

Plus, what kind of little bitch walked out with two burly security guards to the cage? Erika went to the Octagon with just herself, and she was as battle hardened as Freya had been all those nights ago in the sand.

As the fury, her head shaved and talons extended, swept into the cage, the door was locked and Erika readied herself, inhaling and exhaling as her own music, "Bodies" by Drowning Pool pounded from the speakers. No matter what she thought about humans on Midgard, at least they got music right... well most of the time... Justin Bieber was still breathing.

"And now the woman you have all been waiting for. The stuff of myths and legends. Carrier of souls and decider of fates. She will distract you with her beauty as she rips your soul from your body, and you will only smile. Ladies, gentlemen, I give you to the only female to suffer no losses in her last fifteen fights, ten knock outs, three deaths, and two submissions. I present to you, the Valkyrie."

A hush descended over the spectators as Erika eased herself up onto the balcony, all eyes on the cage below as she dropped off the two-storey height with ease and landed deftly on the top of the cage, her feet balancing on the ledge as the fury hissed in her direction. Face a mask, Erika back flipped, landing with grace in the centre of the cage.

She refused to flinch as she heard them question if she really was a Valkyrie. The commentary continued. She was too small, too curvy to be any kind of warrior. Those were the fools who had not seen her fight before, who had come tonight for the first time to behold the bloodthirsty warrior everyone was whispering about.

"Remember my sweet baby girl, that it is not the size of the girl in the fight, but the size of fight in the girl."

Her mother's words rang in her head as the music died, the bell chimed, and the fury came at her, talons striking to remove one of her eyes. Erika deftly side stepped the fury, kicking backward to send her opponent straight into the metal of the cage. The fury shrieked in frustration and came back at Erika, who clenched her fists and waited as the fury telegraphed her punch. Erika reached out, grabbing the fist and stopping the fury in a skidding halt.

The fury tried to yank back her fist, to flex her talons, but Erika had her in an iron grip. The crowd gasped in shock, and hopefully awe, at Erika's display of strength. With a quick yank, Erika snapped the fury's wrist, and the creature yowled in pain. Erika began to bounce from one foot to another as the fury's wrist healed enough for her to try and punch Erika.

Moving her head side to side, Erika flexed her foot, kicking out and landing her heel in the fury's stomach, even as Erika dropped to her knee the next second and swept out her leg. The fury crashed to the ground as Erika wrapped her thighs around the creature's head, grabbed her arm, the one that was already broken, and yanked it back.

The fury tried to overpower her, but Erika had trained until she, the smallest of the Valkyrie, could make Danae, the biggest of her sisters, tap out of a fight. The fury had balls, Erika could give her that, but having balls only meant you got dead faster.

Erika was hoisted up on the fury's shoulders as she stood, Erika's grasp on the fury's head and arm not loosening an inch. Erika caught sight of Freya, whose power was a beacon to those who knew exactly who and what she was. She gave Erika a bow of her head, and Erika snarled as the fury's free fist punched her in the face, blood sprouting from her nose and lip as the skin split apart.

Cursing Freya for the distraction, Erika leaned her body downward and grinned, knowing she must look like something from

Carrie with blood all over her face. Spinning her body in an inhuman way, her thighs tightened around the fury's neck as she twisted. The sickening sound of bone snapped as Erika broke the creature's neck. Their bodies hit the floor, and Erika rolled away from the dead body and snarled.

There was a heartbeat of silence before the crowd erupted into rapturous applause. Erika, still crouched, wiped the blood from her mouth and spat on the canvas floor. The cage door opened, and Felix sauntered in as Erika rose to her feet.

Raising her hand in the air, Felix grinned at her, even as he whispered. "You could have drawn that out a little longer, darling."

Erika snarled. "I did. Bitch was all claws and no bite. I didn't even break a sweat."

Felix gave an exaggerated laugh as the gathered folks continued to clap. Erika's eyes darted over to where Freya had been standing, but the woman was gone. Erika pulled her hand out of Felix's grip, spat on the floor again, and grinned, showing him teeth.

"Next time, give me more of a challenge."

"Oh, it will be my life's mission to find someone who can take you down, Valkyrie."

Erika flashed from the arena and let out a scream of frustration in the confines of her room. She had far too much adrenaline in her veins. She needed to either fight or fuck. Her body clenched as she felt Loki's eyes on her, but despite the lust circling in the air, the bane of her existence remained invisible.

The door to her room opened and a scantily clad nymph came in, stripping off her bra as she closed the door with a snick.

Erika rubbed the blood from her nose as the ruby haired nymph gave her a hungry smile.

"The boss said you might need to work off some of the aggression."

The nymph was taller than Erika was, but that didn't stop her from slamming the nymph against the wall, dragging down her head and claiming her mouth. The nymph opened her lips eagerly, and Erika assaulted her mouth with as much passion and fury as she had expelled during her fight.

Erika felt his eyes watching as she broke the kiss and shoved the nymph to her knees, the woodland creature obeying with an eager lick of her lips. Glancing over her shoulder, Erika grinned into the air, her mouth speaking of its own accord. "You could join us."

An invisible hand wrapped around her throat, and Erika moaned at the possessiveness of the touch, even though it was just a brush of air against her neck. Erika let herself be stripped of her shorts, and then the nymph did something incredible with her tongue that had Erika jerking her hips forward.

And not for one second, as Erika rode the waves of her climax, did the pressure ease off her neck. It only made her crave more.

CHAPTER TWO

Ricky

Leaning in the doorway of his front room, Ricky looked at the boy who was his son and tried to work out how he could get the kid to talk to him. When Fionn had left Zach with Ricky, the boy had clammed up and barely looked at him. Not that he blamed the poor kid; he'd just lost his mother and was saddled with an old man who didn't know a thing about him. Now Zach sat on the floor, reading a battered comic book, as Ricky took him in.

Hair of midnight black, Zach was the spitting image of Ricky, apart from the thick-rimmed glasses that kept sliding down his nose, emphasising the deep emerald of his eyes. When Fionn had brushed past him, heading straight into the house that Ricky had wrecked minutes ago, he barely looked at the mess. Fionn told Zach to go into the living room and watch TV. The boy glared at his uncle, causing Ricky to grin, because it was Ricky's own face that looked at his uncle with contempt.

Fionn had ushered Ricky into the kitchen and proceeded to tell him why Sadie had lied to him for five years.

"That kid might be the spit of me, Fionn, but I'm gonna need a little bit more to understand why Sadie simply forgot to tell me I had a kid out there."

Fionn folded his arms across his chest, his mouth pressed into a grimace before he sighed and said. "Sadie made a mistake in not telling you, there's no doubt about that. But I made a grave error in keeping her secret. We thought Zach might have been ... not yours. Sadie came clean just before her fight and told me what went down before the wedding. I'm sorry. You should have said something."

Ricky scrubbed a hand down his face. "Not my story to tell, mate. It was between me and Sadie. But, that kid did not deserve to spend the last five years thinking he had no dad. I understand he's a shifter, but I deserved to know he existed."

"I agree, but she told him all about you, Ricky, and he had a picture of you in his bedroom. Sadie did not want to tell you about him until we were sure he was yours, and that he was not just a shifter."

When Ricky said nothing, Fionn continued on. "Look, I know I'm dropping this in your lap, but Zach is not safe within the pride. Sadie lost a dominance fight and died because the females did not want an abomination in the pride. I was out voted, and he needs his dad now."

Ricky wanted to smack the shit out of those bigoted bastards, but asked Fionn, "Why call him an abomination? I can tell he's a cat by the way he walks."

"Come with me."

Fionn strode through his house like he goddam owned it and went into the living room. Zach glanced at them as they came in, scowling when Ricky smiled at him. A marching band had started a merry tune in his head as Fionn sat down on his couch and said to Zach, "Hey Zach Attack, wanna show your dad your cat?"

"No."

Ricky had to admit, he liked the kid already.

"C'mon Zach, don't be a brat. Show your dad your cat, please."

A shimmer of light, and then a small black jaguar growled at him, his clothes ripped down around his paws. Ricky came forward and reached out a hand to rub the cat, but Zach snapped his teeth and backed away. Another shimmer of light and a very naked five-year-old sat amongst the ruins of clothing, waiting for further instructions with a very bored expression on his face. Zach picked up his glasses and put them back on his nose.

"Thanks, Zach. Now, can you show your dad some magic?"

Ricky's heart sank into his stomach. Please no, not his kid.

Zach sighed and held out his hand, a flicker of flames sparking before it blazed to life. Ricky could feel flames, his son's magic called out to his, and he stumbled back. Zach quenched the flames, picked up his comic, still starkers, and ignored them both. Ricky wished with all that he had in him that Zach had not been magically gifted, but the boy seemed to have more of a grasp on his magic then his dad did.

Fionn ruffled the boy's hair, got to his feet, and stood in front of Ricky. "That boy is very special, Ricky, and I am entrusting Sadie's most precious gift to you. She might have lied, dammit we know she cheated, but that boy does not deserve to be treated differently because of what his mother did or did not do."

Ricky balked, slightly offended. "Fionn, I'm not petty enough to take it out on the boy, I promise. I'm pissed she didn't tell me, no, scratch that, I'm fucking snapping. But Zach is mine."

Fionn reached out and clasped him on the shoulder. "Good. Before she died, Sadie asked me to tell you she was sorry and to bring Zach to you. I know right now, her words might seem empty and pointless, but I ask one thing from you."

Ricky waited, and Fionn continued. "Promise me you won't let him forget her. Despite what she did, Sadie told him all about you. Dressed him up as a police officer for Halloween so he could be just like his dad. He likes music, comics, and documentaries. He is the sweetest kid you will ever meet. You and I, we didn't have exactly great role models growing up, but you just be the best kinda dad you can for him, for Sadie."

"Christ, Fionn, way to make a dude feel like a complete and utter bollo–" Ricky paused, realizing that he would need to watch his mouth from now on. "You know me, what makes you think that I could be any sort of father to that kid."

"Because you're the same man who let everyone think he ran out on his fiancé days before their wedding because he got cold feet and took all the shite we dealt without saying a bad word against Sadie. That's the man who can raise a boy right."

Fionn had stepped away then, saying goodbye to his nephew with the promise to visit as soon as possible. Zach's lips had quivered slightly as Fionn walked out the front door, leaving Ricky staring at the miniature version of himself.

Ricky had tried to get the young fella to speak to him, but Zach had chewed on his lip, only stopping to ask in a small voice where he was going to sleep. Ricky showed him to the guest bedroom, stating Zach could tell him how he wanted it decorated.

But his son had shifted into his cat form and curled up on the bed. Ricky told him he would be across the room and pulled the door, leaving it slightly ajar. When Ricky had woken the next morning, Zach refused to change back to human, and Ricky had spent most of the day banging his head against the wall trying to make conversation with a jaguar cub.

Even cleaning up the mess Ricky had made on his path of destruction hadn't even drawn a reaction from the little boy. Zach didn't even bat an eye as Ricky chucked broken pieces of furniture out into the back garden.

Now, as his son watched some documentary about a lost city or some shit, Ricky braced himself for more of the silent treatment. Zach knew the moment Ricky had walked into the room, ignored him when he set a glass of milk down on the ground, putting two cookies on the arm of the chair.

"Your mom used to love a glass of milk when she'd been shifting a lot. Not sure why, but I..." Ricky sighed, not really knowing what to say next. "The cookies are just because who can have milk without cookies."

When Zach continued to ignore him, Ricky sank down into an armchair and grabbed his guitar. He strummed the strings softly, so as not to interrupt Zach, and closed his eyes, trying to push down the voice inside his head begging him to take some more pills, to stop the magic that was building inside of him. Ricky knew he needed to get help, because there was no way he was gonna be off his face in front of a five-year-old.

Ricky shoved down his magic, using music as a crutch to ease his troubled mind. Maybe he should call Caitlyn, ask her what in the hell he could do with his kid. Ricky really wished he could call his mam right now, ask her advice. But his Da was dead, Sadie was dead, and there was nothing at all he could do to make it better for himself, never mind Zach.

He played the first few chords of Linkin Park's "Numb" with his eyes closed, the melody soothing his soul, popping his eyes open when he heard a distinct tap, tap. Low and behold, Zach was drumming along to the beat with him. Ricky continued to play a little bit longer, and then stopped.

"You know, I have a drum kit lying around here somewhere if you want me to try and dig it out. But, if you like the drums, my buddy Donnie is wicked on the sticks. We could invite him over, but a little later, he is a vampire."

Zach's head spun in his direction. "You know vampires?"

Ricky glanced down at the strings of his guitar so that Zach would not see the grin the size of Texas kick up his lips. "Sure do. I know a few, work with them. I also work with a werewolf who is my best friend and a bear who is my boss."

"Vampires are so cool."

Who'd have thunk that vampires would get his son talking to him?

"You can come with me later while I check up on things at work, and I'll introduce you."

The boy's eyes widened, a twinkle brightening the emerald in them. As his face lit with a brilliant smile, Ricky felt as if he had been punched in the gut. He wondered if his Da had ever felt this way, like his heart would explode simply because he had made his boy smile.

"Really?" the little boy asked.

"Sure, no hassle. I need to try and take a few days so I can sort you out with school and stuff. But, these vampires are pretty cool. They will love you."

Zach scrunched up his nose, and his glasses slipped down. Ricky reached out and pushed them back up the bridge of his nose. "We'll go later. First, you gotta have a shower and change your clothes." When Zach frowned, Ricky tilted his head to the side and tapped his nose. "Vampires sense of smell is just like a cat's, if not better. You don't want to meet your very first vampire and smell, do ya, kid?"

The boy shook his head, heading for the door. "You need some help?"

Zach shook his head. "I'm a big boy. I can shower by myself."

Ricky went back to strumming the strings as he replied. "No hassle, Zach. You need anything, you just shout, okay? I won't play too loud."

Zach hesitated for a moment in the doorway and looked back at him. "Hybrid Theory was their best album, but I liked what you were playing. Not sure about the new material, so don't play anything from that."

Zach slipped out of the room and into his bedroom, with Ricky's jaw on the floor. If there had been any doubt before that Zach was his son, the niggling sensation had been smitten in that one sentence. Ricky began to play "In the End" from start to finish without singing. He played it until Zach came back out with his hair washed, dressed in black jeans, an old Metallica shirt Ricky was sure used to be Sadie's, and a little leather jacket.

His hair was a tangle of mess, and Zach had a brush in his hand. Ricky set down the guitar, and Zach climbed into his lap, giving the brush to Ricky. Ricky found that his hands were shaking, but this time it was in nervousness. Brushing the strands of his son's hair was the most surreal feeling in the world, and his chest felt heavy as Zach handed him a black band. Once he had finished brushing the knots out of Zach's hair, he stumbled as he tied it up into a ponytail.

Satisfied, Zach hopped back down off his lap and went back to his documentary. Ricky wasn't sure how long he simply sat there and watched Zach, but it must have been awhile, the sound of his phone ringing taking his attention away from his son. Glancing at the screen, Ricky cringed when he saw Sarge's name on the screen, his boss no doubt having heard about his Da's death, or maybe Sadie's.

Slipping from the front room, Ricky pressed answer on his phone. "Sarge?"

"Ricky, how you holding up?"

"I'm grand, Sarge."

"Don't you go all Irish and tell me you're grand. He might not have been one of my favourite people, but Xavier was still your father."

Ricky rubbed his temple, sighing as he said in truth, "I haven't had a second to think about him to be honest, Sarge. Things have been a bit ...weird..."

Ricky explained to Sarge about Sadie, and about Zach, and how things had gone down. The bear listened intently as Ricky ranted on for a good few minutes. When Ricky stopped yammering, Sarge gave a low whistle and said, "You don't do things by halves, do you, son?"

"Not a chance."

"Well you bring your boy to the station and introduce us. You bring him in now, Ricky."

"Yes, sir."

The bear hung up with a grumble, and Ricky grinned.

"Hey Zach? You ready to go, dude?"

The little boy was next to him then. "Are we going to see the vampires?"

Ricky brushed his own hair from his face, then patted Zach on the head. "Ya, we're off to see the vampires."

Ricky made it to the car before realizing he did not have a goddam car seat for the kid. Glancing down at Zach, he put his finger to his lips. "Our little secret, just for today. Tomorrow, I'll get a booster seat, 'kay?"

The small boy nodded and slipped into the back seat. Ricky triple checked that the belt was tied, earning a small puzzled look from Zach. "Safety first, kid."

Backing out of his drive slower than a fucking snail, Ricky was suddenly aware of how reckless he had driven in the past. Now, with Zach inside this hunk of metal, Ricky could hear every beat of his heart on the drive to the station. Zach seemed oblivious to Ricky's panic mode, having pulled a hand-held console from his jacket pocket.

Arriving at the station, Ricky pulled his Focus into his usual car park space and turned off the engine. He peered in the mirror and sad eyes peered back at him.

"Ricky? Is my mom really dead?"

"Ya, kiddo. She is. I'm real sorry about that. I loved your mom once."

"Can the vampires not bring her back for me?"

Ricky heard the tears in Zach's voice, and Ricky took off his belt, turned around. "No Zach. The vampires can't bring back the dead; that's not how it works."

"Okay."

How the hell was he supposed to do this, be a dad?

Opening the back door, Zach slid out, waiting while Ricky closed it. He made to walk into the station, pausing when he realized the boy was not by his side. Zach chewed on his lip again, pushing his glasses back up his nose. When Ricky had asked Fionn why a shifter whose senses were meant to be 20/20 had glasses, Fionn had shrugged, telling Ricky that Sadie said the pride's doctor explained that Zach's eyesight in jaguar form was as good as any shifter. Yet, perhaps because of the genetic anomaly that made him half warlock, it might have affected his eyesight. The doctor had also told Sadie, before Fionn had a word with him, that this was why you needed to stick with your own species.

Ricky scooped up Zach, and he leaned his head against the curve of Ricky's shoulder. Striding straight through the station, Ricky ignored the stares and questions as he walked right into the P.I.T office. Sarge stood with his back to them, turning around when the door closed behind them. Small hands clutched Ricky's tee tightly, hair dropping in front of Zach's face.

Sarge came forward as Ricky shifted his weight slightly. "Apparently, he's a little shy."

"That's okay Ricky. Hello, Zach, welcome to the family."

Zach moved the hair out of his line of sight, and scrutinized the bear, whose face softened for the first time since Ricky knew him as he looked at Zach.

"You did good, son."

Ricky snorted. "I had nothing to do with it. Sadie was the one who raised him. I'm just the consolation prize."

Sarge gave him a stern look, but said nothing. Ricky moved away from the door, his arms burning, with Zach still clinging like a leech. Damn, if the kid wanted to be carried around like this, he'd need to hit up the gym, for real...like lift some weights and shit.

"When are the others due in?"

"The happy couple should be here just after sunset. Melanie and Kenzie stayed in the bunker last night to give them some privacy. Those two have been as thick as thieves today in the gym. I even think Kenzie smiled a little as Melanie landed on her ass."

The door behind him opened, and Ricky felt his stomach lurch. He'd been a dickhead to Melanie at Caitlyn and Donnie's shindig, and now he was going to flaunt Zach in her face. His mouth dried up. She came to a halt as he turned, spotting the boy in his arms.

Some catch he was, right?

Puzzled, Melanie stepped forward and wiped a towel over her face. He knew the moment she inhaled, she would pick up the familiar scent that marked Zach as his.

Ricky cleared his throat. "Hey, Lanie, let me introduce you to Zachary Spencer Moore. Zach, this pretty lady is one of the coolest people I know." He nudged the little boy with his elbow. "And she's a vampire. Zach, this is Melanie."

The little boy lifted his head and stared at Melanie. "Are you really a vampire?"

Melanie skipped over the blunt introduction and gave her best smile to Zach, and by gods, Ricky's heart kicked a little. "Sure am, lil' man." Holding out her hand, she waited until Zach reached out and shook it before she leaned in with a wink. "It's so good to meet you, Zach. Wanna come on a tour with me around the station?"

Faster than Zach had warmed to Ricky, his son all but leapt out of his arms and into Melanie's. Ricky let out a sigh of relief, not realizing how tired he was. Melanie balanced Zach on her hip like he weighed nothing.

"I'm just gonna take Zach here to meet Kenzie, if that's okay with you, Dad?"

It took Ricky a second to realize that Lanie was talking to him, and he flushed. "Yeah, sure. I'll be here if you want me. Okay, Zach?"

The little boy nodded. As Melanie began to walk out, Ricky whispered very softly so that Melanie would be the only one who heard him...he hoped. "Lanie, his mom just died. And I only found out about him 36 hours ago. Thank you."

Melanie gave him a small smile. "We'll talk later."

His son vanished with the girl he would never be good enough for. He heard Zack laugh, a sound so innocent and pure, and he fell in love all over again with his vampire girl.

Turning to Sarge, who watched him eagerly, Ricky rubbed the stubble on his chin.

"How in the fuck do I do this, Sarge...how do I do this?"

Ricky heard the crack in his voice and felt the tears stain his face as Sarge pulled him in for a hug. "You depend on family, son. We got you."

CHAPTER
THREE

Ever

Morning came around again too quickly. The broken sleep Ever had gotten did little to ease the tiredness in her bones or quell the overwhelming feeling that she was being followed. Stretching out her limbs, she groaned, pulling back the curtain and surveying the street outside. It was still rather early; the sun had barely risen. It would be another hour or so before the residence of the Wigan suburb rose, going about their weekly routine of work or school. The local school was a stone's throw from Ever's rented apartment.

The memories of her past lives continued to unfold, like a video reel that would not stop playing. It kept her awake at night, caused her to freeze up standing in a crowd, and she even caught herself speaking in a foreign language that she did not speak on the train to work yesterday. Her mind remembered being a Valkyrie, remembered that she had fought and died many a time. Yet, the Ever she was now felt separate from the memories that became part of her entire fibre of being.

Huffing out a breath, she pulled her knees to her chest, palming the dagger that she'd hidden under the cushion on the couch. Her other hand played with the wolf charm bracelet at her wrist, the magic contained in it giving her an electric shock. If she removed the bracelet right now, then Derek would be able to find her. As lonely as she was right now, Ever wanted to snap the bracelet in half and fall into the arms of the man she loved.

But it was more than that, wasn't it? Derek Doyle–the man, the werewolf–the one she had fallen for was bound by a curse, meaning that their souls were linked. Ever considered that Derek had no choice but to love her, yet she hoped he saw beyond the confines of the curse. She prayed he had fallen for her because of who she was now, not what she had been.

Not bothering to change from the sweats and hoodie she'd slept in the previous night, Ever grabbed her second hand MP3 player and summoned the wavering power, disappearing from the comfort and security of her apartment, and landed smack bang in the middle of The Three Sister's and the woods that surrounded it.

Popping the earbuds in place, Ever turned up the volume, but her supernatural hearing meant she could hear over the music. Stretching out her limbs, she checked to ensure she was alone on the path, surrounded by the shade of the trees, a light mist and fog chilling the early morning air. Without Erika to run drills with her, Ever had taken it upon herself to go for early morning runs to maintain the fitness she had begun to build up before she had opened her mouth and become Other.

Ever set off at a steady pace, inhaling the scent of the trees and earth. There was another reason she decided to run here, having stumbled by the pond and forest while out wandering the streets of Wigan. The smell reminded her of Derek's scent, and it almost felt as if he were here, and she was surrounded by him. She knew that he would have loved this place; it was so calm and serene.

As she picked up the pace, Nothing but Thieves played in her ears and another memory hit her.

The roar of the monster made Ever want to slap her hands over her ears to protect them from the enraged beast that stalked her. Freya yelled at her to get up, to fight. Ever did not want to fight, for she was only little and the monster terrified her. Her mother's prized Svinfylking—a boar-like creature that was actually made up of two boars bowed its head and bouldered toward her, its head lowered in a ramming manner.

Ever's heart pounded in her chest as the beast, a master of disguise, morphed into a bigger and badder beasty, horns protruding from its temples, teeth bigger than glaciers, and claws that would rip a puny girl like her to shreds.

"If you do not fight like a Queen should, then you will never wear the crown!"

Freya's fury dripped from every single word, a snarl of disappointment curling her beautiful features, marring the ethereal face that had seduced a world, even seduced Ever's father, Odin.

All of her Valkyrie sisters were watching, studying the child that would be forced to lead them, all except the newest addition, Erika, who Ever knew had been at the receiving end of a tough-love lesson from Danae, her eldest systir.

The boar charged again as Ever stumbled back, almost tripping over the sword that lay in the sand. Ever kicked it up, felt the power in the blade as she grasped the hilt, and knew that this blade, and this blade alone, was meant to be wielded by her. Above her hand, wings of solid metal etched out from the blade, and blue gems the colour of her eyes adorned the hilt along with Norse warrior markings. The blade's power surged through her, and Ever let loose a battle cry that sang through the trees and echoed back at her.

Charging through the sand, Ever met the beast head on, her hand striking out to slash it above the knee. She slid in the sand before getting to her feet and running the beast through from behind with the sword. The blade sang out, vibrating in her grasp as the beast's blood drenched it. The monster roared, this time in agony, before dropping to his knees, the blood spilled not enough to sate Ever or her new blade.

Rage, white hot and directed at her mother's prized fighter, coiled in Ever. She slashed and sliced through flesh and bone until blood sprayed her face and body, her anger leaving her in a screech. The beast moved no more, and Ever knew she had killed him. It was her first kill, and her stomach revolted as she stared down at the slain creature.

She expected Freya to be angry, but she appraised her with a look that might have been considered pride, if you did not know Freya in the slightest. Dropping the now sated blade onto the sand, Ever found herself staring at her bloodstained hands as she backed away from the body.

"I'm sorry," she whispered, as the realisation of what she had done caused silent tears to run down her cheeks. "I'm so sorry."

Ever did not know who she was apologizing to—the dead beast or Freya. But Ever was now a murderer, exactly what Freya had intended her to be. It was everything Ever had fought against from the moment she had been informed of her destiny.

With her entire body quivering in shock, she spun on her heels and bolted from the training sands to the sound of her mother calling her back.

Ever came back to reality when she stumbled over a large branch. It must have fallen down in the recent storms caused by her frequent lightning hops. Managing not to fall on her face, she shook off the memory, but couldn't stop the bile creeping up her throat. Despite the early morning, she had to suppress a scream of frustration. Closing her eyes, she inhaled the scent of wood and rain and breathed out.

It did little to calm the chaos in her mind, yet she glanced around to ensure no one could see her summon the lightning. When she had first spoken the words, and was struck by the bolt of lightning, it had hurt. By the gods, it had hurt like she had sucked on an electrical pole. Now, having used the lightning to spark from place to place, it felt like an extension of her body, as easy as breathing.

But damn, she wished for Erika's ability to flash from place to place without breaking a sweat.

Flashing back to the apartment, Ever dashed into the shower and washed away the dirt and grime from her quick jog. Dressing in jeans and a checked shirt, she gathered her towel dried hair into a bun and reached for her wig. It was a dark brown shade, non-descriptive, and would not stand out. Odin's spies were looking for a girl with sun kissed hair, so disguise was necessary. Pulling on a slate grey hoodie, she pocketed her MP3 player for the train ride and shoved some money into her pocket.

Stepping outside, Ever nodded a hello to her neighbours before descending the stone steps and plodding down the road. She walked through the housing estates with her headphones on, but the music at a bare minimum. Unable to shake the feeling that she was being watched, she glanced suspiciously over her shoulder as she strode into Garswood station and awaited the train to take her into Wigan town.

Some might say she was foolish, hiding so close to Ireland, but hiding in plain sight might work to her advantage. The train whistled as it came to a halt, and Ever gave one more look behind her as she ducked inside the doors. It took just under twenty minutes to arrive at Wigan Wallgate, but she continued to feel as if someone was on her tail.

Switching trains, she hopped onto one that would take her directly to Manchester's Victoria station. That train journey was an agonising forty minutes of tension as she refused to sit down, eyes darting between the doors of the train and the adjoining carriages. When it finally chugged into the station, Ever fled the metal carriage and shuffled her way around the commuters.

Once outside the station, she pressed her back against the wall and waited to see if anyone suspicious followed her out. After a while, she chided herself for being so jumpy. Placing her hands in her pockets, she strode away from the bustling city centre and down a tiny narrow side street off China Town. Manchester was, Ever had come to understand, a city where you could lose yourself in the moment, yet, even an outsider like her felt as if she belonged.

It was a city that had a heart beating within the confines of its borders, and nothing and nobody could harm it, for those who called themselves Mancunians would stand together, stand strong, and face down those who threatened to disturb this wondrous city.

Ever had arrived in the city shortly after the Manchester bombings and had witnessed just how strong the community was. Perhaps, because she had been among those here, it happened to be why she felt like this. If she had been in London, Paris, or even in war-torn Syria, and saw how people reacted to attacks there, then the same could be said.

In truth, the human race had more power within themselves than any god or gods who aimed to strike them down. Maybe this was the very reason her brother, Thor, loved the Midgardians so very much.

Oh, she missed her big brother. He might not be the sharpest of the gods, but Thor never made her feel anything other than his little half-sister. Spending so much time by herself, Ever even missed Loki, just not the trouble that seemed to follow him around.

She came to a stop outside a small café, pushed open the door, and went inside. The café had only a few patrons, the early morning rush already gone, and Ever slipped into the staff cloak room and put away her few bits. Yanking the sleeves of her hoodie up, she went into the back and began to wash the dishes piled next to the sink.

"Morning, Kira."

"Hey Stan, busy morning?"

Her boss, a small human man of about sixty, with a rounded belly and a happy face, grinned at her. "Same ole, same ole, Kira. Those millennials love their coffee."

Ever laughed as she rinsed the dishes and set them about to dry. There would be a lull now, the clock just ticking by to nine-thirty, and Ever went outside, pulling up a chair so she could prop it against the counter. Stan paid her under the table, so she only worked a couple of hours every day, more when needed. Stan normally worked all the hours himself, since his daughter Sally was now pregnant with twins. When Ever had stumbled in, starving and drenched to the bone, Stan had given her a cup of warm coffee and a bacon sandwich, glaring at her in a way that reminded her of Tom Delany, her godfather. She had polished off the sandwich.

Then, he told her food wasn't free and sent her into the kitchen to wash dishes.

"So, Kira...I have a friend whose son is a doctor. I think you two would make a good match."

Ever gave him a small smile. "I've sworn off men, Stan. More trouble than they are worth."

"Nonsense!" The man exclaimed, but the smile did not waver from his face. "We need a good woman, or a man if that's your cup of joe, to keep us in check. I know some of those lesbians, if that's more you, Kira."

Ever let loose a whoop of laughter. "Nope, but thanks for thinking of me. I'm just going to check and make sure you paid all the bills this week."

"Sally told you I forgot to pay the electric bill? That girl should be more concerned about those two boys in her belly and forget her old man."

Ever pressed a kiss to the man's cheek, grinning as he blushed. "Your daughter only worries about you. I think it's sweet. Not everyone gets to have that kind of relationship with their parents. You should cherish it."

"Who hurt you, Kira Doyle? Your parents?"

Ever dismissed him with a wave of her hand. "Let's just say my parents are not the most affectionate in the world. Never mind me, go serve the customers and I'll check the paperwork."

Ever bounded up the stairs and into the small office, which gave her a glorious view of Faulkner Street and the Archway. The structure was a gift, Ever learned, from Manchester City Council. It was beautifully adorned with depictions of dragons and phoenixes. In all of her lifetimes, Ever had only come across the creatures in death, when she or one of her sister's had escorted the souls of the slain warriors to Valhalla.

As rain trickled down the windowpane, Ever closed her eyes and imagined she stood with the sand between her toes, the sun shining down to heat her skin, and the sound of waves lapping against the shore. The vision was comforting to her, even as she waited for certain death. It was not that she hated being a Valkyrie. No. Rather, she detested being a Valkyrie Queen. Despite her earlier memory recollection, Ever understood that in war, there would be death, there would be loss, and most often, there would be suffering.

If all that Ever was in life was a Valkyrie soldier, it might have been enough for her. Yet, being a leader was not something she wanted, even if it was etched into every fibre of her being.

"Kira? Could you give me a hand, please?"

Ever trudged down the stairs, jumping the last two in an effort to drag herself out of her pity party. She came around the corner and asked Stan if he was quite all right. The man had paled ever so slightly.

"I'm fine, Kira. Would you mind serving the gentleman in the corner? I find myself unable to move just now."

Ever crouched down, flicking a stray bit of fake hair from her face. "Hey, you want me to phone Sally? I'm sure Maureen could come in and cover for a bit if you want to rest."

"Stop fussing, woman. I'll be fine. Just go serve the customer."

Ever frowned at him, rising to her feet and grabbing a pad and pen from the counter. She strode around the L-shaped corner, a smile on her face. Her eyes watched Stan as she said, "Hey, what can I get you?"

Silence greeted her. She turned her attention to the customer, and the air left her lungs. Eyes of deep hazel, tinged by amber watched her like a predator stalks its prey. Full lips pressed together, a muscle ticked in his jaw. His blank expression reminded Ever of the first time she had literally run into the gorgeous Derek Doyle on the campus where she taught.

He was as handsome as she remembered, angular jaw line, strong features emphasised by the stubble grazing his chin. It made Ever want to reach out and run her knuckles over it. Dark brown hair tumbled into his face as he leaned back, his arms stretched out on the back of the seat to appear non-threatening, like he was totally comfortable where he was.

But Ever could see the coiled tension in his muscles, knew the animal that prowled under the skin of the man, a man who was hers as much as she was his. As he held her gaze, his nostrils flaring at the scent of her, Ever's heart kicked a snare drum in her chest.

Derek gave her a smug smile as he spoke, each word like a caress. "I'm sure you remember how I like my coffee, Kira *Doyle*."

Damn, so he'd been listening long enough to know she'd been using his surname.

"What are you doing here?"

Derek's hands clenched into fists at her question, as if he really was trying not to lose his temper. "Is that anyway to greet your mate? I should bite you and remind you where you belong."

And if that did not send warmth flushing to the most feminine parts of her, it was obvious Derek knew it as well when his lips kicked up into a satisfied grin.

"I'll have a coffee and a half dozen bacon sandwiches, please, Kira."

Ever spun round, unable to say another word as she stumbled toward the kitchen. She should run, she should bolt out of the café right now, but only a fool would run from a wolf when it had caught the scent of its prey.

So she made the goddamn bacon sandwiches and piled them up on the plate. She waited until Stan came to the kitchen, steadying her hand as it shook while pouring Derek's coffee.

"Who is he, Kira? Is he the man who hurt you and put the sadness in your eyes?"

The growl that sounded in the empty café caused Stan to freeze. Ever patted him on the cheek and sighed. "No, Stan, I promise Derek never hurt me. It's rather the other way round."

Stan narrowed his brow, asking Ever again who Derek was.

"That man is my mate, and he's just a grumpy old werewolf who gets a little growly when he doesn't have a bacon sandwich. I promise, Stan, once I feed him, Derek will roll over and expect a tummy rub. It's quite embarrassing really."

Ever grabbed the sandwiches, ignoring the rumble of laughter coming from Derek. Walking on shaky legs, she balanced the plate and the coffee before setting them down on the table. Averting her gaze from the steely watchful eyes of the wolf, Ever said, "Here's your sandwiches, please don't choke on them. I'm not sure Stan has paid the insurance this month."

She made to move away, but a hand wrapped around her wrist as Derek growled, "Ever, sit the fuck down or I will throw you over my shoulder and march you out of here."

In her mind, she saw a variety of different ways to break free of Derek's hold, but found that she did not want to. The hand, roughly but gently stopping her from moving away, branded her, just like every kiss, every touch, and every laugh had done many lifetimes before this.

She had run, and she had been found. She would not have the element of surprise again, so Ever sank across the way from her mate, mourning the loss of his touch when he let her go to drink his coffee, all the while watching her.

This was going to be a long day.

Felix Grande, or rather the persona he went by in this century, kicked the fury from the back of the truck and inhaled the scent of fear that clung to the dead body. That beautiful Valkyrie brought in more cash in the last week than he had made the previous month. She was a ball of chaos that he drank from nightly, which was why he invited her to stay within the confines of the arena. The girl held so much anger and hatred for herself that it fed the demon in him and kept him sated for days.

Supernaturals came from near and far to catch a glimpse of the Valkyrie warrior in action. It was a magnificent thing to behold, the keeper of souls in action. She was as bloodthirsty and vengeful as legend proclaimed, and that was worth a lot of money to him.

His bodyguard, a former Berserker who Felix managed to lease until he wanted the animal unleashed, picked up the fury with one arm and tossed her down the ravine. Felix tried to dump the bodies where those pesky agents that belonged to P.I.T would not find them, but it was getting harder and harder to hide the trail.

If the Valkyrie kept killing at this rate, she might outgrow her usefulness.

However, for now, he would feed off her chaos...for she was chaos in a human shell.

When she wore out her welcome... well, Valkyries bled like the rest of them.

CHAPTER
FOUR

Caitlyn

C aitlyn shut the door to her new apartment, the top floor of a warehouse that she and Donnie were converting into living space for them, as well as Melanie and Kenzie. Although at the moment it was nothing more than a shell, Donnie had requested she meet him here, that he had something to show her.

"Donnie?" she called into the quiet, her senses on overdrive as her heels clicked against the hardwood floor. When she received no answer, Caitlyn went in search of her mate, a smile ghosting her lips as she spied the picnic blanket, the candles and the food laid out with care on the floor. There had been little time for romance over the last few days, and Caitlyn felt a little twinge of guilt.

She pondered a way to make it up to the man who had waited twenty years to be with her, and then froze when the voice from her nightmares said from behind her, "Hello, my rose."

Caitlyn turned around slowly. Cautiously, she said, "You are dead. You cannot be here."

Her words dried up in her mouth as Cain stepped out of the shadows, Kenzie's scythe cupping the neck of the man she called hers. Donnie's face was battered and bruised, and his eyes seemed unfocused as he said, "Run, Cait."

"Do, Cait, run from me so I can hunt you down."

Caitlyn's body began to shake She stepped closer to the monster from her nightmares. Cain pressed the tip of the scythe against the crook of Donnie's neck, causing Caitlyn to pause her movements.

"Take a step closer, my rose, and I will divest Donald of his neck, just like I did poor Kenzie."

Horror washed over Caitlyn as she tried to wake herself. It had to be a dream. A nightmare.

"You are dead. You are not here. This is not real!"

Cain, the face of an angel masking the monster Caitlyn knew lurked beneath the surface, gave her a feral grin. He sliced the scythe across Donnie's throat until his head fell, making a sickening thud on the ground. Caitlyn's scream raged through the abandoned warehouse.

Tossing Donnie's body aside, Cain had his hand wrapped around her neck a second later.

"You're dead. You are not real," she whispered.

The words were spoken more to convince herself of Cain's demise than to remind him that he was no more, that he had no claim on her.

"Perhaps I am dead, but as long as you dream of me... as long as you remember me, my Caitlyn, I will always be alive to you. You keep me alive, my love."

Caitlyn sat up straight in Donnie's bed and clasped a hand over her mouth to suppress the scream that lingered in her throat. Her eyes wandered over to where Donnie lay on his stomach, an arm tossed off the side of the bed, the other resting above his head. He looked so peaceful, her dreams not invading his sleep this time. Caitlyn reached out to touch him, but she snatched her hand away, slipping silently from the bed and out into the hallway before she woke the sleeping vampire.

Heading into the kitchen, Caitlyn opened the fridge and took out a bottle of blood, drinking it down until every drop had been drunk. Setting the bottle on the counter, she placed both hands on the countertop to steady herself. The dreams of Cain, the ones where he succeeded in taking everything she held dear from her, had begun on the night Kenzie had taken his head. Nothing she did could rid her of the dreams.

Donnie knew something wasn't quite right, because Caitlyn avoided his touch, avoided being intimate with him, since they had returned home from their mating party. She did not want to taint him with her darkness.

It was stupid, of that she was certain. Yet, she found that she could not help herself. Nor could she help the nasty twist in her stomach whenever Donnie tried to get her to settle on some of his ideas for their new place. Caitlyn had shrugged off decisions about flooring, paint colour, even the type of granite she wanted for the kitchen counters. Every time the renovations were brought up, she felt angry for reasons she had no clue of herself. In her mind, Caitlyn understood she was being unreasonable, yet that did nothing to curb her emotions.

Careful not to disturb Donnie, Caitlyn showered in Melanie's bathroom, knowing their youngest family member had chosen to sleep at the station with Kenzie, so they could train together. Once Caitlyn had dried off and dressed in denim jeans, one of Donnie's t-shirts knotted at the waist, and a pair of her favourite boots, she quietly fled the house and ran toward the station. The sun had barely dipped behind the horizon.

Arriving at the station, Caitlyn strolled through the building and was headed for the squad room when she heard a squeal of childish laughter coming from the gym. It beckoned her closer. Pushing open the double doors, she stood on the outskirts, watching as Melanie and Kenzie chased after a little boy with shoulder-length black hair, his eyes as green as his father's, the scent of him mirrored the one that was Ricky. Oh, she would have known the child was Ricky's on a first glance, even without the other clues. The warlock turned to face her, walking over to stand beside her, his body tense.

"You have a son." Not a question, simply a fact.

Ricky sighed, dropped his eyes as he replied, "Ya, I guess I do. Only found out about him two days ago. My Da's dead... so's Sadie. And I got a son that I have no right to be raising."

"Children are a blessing. You will do just fine."

Ricky glanced sheepishly at her. "I'm sorry, Caitlyn. About everything. I know I'm an ass most days and say shite I really shouldn't, but what happened to you... it wasn't right."

Caitlyn closed her eyes, not wanting Ricky to see the sadness lurking there. "Thank you for your words, and thank you for defending me to Cain. I am sorry for those you have lost also. Now, let us forget about sad things and introduce me to your son."

In a rare gesture, Ricky grazed his knuckles on her cheek, earning a frown from Caitlyn. The warlock grinned. While Caitlyn could still smell some sort of narcotic in his body, it was clear that since faced with his child, Ricky had managed to stay away from the crutches he used to block out his pain.

"Hey, Zach, can you come here a minute? There's someone I'd like you to meet."

Melanie and Kenzie stopped chasing the boy around and took his hands, swinging him backward and forwards as they came across the gym floor. They stopped a short distance away, the little boy glancing warily at Caitlyn as he approached to stand in front of her.

Caitlyn dropped to the ground, folding her legs under her so that she would be face to face with the small boy. Jessamine had barely been older than this child when her life had been snuffed out, and Caitlyn knew, without speaking a word to Ricky's son, that she would die to protect him.

The little cat, if her nose was correct and it mostly was, reached out a finger, which was when Caitlyn realized that she had begun to cry.

"Why are you so sad?"

The innocently spoken words allowed her to smile. "You remind me of a little girl I once knew," Caitlyn reached out and twirled his hair in her fingers. "Her hair was the same colour as yours, and when she smiled, Jessamine lit up the room, just as you do, little cat."

He pushed his glasses up his nose, tilted his head to the side, and assessed her. "What happened to her?"

"She died."

"My mom's dead."

Caitlyn cupped his cheek. "I am sorry to hear that, Zach. I am very sorry to hear that."

The room gasped as Zach climbed into Caitlyn's lap and threw his arms around her neck. No one, especially not Caitlyn, knew exactly what to do. The boy hugged her tightly and said very matter of factly. "It's okay, pretty lady, we can be sad together. I don't mind."

Mon Dieu, how to respond to that? Caitlyn took the boy in her arms and simply held him, as if one hug from this innocent child could save her from herself. The room was silent for many heartbeats, as Zach leaned out of her embrace, gave her a smile, and said, "I'm Zach."

"And I am Caitlyn. It is a great honour to meet you, Zach."

Zach grinned. "You have a funny voice."

Caitlyn chuckled and felt the knot in her chest ease just a smidge. "I was borne in Paris a long time ago. Do you know where that is?"

"Sure, it's where Disneyland is."

"So it is."

The others in the room laughed at Zach, who seemed perplexed about what he had said to make everyone laugh. Caitlyn found she did not want to let the boy slip from her arms. She ran a hand over Zach's hair and chuckled as he purred. Such a cat.

"Hey, hot stuff, if someone did that to you would you purr, too?" Kenzie teased Ricky, who looked scandalized by her words. It took a moment for him to recover, before he wiggled his eyebrows.

"Depends on who is petting me, Buffy."

Zach held Caitlyn's gaze as he frowned. "Ricky's not a cat, only me. He probably doesn't like to be petted."

Melanie snickered, while Kenzie coughed a laugh. Ricky looked up at the ceiling, muttering, "I'm gonna end up grey from this."

Caitlyn smiled a genuine smile, feeling light in her heart for the first time in days. Aware that Zach was studying her with inquisitive eyes, she tapped him on the nose. The boy grinned and asked, "Are you one of the vampires?"

Caitlyn flashed her fangs, but the little boy didn't even flinch, simply widened his eyes, his small hands reaching out.

Ricky made to stop him, but Caitlyn held up a hand to assure them she was fine. His tiny fingers touched her fang, and then he said, "Cool."

Caitlyn, who saw herself as the worst of the monsters, had never heard a vampire described as cool. She continued to stroke his hair, felt his body vibrate against hers as he purred. Ricky bantered with the girls, and Caitlyn felt her troubles subside with each stroke of Zach's hair.

"You're pretty when you smile, Caitlyn."

"Hey, short stuff, that's my lady you're flirting with. I see you've inherited something else from your dad."

Caitlyn had felt it the moment Donnie had walked into the station, heard him come in, but it had been centuries since she had held a child in her arms. She was having too much of a peaceful time. Zach, bless his soul, growled at Donnie as if he were a full-grown wildcat, his hands clinging to Caitlyn's shirt, well, Donnie's tee.

Caitlyn kissed Zach on the forehead, lifting him up with ease as she got to her feet. "It is okay, Zach, that vampire is my mate."

Zach scrunched his nose. "Another vampire?"

Donnie came to stand beside Caitlyn, a lopsided grin on his face as he regarded Ricky's son. "Hey Zach, I'm Donnie. Your dad and me go way back."

"Don't make the pretty lady sad again. Or I'll use my cat claws."

Donnie chuckled as Ricky scooped Zach from Caitlyn's arms. She instantly felt the loss of him. He scrambled down his father's body and scampered over to Melanie, turning to growl again at Donnie.

"It appears, mate, that my son isn't your biggest fan," Ricky said with a chuckle.

"Nah, mate. Your little cat just has a soft spot for my other half. Not that I can blame him. She's hot."

"Dude, he's five."

"Dude, he's your kid."

They both laughed as Caitlyn bristled, and the momentary peace in her soul evaporated piece by piece. Zach ran back over and grabbed Ricky's hand.

"Ricky, I'm hungry."

Melanie and Kenzie came over and ushered Zach out the door, Caitlyn having to decline the invitation from the little cat to go eat with them. Ricky waited until Zach was out of earshot, and he let go of a sigh.

"Caitlyn, that was...damn that was impressive. Kid hasn't spoken more than a handful of sentences to me in the last two days, and all y'all have him chatting like he's a guest on a chat show."

Caitlyn ran her hands down her jeans, giving Ricky a sad smile. "It is easy, when Zach is such a wonderful child. No matter her faults, Sadie raised him well."

"Yeah, let's just hope I don't manage to fuck it up now."

"You come to me if you have trouble...would you consider coming to stay with us, even for a while."

Ricky thought over her offer, but shook his head.

Good, Caitlyn thought. *Good choice.*

"Thanks for the offer, but right now, me and Zach gotta get used to each other. To be honest, I dunno what to feel right now...my Da's dead...Sadie's dead, and I just found out I have a five-year-old son who is being forced to live with a stranger." Ricky hesitated, and then blew out a breath. "Sorry, rambling. I'm gonna need some help here folks."

Donnie clasped a hand on Ricky's shoulder. "Anytime buddy, day or night."

Ricky rubbed the back of his neck, quickly leaving the gym. All that remained was Caitlyn, Donnie, and a cavern of silence between them.

"He's got a tough road ahead of him."

Caitlyn nodded, wrapping her arms around herself. "He has a lot of help. The child is something else."

She stepped around Donnie, who stopped her with a gentle hand on her arm. "Hey, what's going on?"

"Nothing."

Donnie growled low in his throat. "Don't 'nothing' me, Cait. Not anymore. Please stop shutting me out."

Caitlyn rubbed her arms, more for something to do than any chill she might feel. When she kept her mouth shut, Donnie wrapped his arms around her, and she went to him.

"Whatever it is, Cait, that's bothering you, we can deal with it. You and me. It's ride or die, remember."

"We are not Dom and Letty, Donnie."

"Nah, I'm much better looking than Vin Diesel. But maybe I need to shave my head again, because bald is sexy."

Caitlyn slid her hand up to drag her fingers across his scalp, pulling a groan from her man. It puzzled her, this delight inside that she could exact this response from him. It felt wrong, almost shameful. Caitlyn ran her nails through the blond, trimmed hair, slightly scraping the scalp.

"Damn, Cait, do that again."

When she complied, Donnie pressed closer against her body.

"I like your hair like this, please don't cut it."

Donnie cupped her face and winked. "Your wish is my command."

He kissed her then, a quick press of lips before he stepped back, wrapping his arms around her waist. "You gonna tell me what had you running from bed this evening?"

She considered telling him she was fine, but she refused to lie to him.

"I have been having nightmares and did not want to disturb you."

"Christ, Cait, shit like that wouldn't disturb me."

"I am not used to being so open with anyone... I am used to dealing with things on my own."

Donnie sank to the ground and dragged her down, so she had no choice but to go with him, sitting astride his lap. Hands folded in her lap, Caitlyn looked at the ground until Donnie lifted her chin with his finger, the intensity of those blue eyes drawing a sigh from her.

"Tell me about your dreams, Cait."

Placing a hand on his chest, Caitlyn spoke her fears aloud, giving them power over her, or so she felt. "I dreamt of the warehouse, and of Cain taking your head in the home we were making our own. In my dream, he told me that Kenzie was dead, and then he took you from me."

"Cain's dead," Donnie assured her in low tone, clipped with a possessive edge that did not calm her mind. "Cain is dead and we are not. He cannot hurt you anymore, Cait. You are free."

Caitlyn shook her head. "I do not feel free. In my dream, do you know what he told me? *'As long as you dream of me... as long as you remember me, my Caitlyn, I will always be alive to you. You keep me alive, my love.'* There is power in dreams, Donnie, for they show us what truly matters to us. Is it wrong of me to feel so numb, so incomplete, because my very reason for existing is gone, and I am struggling to find my purpose?"

Donnie slipped his hands onto her ribs, the pads of his thumbs grazing the underside of her breast. "No. but your sole purpose in life was not to kill Cain. Your calling is defending those who cannot defend themselves. It's bringing to justice those who would hurt the innocent. It's being part of this big, dysfunctional family, Cait. I have no control over your dreams, or over you. But, baby, maybe you need to talk to someone about what's going on in that beautiful mind of yours. Someone impartial who isn't me, or Derek, because I know those midnight strolls you two go on are more like therapy sessions anyways."

Caitlyn, under no circumstances, wanted to tell a stranger her life story and be judged. Scrambling out of Donnie's lap, she stood and made for the door, pausing when Donnie clasped a hand on the back of her neck in a pure sign of possession.

"Remove your hand." The words bit out, sounding cold and disconnected, and Donnie did as was asked of him.

"I'm not really sure how I became the bad guy in all of this, Cait, but shutting me out hurts me. Like physically. Every single time you flinch when I touch you makes me want to punch a wall. I can feel you, icy cold, through the mate bond, and all I want to do is help."

Folding her arms over her chest, Caitlyn wanted to hurt him, make him leave, because he did not deserve this... this shattered version of a person.

"If this is all about sex to you, then I'm afraid I cannot help you with that."

Donnie growled, a feral sound that made the hairs on her arm rise to attention. His entire body shook with rage, and Caitlyn knew she had gone too far.

Good. He might realize now that I can never be what he needs.

A stony calm washed over his handsome face as the thought slipped through the mating bond, and he understood that she was, in essence, trying to piss him off.

"I know what you're doing, Caitlyn Hardi. I fucking see you. If all I wanted were a few quick fucks, then I would just go out and get them. This thing between us is about much more than sex and you know it."

A throat cleared behind them, and Ricky had the good sense to look uncomfortable. "Sorry to interrupt, but we caught a case. I have Zach, so I can't go. Sarge wants to know if you two can head up to check out the body. I'll tell him that's a no...?"

Caitlyn faced away from Donnie. "You go with Donnie, Ricky. I will stay with Zach and make sure he is taken care of."

Ricky's brow rose. "You sure?"

"Certainly."

Striding from the room, Caitlyn leaned against the wall outside, ignoring the mumbled conversation that was taking place in the room. She hated herself for not being able to tell Donnie that every single time she considered some enemy may come for him to get back at her, it almost caused her to become undone. Perhaps she could find a way to break the mating bond.

Maybe it was time for her to start over afresh... somewhere new.

CHAPTER
FIVE

Erika

C omplete and utter chaos lay at Erika's feet as she surveyed the battle of death that played out before her. There to reap the souls of the brave, the hum of battle sent little shivers of pleasure along her skin, the urge to wade into the fight and lay waste to the unworthy more a compulsion than a necessity. Casting her gaze outward, she was invisible to the combatants around her.

The Battle of Clontarf, where the High King of Ireland, Brian Boru, fought against the warriors of the Viking-Irish alliance, which roughly consisted of Sigtrygg Silkbeard, King of Dublin, Máel Mórda mac Murchada, King of Leinster, and a Viking contingent led by Sigurd of Orkney and Brodir of Mann, had been waged from sunrise until sunset.

The body count was immense. Erika estimated that close to ten thousand men were slain on this day. Their souls called out to her, begging to be carried off to Valhalla or escorted to Fólkvangr.

Having spent the day carrying souls to their final destinations, dusk began to settle over the coast. The Viking ships that had lingered on the fringes were now retreating, the battle over and the victors emerging. Though the High King of Ireland's side had been successful, Erika knew that Boru's son had been slain, along with his grandson. On the other side of the battle, Leinster king Máel Mórda and

Viking leaders Sigurd and Brodir had also been slain, their souls fine additions to the army of Valhalla.

Surely, when most of those who had called these people to arms had been killed, did it really matter who had been victorious on this day?

Erika stepped over a corpse, unsure of which side the slain man had fought for, and made her way to the warrior who called out to her the most.

Brian Boru lay on the ground, his beard a shade of grey time leached of color, his face wrinkled with age, and his body that of a man who had fought many a war. His final sun had set. He would make a fine warrior to command. For now, he would join the ranks of the Valkyrie's army and help win the war that Odin had forced upon them.

The High King of Ireland opened his eyes to peer up at her, as Erika allowed him to see her face. He imagined what the Irishman saw; a woman of strength and power, a sword grasped in her hand, a shield attached to her hip.

"Be at ease, Brian Bóruma mac Cennétig," Erika said, speaking to the king in his native tongue. "Death has come to claim you, and I am here to deliver your soul."

"Are you an angel?"

Erika laughed at the king's words. "For certain, I am no angel. I have come to take you to Valhalla, where you will be blessed to join my queen's army."

The man coughed out a laugh, blood trickling from the corners of his mouth. "I am a king, I bow to no foreign queen or gods."

Erika saw it in his eyes, felt the truth as he spoke it. This king would not get on bended knee and show Ever the respect she deserved, what Erika demanded of her soldiers.

Erika dropped to her knees, right there on the blood soaked bogside, the muck drenching her skin. Sheathing her sword into the holster at her back, Erika leaned down so that her lips were a breath away from the king's ear, a small smile playing on her lips as she said, "Fear not death, for the hour of your doom is set and none may escape it."

Lowering her voice to a mere whisper, Erika continued, "Hel, great goddess, daughter of Loki, she who guards the spirits of the dead. Take my offering, he who fought bravely, but chose unwisely. Take him as my offering, one warrior to another. For this man is not worthy to walk the shores of Valhalla, or grace the beauty of Fólk-vangr. Take this son of Ireland, Brian Bóruma mac Cennétig to Hel."

The High King of Ireland inhaled sharply, and then his chest rose no more as Erika shoved off the ground and waded through the mangled bodies. Catching sight of Ever, Erika jogged forward, coming to stand by the future queen who dared to name a small Valkyrie girl as her general.

"I did not realize that you and the goddess of Death were such good friends," Ever said with a chuckle.

"I send her the unworthy sometimes, so that when my time comes, I will not be sent to Hel."

"Death is not foolish enough to come for you, Erika. It is too afraid of you to even dare."

Now it was Erika's turn to chortle, nudging Ever with her shoulder. When Ever returned a small smile, Erika asked what was troubling her. Ever said nought for a time, then she began to walk toward the shoreline, where some of her sisters were claiming the souls of the fallen.

"Odin states that he wishes to reclaim control over Valhalla. That he needs the army to stand against those who would smite him."

Erika clenched and unclenched her fists. "The Valkyrie will not follow Odin. We are loyal to you and only to you. And if any of them decide to waver, I have no problems in persuading them otherwise."

Ever put a hand on her shoulder, sending a shiver down Erika's spine. She had perfected the ability to not allow her emotions to show on her face.

"And then it will end only when blood is spilled, and not from you, Erika."

"Fools need to have their blood spilled if they follow Odin."

Ever squeezed her shoulder, and Erika could feel her cheeks heat.

"At least I know I always have you at my back, Erika."

"In this lifetime and the next."

Ever removed her hand, and Erika felt the loss of her touch, cursing herself for these feelings that had welled inside of her without her consent. The only other being that made her feel this way was Ever's adopted brother of sorts, Loki, the Trickster god. And that made Erika believe that she was screwed up on the inside, having feelings for the woman who was her best friend and for the man who could never be hers.

Erika opened her eyes in the dark, a sliver of light creeping in through the curtains. She had awoken because of the dream, and because she was acutely aware that she was no longer alone in the room. Having tossed and turned for most of the night, she remained calm. Her senses reached out and halted on a familiar aura.

"Don't you know it's creepy to watch someone sleep?"

"You look so peaceful when you sleep, General. Almost feminine"

Erika snorted. "I think the word you were looking for was fero-cious, not feminine."

"That too."

Slipping her legs out of the bed, Erika turned on the bedside lamp, and Loki came into her field of vision. Dressed simply in a pair of ripped jeans and a plain black tee, he sat with his arms clasped in his lap, his hair shorter than he usually liked to appear in, one knee resting on top of the other. He looked the epitome of sexual seduction. Tall, dark and handsome were words insignificant to describe him, but the god was a cocky bastard who had women, and men, lusting after him. Erika would be damned if she was going to be one of the groupies that fawned over him.

A smug satisfaction rushed through her as Loki's eyes roamed over her bare legs. The tee she had thrown on before trying to get a few hours kip was barely long enough to cover her back-side. Erika stretched the tired muscles in her neck before rising and striding over to sit on the chair opposite Loki.

Lifting her legs, she placed her feet on the arm of Loki's chair. Between one breath and the next, Loki had dropped his leg, propped her legs onto his lap, and began to rub the soles of her feet with those sinfully good hands of his. It took every ounce of willpower not to moan at the intense pleasure that tingled from her toes, right up to her brain, which almost went to mush.

"You'll get yourself killed if you continue down this path, General."

"Well whatever doesn't kill me had better start running. They won't get a second chance."

Loki sighed, yet continued to massage her tired feet. "Freya has sent you on this mission to keep you distracted, stop you from racing off to find Ever, or going to find Odin before Ever can break the curse." Loki lifted his eyes to meet hers, his lips tugging up into a sly grin. "But, I have more interesting ways to distract you, Erika."

The way Loki said her name made her want to slither into his lap and indulge her wildest fantasies. However, since Erika held on to some of her common sense, she tried to disguise her thoughts with sarcasm.

"That has got to be the lamest pickup line in existence."

With a grin so wide that Erika could see his perfectly white teeth, Loki shrugged. "Don't worry, that's only plan A."

Lifting her eyebrows in suspicion, she took the bait and asked, "What's plan B?"

Pressing his thumb hard against the underside of her foot, Loki continued. "To take you hostage. I've had many a fantasy where I get to tie you up, General."

Loki snaked his hand up to rub her calf, and Erika couldn't stop the moan that escaped her lips. If he kept working those magic hands, she'd be begging him to bring them up a little higher.

"Do you remember the first time we met?" Loki queried, his hand still massaging her calf.

"Ya, I was about fifteen, and you'd been off sowing your wild oats and being a manwhore."

Loki chuckled. "You gave me so much sass that I did not know what to do with myself. There you were, this beautiful young woman, a warrior, and you did not fall at my feet like most do."

Erika slouched lower into her seat, allowing Loki to roam his hand over her knee. "As I recall it, you showed up in Valhalla to see Ever and expected me to bow down to you."

"I knew, even then, that I had to have you."

Erika snorted, closed her eyes, and let the memory play out in her mind.

It had been a long day of training and all Erika wanted to do was to sneak off to have a long soak in the hot spring she had found on the far side of Valhalla. Her other sisters had already traipsed back to their huts, but Ever had remained on the training sands, trying to perfect a combination of moves that she had a little trouble with. As her general, Erika had sworn to watch over Ever until the blood failed to flow in her veins.

Ever slashed out with her sword, her feet stumbling slightly as Erika cringed, suddenly coming to attention when a dark mysterious stranger appeared in the sands behind her. Erika lunged forward, reaching for the short daggers on her hip. She barrelled into the stranger, a dagger to his throat, and was puzzled when the man smiled. Her heart pounded.

Erika took stock of him, this man that lay beneath her in the sand, her thighs pressed on either side of his shoulders, her blade at his throat. Power, pure and unbridled, coiled inside him, called out to her in the most intimate of ways. Most men would scowl if you said that they were beautiful, not handsome, yet from the smug smile on his face, this man who snuck up on her queen made Erika think that he would not mind being called beautiful.

His face was all sharp angles and high cheekbones, and his skin was fair, a stark contrast to the rivets of black hair that hung loose. Splayed in the sand, Erika fought against the urge to stroke his hair, to see if it felt as soft as it looked. His lips looked sinfully full, yet she was beginning to think her hormones were overreacting to the first good-looking man she'd laid eyes on in months.

Ever, having realized what had happened while she'd been distracted, clasped a hand over her mouth and laughed, leaving Erika to snarl back at her best friend and queen.

"I do not think it is funny to have someone unknown sneak up on you, Ever."

Glancing back at the gorgeous man beneath her, Erika eased up, yanking back her blade and rolling away from the stranger. The man rose without much effort, as she took in his clothing. He wore the finest of Asgardian leathers, black with a slight stripe of green on the sleeves. His long coat, which he dusted free of sand, was out of place here in Valhalla. The cropped top and short skirt she wore seemed insignificant compared to this man's finery. Her heart almost stopped when she spied the emblem of the royal house of Odin embossed on the chest.

"Erika," Ever began, but Erika held up her hand. She continued to watch the man, who leaked power from his pores, even as he grinned like an imbecile.

"You really do not have a clue who I am, do you?"

Erika lifted her brows. "You would think the confused looks, blank stares, and your ass hitting the sand would have answered that for you."

The beautiful stranger laughed, stepped closer, took hold of Erika's right hand, and lifted it to his lips. Still holding onto her hand, the man said with great pride in his voice, "I am Loki, son of Laufey, adopted son of sorts of Odin, and therefore half-brother to Thor Odinson, and Ever, daughter of Odin and future Queen of the Valkyrie. And who might you be, little warrior?"

Erika schooled her expression, but could not disguise the jump in her heart. This man, this god, was renowned for his many exploits in mischief, his escapades in trickery, being the father of many feared beings like Fenrir and the goddess Hel, as well as, according to a few, many sexual perversions.

Instead of dwelling on the fact she faced a god, Erika squared her shoulders before saying. "I am Erika, born of the sands, daughter of no one, destined protector of the future Valkyrie Queen, and General to the armies of Valhalla."

She snatched back her hand, rubbing it on her skirt. She held the gaze of the god, whose eyes seemed to hold the universe within them, a collision course of stars and galaxies. After not backing down from him, he gave her a quizzical look.

"Why are you not worshipping me, General?"

With a shrug, Erika replied. "Not interested, thanks."

Ever, who had been watching the exchange with muted amusement, hurried over to Loki and threw her arms around him. He spun her around as if she were five. Erika cringed at the jealousy that sparked inside her, yet, if she were being honest, she was not sure if she was jealous that Loki was hugging Ever, or the other way around.

Erika spun in the sand, as Ever chatted unreservedly with Loki, and proceeded to storm away from them. The sand pinched her toes as she bolted from the lovey dovey scene on the beach. She had barely made it across the sand before Loki called out to her.

"I look forward to speaking with you again soon, General."

The sexual undertone in his words caused a shiver to dance up her spine, like an invisible caress.

Erika's last sight of Loki, before she disappeared into the trees, was of the god watching her walk away, like he had found her interesting and alluring. And not surprisingly, Erika felt the same.

It would be months before she saw Loki again, yet he managed to pop in more often than Erika liked, chuckling when she snarled at him. It infuriated her.

"It infuriated me also. The fact I could not even get you to smile at me."

Erika pulled her legs from Loki's grasp and hugged her knees to her chest. "I had other duties to attend to than to think of upsetting the infamous trickster god. Ever has always been my top priority. That will never change."

Loki tilted his head, his lips pressing into a firm line before he clasped his hands together. "Would I appeal to you more if I were a woman? I can do that for you, if it is what you prefer."

Erika glared at him, but her expression softened when she saw that Loki was not teasing her, simply wondering if she would have succumbed to him sooner had he worn the guise of a woman.

"No," Erika replied, softening her voice just a little. "I do not prefer women over men. Or vice versa. I just like who I like. If it massages your ego, oh glorious one, I think you, as you are, are plenty hot for me."

"Good."

The smugness in his tone nearly eviscerated all the good work Loki's magic hands had made by relieving some of the tension in her muscles. Erika hopped off the chair and stood, walking back toward the small bed in the corner.

"Now that I've stroked your fragile little ego, perhaps I can get some sleep. There is a big fight tomorrow that I need to rest up for."

Folding his arms across his chest, Loki frowned at her, the expression marring his beautiful features. "There are many out there that would relish the chance to slay a Valkyrie. Without your sisters, even without the P.I.T team, you are vulnerable. Even I cannot protect you without incurring the wrath of Thor."

Erika snorted. "I can look after myself. Have done so since the day my mother abandoned me on the sands of Valhalla. I am a Valkyrie General who has clocked up more battle miles than all her sisters combined. Those who would strike out at me, they know who I am, what I am. Let them come if they can find the courage. I will bathe in their blood with a smile on my face."

"Damn woman, that is sexy as sin."

Erika waved him off, sitting on the edge of the bed. She gave him a little wicked grin. "Now unless you want to sex me into slumber, I suggest you leave so I can rest."

Loki vanished, leaving Erika alone... but she could sense him lingering around the room. Snuggling down onto the mattress, she pulled the blanket to her waist.

The side of the bed dipped as Loki reappeared, pulling the blanket up to her chest as he held her gaze.

"How about a kiss goodnight?" Erika asked sleepily.

Loki leaned down, his lips inches away from her own. Her pulse quickened and she fisted her hands in the sheets.

"The problem is, Erika," Loki said as he leaned in even closer, his breath on her lips. "If I kissed you, I don't think I'd be able to stop."

He disappeared a moment before his lips would have grazed hers, and Erika growled in frustration. Her growl went unanswered; the aura that inevitably came with Loki had gone from the room.

Erika tossed and turned before falling into a fitful sleep.

And when she did dream, it was of a god with sinfully good hands.

CHAPTER SIX

Ever

Sitting in silence, Derek munched away on his bacon sandwich, his eyes never once straying from hers. When he finished, Ever studied him as he wiped his mouth with a napkin, leaned back in the chair, and gave her a wolfish grin.

"So, you're a Valkyrie?"

"Ya."

"You don't sound too chuffed about it, Ever."

With a sigh, Ever rested her elbows on the table and then perched her chin in her hands. "It hard to explain, Derek, it really is."

"Try me." The gorgeous man across from her growled, the only thing betraying the cool exterior of his expression.

"When I accepted who I was, when I spoke the words that broke me free, it was intoxicating, overwhelming, and unexpected. I remembered everything about my other lifetimes–my lifetimes with you–and then I remembered just being me, Ever Chace. I may be a Valkyrie, but I am also the woman who never felt whole until I met you."

"Then why did you run?"

Ever gave him a small smile, thinking over her words before she spoke again. "I got all of these flashes of memories when I became my Valkyrie self, and after my father's ravens came to chat with me, I wanted nothing more than to keep you safe, keep you all safe. He showed me a vision of his path of destruction and the countless, pointless deaths because I–her–me, is too proud to hand over the keys to a kingdom I never really wanted in the first place."

Cracking his knuckles, Derek narrowed his gaze, and Ever felt a strange sensation, a wave of lust that sparked from the unbridled aggression that lurked as Derek's eyes flashed to amber before returning to their oceanic blue.

"If there is one thing I learned from being part of a team, it's that we are better together rather than by ourselves. When you are within a team, you have people watching your back, keeping you safe. It works both ways. If you had come to us, come to me, then you wouldn't have run off, dividing up the team and making us all easier targets."

Stan ventured out to glance around the corner, and Ever turned to wave him off. Thankful for the few minutes to collect herself, Ever wet her lips, conscious that Derek still watched her as if he suspected she would bolt at any second.

"At the time, I felt I was doing the right thing. Maybe I was wrong, but what's done is done. I went from being a woman in love with this amazing man, and having a fantastic career and friends, to being a fucking Valkyrie warrior who held the fate of the world in the palm of her hands, held *your* fate in my hands. I didn't want it back then, all the responsibility, and I still don't."

"And so, you ran."

There was no question in his words, just the simple truth of the coward she had been, running away to try and solve her problems. Deep down, since she had first rode the lightening and vanished from Cork, Ever knew one day, and one day soon, she would have to return and face the music. But the music had come to face her and by the gods, she felt relieved.

"Look, Derek," she started, her fingers dancing over the bracelet. "I know I messed up. I had to come to terms with who I was in order to be ready to fight my father. I never meant to hurt you. That was never my intention."

Derek's entire body trembled as the rage he had on a leash slipped. Amber pierced his eyes, his hands gripped the table, and the table groaned under the pressure of his grasp.

"If you could not break Stan's furniture, I'd be ever so grateful. He's been good to me, Mr Broody."

"You told me... you said we would do this together. You said that you needed space, making it sound like it was because of me and who *I* was. Ever, you told me that we were in this together. After everything we shared, after everything we'd been through, you said you wouldn't and you *fucking* did!"

The last few syllables came out in a roar, and she fought not to cover her ears. She supposed it was lucky that it was midmorning and the lunchtime rush had not started, because she was not certain that Stan would have any customers left if an enraged werewolf went on a rampage in his café.

Shoving the fake hair from her face, Ever reached over and grabbed Derek's coffee cup, lifting it to her lips and taking a huge gulp. His attention now on her, Derek released his grip on the table and grasped her hand holding the cup in his. The moment their fingers touched, a spark of electricity shot through her, and from the growl in Derek's throat, he felt it too.

"I understand why you are angry, Derek. I would be too if the shoe was on the other foot. But I can't do anything to change the past, even if I wish I could. I'd go back and let him have Valhalla and stop this sorry family feud that could get everyone killed."

Derek closed his eyes, not removing his hand from hers, and she saw him breathe in and out a few times as if trying to reign in the beast that was his other self.

"I take it," Ever said, giving him space to calm himself. "That Erika filled you in on the whole sorry story of it. So, you know by now that I am the daughter of a god and a goddess, half-sister to only half a dozen gods, and I used to, before this all started, ferry souls of the fallen to Valhalla."

Without opening his eyes, Derek asked. "Do you know what you did, the night you stopped me from dying when Donnelly stabbed me?"

Thinking about it, Ever shuddered. When Stephen Donnelly, a very sick human, denied the change numerous times and facing death, had kidnapped, harvested, and killed supernatural teenagers, as well as ended Melanie's mortal life by forcing Caitlyn to make her a vampire. In the end, when Donnelly had sensed something other in her, she had come face to face with him and held her own, until Derek in wolf form had taken Donnelly down. Derek almost died in the process. Only Ever claiming his soul had stopped him from dying.

"I claimed your soul as mine. It means that in the event that you do die, I will feel it, and it is my duty, and mine alone, to escort you to Valhalla. It means that any supernatural out there who can see auras or souls will know that you have been marked and that you belong to me."

Her words came out a little husky, and Derek grinned. "I like the way you claim me."

Ever chuckled, reluctantly slipping her fingers free of Derek's hold. "You're such a wolf."

"Guilty."

They shared a smile, and then Derek's eyes darkened. "Can you take off that goddamn bracelet already? I want to be able to feel you, feel the bond. Do you know how much it hurt when you put on that goddamn hocus pocus crap? It felt like claws inside my mind, ripping away the part that connected me to you."

"I'm sorry, Derek. I really am."

"I don't want your apologies, Ever," Derek said, his lip curling slightly into a snarl. "I wish I could hurt you the way you hurt me. But I know that if I had the chance, I wouldn't do it. I love you. What I want is for you to drop this whole woe-is-me attitude and man up. My timeframe has moved up, I need to get back to Cork. There are people back home that depend on me, depend on us. Let's go home."

Panic welled inside her chest at the thought of going home. What would she say to Erika, the loyal soldier who would step in front of a blade for her? What would she say to her parents, the ones who raised her? How in the hell would Samhain react to the fact that the daughter she had raised as her own was not human and more powerful than Samhain would ever be? Derek had fallen in love with the intelligent, human Ever Chace. Would this affect how he felt about her, like she had dreaded from the start?

"Tell me what just ran through your head." When she hesitated, he growled. "Tell me."

Ever blurted out all her fears, afraid that if she didn't get them all out, then she would not be able to again. Derek was safe, and he wouldn't care for her show of weakness.

"Ever," Derek said in a soft voice. "I love you. I love all of you, baggage and all. I don't care whether you are human, demon, half of something I can't even pronounce. Once I had gotten through the fog of rage and hurt, do you know what I felt? Relief."

"Why?" Ever queried, a little stunned by his words.

"Because you became less breakable." A statement of fact. "The fears I had that I would somehow get you killed, or you would grow old and die and I would be alone. That's all gone. You are an immortal warrior who could take me down with the flick of her wrist. I might not remember anything about our supposed past lives, but I'm sure as hell that even the past me would've found that sexy."

Ever assessed him, tilting her head to the side, her heart beating a mile a minute. "So basically, you're telling me I'm worried over nothing, and that I should've just stayed put."

"Basically."

Ever slunk down into the booth, hanging her head as tears pricked her eyes. "I don't feel like her, Derek...the girl who made the bargain with Odin. I still feel like I'm Ever Chace, the girl who you ran into that day at the college. But this power in me, it terrifies me. I'm afraid I'm going to hurt someone."

"I may have only known you for a short time, but you could never hurt anyone, Ever."

"I've killed people, Derek."

"So have I. Do you feel any different about me knowing that?"

Ever shook her head. "No, I don't. I still love you. But I regret dragging you and the team into my horrible family issues. Erika, she was borne into it, but you guys had no choice in the matter. If I go back," Derek's snarl made her rephrase her words. "When I go back, if you stick with me, then you will have to deal with my family, the good and the bad."

Derek snorted. "I've already met Loki. That was an experience."

That dragged a smile to Ever's face. "It always is."

Derek leaned across the table and took her hands in his, his gaze pointedly glancing at the wolf charm on her bracelet, before dragging his gaze up to meet hers.

"I get it, Ever, I really do. The rational part of me understands why you ran rather than stick around. You tried to lone wolf it, but you forgot that you had a mate, and a new family who look after our own." Derek rubbed his thumb over her knuckles, his eyes sparking amber. "I know you regret what you've done, but everyone has regrets, Ever. They regret the career they've chosen, the person they married, or not seeing the world before they settled down. That's just life.

"But, you can't let those regrets stop you from living...really living...in the here and now. You know what I think? Fuck our past lives, and let's live in the moment; let's just be Ever and Derek. Screw destiny, screw the future...C'mon, Ever, what do you say? Will you live in the moment with me?"

Ever swallowed hard, a lump forming in her throat. She realized, there and then, that Derek would have ran with her like he had done so many times before if she had just stopped to ask him. There was nothing she could do about the past. It was time to stop looking at the past and worry about the future.

Her fingers danced over the bracelet as she readied herself to remove it. The air suddenly became too thick to breath and Ever groaned, slapping a hand over her eyes. Maybe, if she wished hard enough, when she opened her eyes, her brother would not be about to ruin the moment with Derek.

"Oh, this is very romantic, isn't it?"

Ever opened her eyes when she heard the scuffle, looking up to see Derek pin Loki to the wall, the trickster grinning like an idiot as Derek's hands turned into claws, digging deep into Loki's charcoal suit.

"Now, look what you've done! You ruined my favourite suit! You can't go around trying to poke holes in people; it's rather impolite."

"I had just about convinced her to come home and you show up and put a boot in it."

Ever got to her feet, aware that Stan had come out at the commotion, and she had little time to defuse the situation. Plus, Derek had reined in his animalistic nature, but Loki had a tendency to bring out the worst in people.

Ever slid out of her seat, strode up to Derek, and ran her palm up his chest. "Derek, please let my pain in the ass brother go. He can't help it, being an idiot is in his DNA."

"Hey...I resent that."

Derek's chest rumbled with a growl, and she asked him again. "Please, Derek. As bad as he is, Loki would never have shown up here unless he thought it necessary."

Releasing Loki, Derek stepped back and returned to his seat. Ever hugged Loki quickly, punching him lightly on the shoulder. "Why can't you do anything normal for a change?"

Loki grinned, his eyes lighting up with mischief and mayhem. "This normal you speak of doesn't sound fun at all."

Ever groaned as she sat down. However, this time, she slid into the seat next to Derek, pushing him a little with her hip. Derek went easily, leaving Loki to adjust his suit. With a wave of his fingers, the suit magically repaired itself, and he took the seat opposite them.

Derek slipped his hand around the back of Ever's chair, his fingers grazing her arm.

"I will cut right to the chase, Kyria. The general is up to her pretty little eyebrows in trouble."

Ever sat ramrod straight. "What's going on?"

Loki clasped his hands together on the table, his face marred with concern. "She is putting herself in unnecessary harm's way, simply because Freya told her to do something. Apparently, since you went walkabout, Freya has taken it upon herself to order everyone around. It's been quite annoying."

Ever gave a startled laugh. "You mean Freya tried to order *you* about?"

"Indeed." Loki quirked his lips. "I was highly amused until she demanded I stay away from the general. I haven't even been very visible. Just insuring Erika does not get killed."

"How close is she to doing just that?"

"Very."

"Explain it to me." Ever almost balked at the sound of the order in her tone, went to apologize, yet Loki didn't even bat an eye.

"There is an underground fighting ring for supernaturals. One of your father's Berserkers is guarding the games master. Erika thinks if she can get her hands on the Berserker, she can find out where Odin sleeps and kill him before he kills you."

Ever laughed. "Is that it? Is that what the big fuss is about? Erika can handle a few fights, Loki. It's in her blood. Erika could go toe to toe with any man or monster and come out on top. She is everything Freya trained her to be. Bloodthirsty. Vicious. She doesn't have a breaking point. Having spent her childhood getting beat on by my bigger and stronger sisters, Erika made it her mission to be the best, and she accomplished that. Have no fear, Erika is perfectly fine."

Loki tapped the table. "I have seen the way she fights. I know she can handle herself. However, when she fought before, she did so to survive. Now, she is reckless as if she doesn't care anymore. It is as if she has given up."

That didn't sound like Erika, Ever's best friend in the world. They had been through thick and thin together, countless trials and tribulations. Ever had to go home, she had to help Erika if she could. Her friend could be stubborn as hell when she wanted to be.

"We have to go back. We have to go home."

Ever slid from her seat, rounded the corner and stood in front of the man who had treated her with more kindness in the last few weeks then her father had for countless lifetimes. Ever embraced Stan, pressing her lips to his cheek in a fleeting kiss.

"I knew you were special the moment I met you."

Stepping back, she pulled the wig off and shook out her hair. Stan smiled as she said, "If I survive what's coming, I'll come back and visit."

Spinning away before she teared up, Ever headed for the door, tossing the wig in the trash as she exited the café with Derek hot on her heels. She strode around the corner, following the path as it swerved around and into an alleyway.

"Ever?"

Checking that they were alone in the alleyway, Ever flashed a big grin at Derek. "One of the positive things about being an immortal Valkyrie, is it has some cool powers. Come here."

Derek came to stand in front of her, and Ever lifted his arms so that they looped around her neck, her own hands wrapping around his waist. Derek shuddered under her touch, and Ever cursed herself again for being so selfish. Wolves needed touch from their mates, and she had withheld it.

"So, it's been a long time since I've done this with anyone. And the last time, I think it was one of your past selves. You need to just let it happen, okay? I got you."

Closing her eyes, Ever summoned the power inside her, felt it the moment the clouds gathered above her, her skin tingling as lightening built in the sky and struck her in one fluid motion. A moan of ecstasy slipped free of her lips as she thought of home, thought of the police station where Derek worked, and willed them to be there.

Between one breath and the next, Derek rode the storm with her, their entire bodies coming together and dissipating before reforming with a loud crack as Ever's lightening shattered the ceiling of the gymnasium. They stood in front of a very startled Sarge, Melanie, Caitlyn, who clutched a little boy to her chest, and a girl Ever didn't know.

Derek staggered on his feet, stepped out of her grasp, and upchucked all over the floor. Ever wavered on her feet, the toll of using so much energy sending black dots floating in her field of vision. Derek puked again as she swayed, her godfather and leader of P.I.T coming quickly over.

Ever felt the exhaustion seep into her bones and gave the spectators a grin as she said, "Hey guys, so what have I missed." The words came out a little slurred as her balance teetered and she slunk to the floor, darkness a welcome friend.

THE BERSERKER DID nothing to temper his rage as he lashed out, digging his fist into the partition wall, cracking the plaster, pieces falling to the ground, leaving bits of the material clinging to his knuckles. Centuries they had waited, centuries they had masked their true selves from the world, until the day that their Master awoke from sleep, and they reined terror down on this world.

Bound as he was to the games master, he could not strike out against the one person whose blood he craved the most, the Valkyrie General.

"You will get your hands on the Valkyrie, Berserker. But right now, that pint-size bally of fire makes me a lot of money. I need her. Once the time comes for us to leave this wretched island, I will give Erika to you. That is my solemn vow."

Growling at the chaos demon, the berserker stomped from the room, the need to quench his rage pulsing in his blood. His boots made a steady thump, thump as he crossed the landing and paused outside the Valkyrie's quarters, the scent of ocean and sand igniting the lust for the kill. He could hear her move about inside the room.

If he flung open the door right now, could he snap her pretty little neck before she recovered from the surprise? This was the Valkyrie who had thwarted his master many a time and had more of a role to play than the false Valkyrie Queen even knew about.

He would take her feminine body against his and inhale the scent of her fear. As she gazed into his eyes and saw her death, he would snap her neck and be done with her.

The shockwaves her death would cause could cripple the remaining Valkyrie while Odin recovered from his sleep. This was about so much more than Valhalla or Odin's madness. This was about showing the world that they were at the top of the food chain, and all would bow down to them.

Controlling the urge to kill, the berserker took off down the hall, grinning like the Cheshire cat as he allowed his mind to imagine all the ways he would kill the Valkyrie.

CHAPTER
SEVEN

Derek

D erek's knees hit the gym floor at almost the same time Ever slumped to the ground, and his stomach rolled, another wave of nausea springing forth as he vomited all over the floor. Sarge darted over to Ever, checking her pulse, and Caitlyn handed the little boy–Ricky's if his nose was right–to Melanie, before coming to crouch in front of him.

"I'm okay." The words came out hoarse and unsure as Caitlyn helped him stand. "Ever's okay too, she just wiped herself out flashing us here."

Sarge yelled out a command, and a poor uniform came to clean up Derek's mess. The entire room waited for the uniform to vanish before they all began to talk at once. Derek massaged his temple, his head still spinning a little. A shrill whistle sounded, causing everyone to halt their questions. Derek tilted his head to the left and assessed the girl who whistled.

Dressed head to toe in black, she stood with the grace of a fighter, her black hair pulled back off her face, the creamy complexion of her skin so alike to Caitlyn's, it was not hard to see that they were in some way related. Her fingers twitched as if they were used to having a weapon of some sort grasped in them.

The wolf in him rose to the surface, his lips curling into a snarl as he let out a warning growl, testing the girl who was not completely human. Pride rippled through him as the girl slightly adjusted her stance, bending her knees, but casually positioning her body in front of Melanie, who clutched the little boy in her arms. His wolf approved. She defiantly held his gaze for three long heartbeats, before cursing and lowering her eyes, still watching him.

"Ease up, little warrior. I mean no harm."

"Bite me, wolfman. Don't know who the hell you are, but you can't come in here and scare the hell out of the kid."

Derek looked at the kid, who looked the spit of his dad with long black hair, haunting green eyes, and thick-rimmed glasses that dwarfed his face. The kid narrowed his gaze and growled at Derek, and he knew the kid had a backbone of steel.

Caitlyn sighed, giving Derek an exasperated grin when she turned to the girl and explained. "Derek, this is Kenzie Blake, my niece. Kenzie, this is Agent Derek Doyle, who happens to be your supervisor."

Kenzie glanced at Melanie who grinned and handed the kid to Kenzie before she galloped over and hugged him fiercely.

"I got your message. We'll take soon," Derek whispered, his tone low and only for Melanie. As she stepped out of the embrace, Melanie punched him lightly on the shoulder.

"That's for leaving and not telling anyone where you were. How do you think I felt waking up and finding you, Ever, Donnie, and Caitlyn all vanished into the night?"

Derek turned to Caitlyn who shrugged. "A lot has happened since you went after Ever."

Inhaling a calming breath, Derek's nose, now free of the stench of vomit, caught the new layer to Caitlyn's scent. Disappointment flooded his veins as Derek gave her a small grin. "Congrats."

"Many things have happened in the short time since you left."

Waving his arm out, Derek motioned toward Kenzie and the little boy. "I can see that."

"Not to interrupt this happy reunion, Derek, but what am I to do with your sleeping beauty?"

Derek glanced down at the unconscious Ever and his mentor. "She'll be fine. I'll take her downstairs in a minute, and she can sleep it off in the bunker."

"I can take her." Kenzie said, striding over to where they stood, but not before handing Ricky's kid back to Melanie. The young woman bent down to slip her hands under Ever's body, a growl slipping free from Derek's lips.

"You'll drop her, human."

Kenzie snorted and gave him a glare that was all Caitlyn. "Simmer down, wolfman. And I guess at this stage, I'm not entirely human." As easily as Caitlyn or he himself would have, Kenzie hoisted Ever up into her arms and strode to the door, pausing as Derek held the door open for her and pressed a kiss to Ever's forehead.

When Kenzie was gone from the room, Derek turned to Caitlyn. "She smells human...what is she?"

"She is blood kissed. Cain addicted her to his blood to stop her aging and moulded her into an assassin. I've been limiting her vampire blood to see if it will kick start the aging process, but alas, she still looks seventeen."

"And how old is she?"

"Twenty-seven."

Derek snarled. "Damn, someone needs to kill that bastard already."

Silence met him as he glanced around. Caitlyn had tensed, Melanie had tears in her eyes, and Sarge sighed.

"What? What did I miss?"

"Cain's dead. I killed him. And now Caitlyn is Queen of the Vampires," Kenzie said as she strode back into the gym. To his surprise, Kenzie sounded quite proud of the fact that she had killed the monster who had tortured and murdered Caitlyn's family.

When he stole a glance at Caitlyn, the vampire simply shrugged and sighed. "It is a rather long story, *mon loupe*. I would rather tell it over a nice glass of wine."

Caitlyn plucked the little boy out of Melanie's arms, who clicked her tongue at Caitlyn, disappointment all over her face. It seemed that Ricky's little man had all of his father's charm as well. Caitlyn opened her mouth to speak when the door to the gym swung open, and Donnie and Ricky strode in.

One look at Ricky had Derek glaring at the rest of his team. Eyes sunken into his head, sweat dripping from his forehead, Derek could smell the fucking drugs leaking from his pores. Ricky had lost some weight, reminding Derek of the time Ricky thought a liquid diet was all he needed to get over his ex. The chatter between Donnie and Ricky stopped dead when they spotted him, Derek surprised as anger flashed in Ricky's eyes.

Striding over, Ricky took the boy from Caitlyn's arms, ignoring Derek completely and tossed his phone to Donnie, telling him he was going to get some air. The boy struggled to get free and Ricky set him on his feet, sighing as the boy shimmered with light, a small black panther remaining. Ricky gathered up the clothes left on the floor and opened the door so the little cat could pounce out of the room.

As soon as the door slammed shut, Derek whirled on his friends. "Does somebody want to tell me what the fuck happened to him? Anyone with a nose can tell that Ricky's jonesing for a fix. I've been gone just over a week! How the hell did this happen, and why has no one tried to stop it."

Donnie inched closer to Caitlyn, but Derek saw that the vampire did not touch his mate, something that a newly mated vampire would not be able to control, the need to touch and show the world that she was his. As Derek read Donnie's thoughts, the vampire arched a brow as if to dare him to say a word. The silence stretched out for too long, only broken when Melanie spoke.

"That's why he's been acting all weird, isn't it? That's the strange powder smell I keep getting, right?"

Donnie scrubbed a hand down his face. "When we started this team, we made a promise to not get into each other's private business. It wasn't our place to tell you, or anyone, about what's going on in his head. He's coming down hard, but he hasn't taken anything since Fionn turned up to his house with Zach."

Sarge let loose a growl. "Is he a liability to this team? Do I need to bench him?"

Donnie closed his eyes for a second, and Derek cut in before Donnie could say a word. "You bench him, and he could get further into trouble. Hopefully, Zach will keep him from going down whatever rabbit hole he was headed."

"Derek," Caitlyn uttered, her voice low and soft. "Sadie is dead. His father is dead. All in one night, and he learned Sadie kept Zach from him for five years. Ricky is already down the rabbit hole, my friend. He needs to drag himself out."

Jaysus. Derek couldn't believe that Xavier Moore had finally gone and done the world a favour and died. Derek only met the man once or twice, while on investigations for the council, and the man had barely spoken to his son with respect for the office he held. Ricky had ignored his father, simply being more professional that ever. When Derek queried him on it, Ricky had simply said, "If I'd have shown I was pissed at having him order me about, he'd have gotten his rocks off from it. Ignoring him will piss him off more. When Xavier can't get one over on someone, it drives him mad."

"Let's move into the squad room, I'm sure Donnie has some news about the case."

They all filed out after Sarge, Derek studying Caitlyn as she walked beside Donnie, her body stiff, her shoulders heavy with tension. Donnie wasn't much better. Melanie sided up to Derek and shrugged when he looked at the mated pair, then back at Melanie.

Entering the squad room, Derek continued to watch as Caitlyn perched on the edge of her desk, and Donnie gave into his vampire nature and placed a hand at the back of her neck in a possessive hold. Caitlyn closed her eyes, and when she opened them, red tinged the black of her eyes. She blinked, and the red was gone, a mere slip in her control.

Donnie gritted his teeth, removing his hand from her neck, and sat down on his own chair. Once they had all taken their seats, Donnie began to tell them what they had discovered at the crime scene.

"Now, I know we all want to have some chats and go over the gossip, but we've got dead bodies." The former rugby player grinned, sobering as he went on. "Me and Ricky ID'd the body, a Fury from Wexford. Snapped neck was cause of death from what I could see, but without your Anna, Sarge, that's just my guess."

Derek glanced at his mentor. "Where's Anna?"

Folding his arms across his chest as he replied. "She's at a conference in Dublin with the intern, Tadgh. She'll be back next week. Go on Donnie."

Donnie fiddled with Ricky's phone, Melanie tapped the keys on her computer, and the printer whirred. He continued, "The victim was beaten pretty bad, but she had some wounds that were weeks old, barely healed. Her knuckles were split, and there was some skin under her fingernails. We dropped the evidence off at the lab, but we could be waiting days for analysis."

The door to the squad room opened softly. "Did you show them the stamp?"

Ricky came in, a sleeping cat in his arms, and pulled open his desk drawer. Melanie yanked off the hoodie she'd been wearing and threw it at Donnie, who leaned over and put it into the empty drawer. Ricky set his son down with great care and then sank into his own chair.

"I was waiting for you to come back." Donnie replied.

"Vic had a stamp on her right hand, all weird arrows and shit. Did Donnie send it to you, Melanie?"

Melanie answered him with a quirked brow, before she addressed the rest of him. "The image is the symbol for chaos; it's got eight arrows to it. According to the internet, it's also called the Arms of Chaos, the Arrows of Chaos, the Chaos Star, the Chaos Cross, the Chaosphere, or the Symbol of Eight. But, if you wiggle your way through the darker edges of the web, it's also the symbol for an underground fight club that pops up in various cities all over the world."

"Wait a second, an underground fighting ring? Ever's pain in the ass brother told us that Erika is involved in a fight club."

"Ever's brother?"

Derek turned and shook his head at Sarge. "You don't want to know. I'm terrified if I mention him, the asshole will pop up. Oh, and by the way, Erika and Ever are like, weird adopted sisters, kind of."

"Is this about Erika?"

They all jumped, as Ever soundlessly entered the room. She looked tired but no worse for wear after their little flash. Arms folded, hair pulled back, she looked like the warrior she proclaimed to be. Ever glanced at Derek.

"Are you okay?"

Derek leaned back in his chair. "Ya, I'm grand. But I'm not going to want to repeat the experience for a long time."

She gave him a little smile, before she turned back to the team. "Loki told me that Erika is participating in the fights on my mother's orders. Any idea where the base is located? I can get in and get Erika out."

Sarge surged to his feet. "What has Samhain got to do with all of this? And did you just say Loki?"

Ever winced. "Samhain is not involved, Tom. I meant my biological mother, Freya. And yes, my brother of sorts is Loki. I need to go find Erika."

"Ever, wait."

Ever paused at Derek's words. "You can't just drop all these bombshells on people and walk away. They deserve to be told what's in store for them, what's in store for us."

Ever faced them. "My father wants me to relinquish my claim to Valhalla, so that with my death, he can usher in Ragnarök, rebuilding the world so that his beloved wife Frigg can be reborn. This will cause the death of many of the Norse deities, and the world will be reborn again with those who survive. You could all die, if you chose to fight with me when the time comes."

Ricky held up a finger. "Hang on a second. I knew you were supposed to be a Valkyrie, but let me add this fucking math equation up. You are the daughter of the goddess Freya, and the husband of Frigg, who, if my Marvel knowledge is up to par, is Odin, the god of goddamn everything Norse? That means Loki is your adopted brother, and you are the sister of various gods, including Thor? Am I getting this right?"

"Yup, there abouts."

"And how did you not remember that you were a Valkyrie?"

"Loki cast a spell so that I had seven lifetimes to try and stop my father. I have failed seven times to stop him from killing me. If he kills me in this lifetime, I will not be reborn. Odin will control the Valkyrie and use my army to lay waist to the world."

"This is all very Shakespearian," Melanie murmured.

"He sleeps now, having cheated at my last death. I must stand with my champion as the world balances on the edge, and new life will bring new world order."

"And who is your champion?" Caitlyn asked.

"I am." Derek sighed as all eyes turned to him. "Apparently, Ever and I are tied together, have been for centuries."

"Please don't tell me you got amnesia and now think you're a god."

"Nope, that's just Ever. My soul has been reborn, according to Loki, but I'm not sure if I believe him."

"In your first existence, you were a fierce Viking warrior who died on the battlefield."

Ricky rested his head on the desk. "I have no words."

Donnie rubbed his forehead with the palm of his hand. "My head hurts. Okay, so let's say Erika is participating in the fighting ring, then we need someone on the inside as well. Caitlyn is now queen of the vamps, so she's out. Ricky, no offence mate, but this requires a fighter not a lover. Melanie's still too young. So, Derek, that leaves you or me."

"You forget," Ricky snorted. "Derek made himself a reality TV star when he got arrested, he's too famous now for grunt work."

Derek was taken aback by the bitterness that soaked his friend's words, but he kept his mouth shut as Donnie said. "Then that leaves me."

"No."

Donnie growled as Caitlyn dismissed him with the wave of her hand. "You are mated to me and that makes you a target. Any aged vampire who wished to replace Cain, would cement their mark by taking out my consort. I am not questioning your ability to fight, Donnie. Simply pointing out that my new position, which you helped bolster, means we have to change how we go about things."

"I am not going to sit on the side-lines because of what might or might not happen. Goddammit, Cait. Remember what happened the last time you left me behind and ran off to Paris without telling us."

Caitlyn hissed, and Zach clambered out of his bed, leapt across the table and sank his teeth into Donnie's arm. Ricky leapt up and grabbed hold of Zach, who turned back into a tiny human with a growl.

"Stop making the pretty lady sad!"

The entire room quietened as Zach, naked as the day he was born, climbed into Caitlyn's lap, changed back into cat form and curled up in her lap. He purred as Caitlyn ran a hand through his fur. "I am not sad, little cat. But thank you for trying to protect me."

"You're lucky I like your Da, kid."

"Do not threaten him, Donnie." Caitlyn's tone was dead, pure ice.

"Jesus, Cait, I'd never harm a hair on his head. Yours either, if the cat wants to know."

Caitlyn ignored him, as Derek spied Ever attempting to slip out the door. As if she sensed his eyes on her, she turned her face in his direction and mouthed, "I'll be back, I promise."

Then, she was gone and he almost growled, every single cell in his body telling him to go after her. But, he didn't. He turned his attention back to the team and the case.

"So, what are we going to do about the fight ring? Ever will go find Erika, but we still need someone to go in and get information."

"Send me in."

Kenzie had slipped in as Ever dashed out, and now it was Caitlyn's turn to growl. "Absolutely not."

"That's actually a good idea," Mused Ricky, earning a glare from Caitlyn. "It is. I mean, who wouldn't let the blood kissed assassin created by the first vampire to fight. I'd pay to see it."

Caitlyn's eyes turned a vicious colour red that had Derek swallowing hard.

"Absolutely not. I forbid it."

The girl put her hands on her hips, and spoke, and even Derek knew when the words were spoken that Kenzie realized she'd fucked up.

"You forbid it? Damn, you sounded just like Cain right there."

CHAPTER EIGHT

Kenzie

K enzie kept her silence until Caitlin said, "Absolutely not. I forbid it." Then, anger washed over Kenzie. She'd done a lot since coming back to Cork. She'd obeyed the rules, trained with P.I.T despite it being a waste of her time, she'd even become friends with Melanie, a vampire, and one she actually liked. Caitlyn seemed to think she was someone who needed to be coddled, but she was twenty-seven years old goddammit, she wasn't a child.

"You forbid it? Damn, you sounded just like Cain right there."

Kenzie knew the moment she fucked up, the moment when her smart-ass mouth got her into trouble. Caitlyn was nothing like Cain and Kenzie knew that. Donnie growled, a feral sound that sent little Zach clambering out of Caitlyn's lap and back into the drawer. Caitlyn clenched and unclenched her fists as Donnie stood, and Kenzie braced to defend herself.

Donnie, who looked genuinely taken aback, asked. "What? You actually thought I would hit you because of what you said?"

Kenzie lifted a shoulder. "It wouldn't be the first time someone punched or backhanded me for my inability to keep my mouth shut."

"We've all said stupid shit in the heat of the moment. Nobody here is going to hit you because you said something stupid."

"If that was the case, I'd be a walking punchbag." Ricky joked, trying to ease some of the tension in the room. Caitlyn had her eyes closed, and Kenzie felt as if she had struck Caitlyn.

"Caitlyn, I'm sorry, but you are looking at this with your emotions rather than logic. I can't help how much I look like your daughter, and I know that's why you keep me around."

Caitlyn's eyes sprang open. "I do not simply keep you around because you remind me of my dead child, Kenzie. You are family. That might be a foreign concept to you, considering who raised you that last ten years, but all of us here in this room want only to protect you, as I failed to do when Cain slaughtered your family. I will not use you as he did."

"Why not?" Kenzie asked. She was having a hard time understanding why Caitlyn would not use the skills she had. "I have killed over two hundred and fifty vampires for Cain. I killed more for pleasure. You keep telling me, Caitlyn, on those strolls through the woods at midnight that I have a purpose here with you guys. Use me. Utilize my skills. If this was a computer thing, you'd ask Melanie to snoop about, right? Why are my skills any different?"

"It is different when your life is on the line."

"Then make me a vampire if that makes you feel better. This is the kind of thing that gets my adrenaline pumping. I need it. You've kept me away from anything bloody for almost a week. I don't know anything else but kicking ass; I don't know how to be normal."

Her throat caught at the last bit, and Kenzie cleared it. Caitlyn stared at her, and Kenzie muttered. "I could just go anyway, it's not like any of you could stop me."

"Wanna bet?"

Kenzie faced the wolfman. If Ricky was a walking rock-n-roll god, then this man was so good-looking, if he'd been a lollipop, he'd have licked himself. Luscious hazel eyes that reminded Kenzie of chocolate, with hair a darker shade than his eyes, stubble that kissed his jaw and stroked over his mouth, Kenzie knew this gorgeous man was danger in man-candy form. If Jensen Ackles and Jeremy Renner had a lovechild, it would look like Derek Doyle.

"How do you plan on stopping me?"

"I don't."

Kenzie blinked in surprise. "Come again?"

"I don't plan on stopping you, Kenzie." Derek said, his eyes turning to Caitlyn. "She's right. We all come to this team with individual assets. If we don't allow Kenzie to use her skills, then why is she even here?"

Wow. Talk about being direct. She might actually like the wolfman.

"If she were to get hurt…"

"Then we will be there to help her!" Turning back to face Kenzie, Derek ran his eyes over her. "But first I need to know she can handle herself."

Kenzie snorted, a look of arrogance on her face. "How you gonna prove that? You gonna fight me, wolfman?"

"You're damn right I am."

Caitlyn started forward, but Derek held up his hand. "I only mean to spar with her. I assure you, Caitlyn, your little warrior won't come out with a scratch."

"Pity I can't say the same about you, wolfman."

Derek grinned at her. "Let's see what you got."

Kenzie cracked her knuckles and moved for the door. "C'mon Agent Hotstuff, I need a cheerleader in my corner."

Ricky groaned as he scooped up Zach. "You gotta stop calling me that!"

Melanie chuckled, coming to walk beside Kenzie as they strode down to the gym where Kenzie had spared with Melanie the last few days. Nudging Kenzie with her shoulder to get her attention, Melanie looked at her with wide eyes.

"You sure about this, Kenz. I mean, Derek is a werewolf."

Kenzie beamed. "It's not the first time I've fought a werewolf. If I had my scythe, then he'd need to be worried. I got this."

"He'll pull his punches like he does with me."

"Then that will be his fault because I won't pull mine."

Entering the gym, Kenzie yanked off her hoodie and tossed it to the side. She shucked off her boots, and bent down at the knees to make sure her leggings would give her space to move. Twisting her hair up into a bun, Kenzie glanced down at herself to make sure she had nothing on that could be used against her. Stripping herself of weapons, setting them down on the bench, she caught sight of Melanie's shocked eyes.

"Are you always this armed?"

"Yup."

"Even when you're asleep?"

"Especially then. When you are asleep, you are at your weakest. Makes sense to have a dagger or two under your pillow."

As Derek came into the gym, the rest following him in, Kenzie tied a knot at the end of her loose t-shirt, exposing her midriff. Caitlyn came over and frowned.

"You should not expose any weakness."

"It's not a weakness if while he's going for my stomach, I slice his throat. But, as wolfman said, we are just sparing. I promise not to hurt him...much."

Derek barked out a laugh as he stripped off his jumper and took off his boots.

Standing there in a tight black tee, Kenzie assessed him. Predator that he was, Derek would consider her weak from the get go, terribly human. He would forget that she had been broken in the Catacombs of Paris, much like Caitlyn had, and forged anew into a vicious assassin.

Kenzie sank down to the ground, crossed her legs and closed her eyes. Inhaling and exhaling, she centred herself, blocking out the din of those in the room and focusing on the scent of Derek, the sound of his heartbeat, and pad of his feet as he came for her, hoping to catch her unawares.

Just as Derek was about to strike her with his foot, Kenzie rolled, sweeping out her leg catching Derek by the ankle and he stumbled. They faced each other and Kenzie winked.

She could hear Caitlyn mutter for her not to get cocky, but it wasn't cockiness if she was just being herself. For the first time since her scythe had sliced off Cain's neck, Kenzie felt alive, like her life had purpose again.

Bouncing on the heels of her feet, Kenzie waited for Derek to move again, his fist jabbing out as she ducked, kicked out with her right leg, going straight for his stomach. With every punch, Kenzie kicked. She understood Derek was assessing her skills, seeing if she had any physical weakness, but most of her weaknesses came from her mind, the demons that lurked behind her eyes.

Kenzie struck out with a fist to Derek's gut at the same time she kicked out. Her fist connected with his ribs, drawing an oomph from the werewolf, but he grasped hold of her ankle, yanked and twisted so that she went down on her stomach with a thud. Derek twisted her ankle into some sort of old school wrestling leg lock, but Kenzie rolled out of it, pain burning her bones as she tried to balance her weight on it.

With one more trick up her sleeve, Kenzie lunged for Derek, her right fist connecting with his jaw as she leapt and kicked out with both feet, sending Derek to the ground on his back. Grabbing the silver blade from a concealed strap on her leg, Kenzie held the tip of the blade to Derek's throat, the werewolf hissing as the tip of the dagger grazed his throat.

"Kenzie!" Caitlyn exclaimed. "This was a sparring match, no weapons."

Kenzie removed the blade from Derek's throat, slipped it back into its sheath, and rose, holding out her hand to help Derek up. The werewolf grinned as he rose, patting her on the head as he muttered. "Good assassin."

Turing to Caitlyn, Kenzie echoed her stance, arms folded across her chest. "Like fuck it was. Wolfman was testing me to see how good I was. Did I fight like you, or was I a dirty fighter? You never go up against an opponent who could rip your throat out with his teeth without having some insurance. If I'd had my scythe, Derek would be growing back a limb. This wasn't sparring. This was a test."

Derek clasped her on the shoulder. "She's right, Caitlyn. I was testing her. I needed to know that Kenzie could do what needs to be done. I knew she had the dagger all along. You just have to look at the array of blades to know she doesn't turn up to a party empty handed."

Kenzie moved away and slipped her feet into her boots. "At least I took off my boots."

Derek lifted a brow and Kenzie tapped her right boot once. A gleaming blade slid out before Kenzie tapped the boot again, this time on the back, and the blade disappeared.

"Nice." Derek whistled.

"Say what you want about Cain, but he gives kickass gifts. Who knew a psychopath would be good at that?"

Donnie handed Kenzie her jumper, which she slipped into, grinning as he said, "Cain was more of a narcissist than a psychopath. Ricky's a little narcissistic, and he gives awesome Christmas gifts."

"Hey!"

"Are you saying it's not true?"

Ricky grinned. "Nope...just sounded like I should object."

"Oh, do I get a Christmas present, Hotstuff?"

Ricky's cheeks heated at her comment and Kenzie laughed as she started to strap on her weapons, wary as Caitlyn watched her. Kenzie guessed that Caitlyn was worried for her, desperate to see how she was coping with everything that had happened, and surprised that Kenzie had not been struck with nightmares like Caitlyn was.

A couple of days ago, when Caitlyn had woken the whole house with her screams, Kenzie had stormed into Donnie's room with her scythe swinging, Melanie close on her heels. For a split second, Kenzie feared that Cain had somehow risen from the ashes and come to seek revenge. Donnie had lifted his eyes, sorrow and pain filling those baby blues, before Kenzie retreated, taking Melanie with her.

Unable to sleep, Melanie and Kenzie had hunkered down on the couch to watch a movie. When Kenzie asked if that happened a lot, Melanie shrugged, advising Kenzie that she'd get used to it. Kenzie cursed Cain, hoping that the bastard was being tortured by some hell demons who made him their bitch.

Kenzie lifted her head when she heard a strangled cough, and Donnie grinned at her. Sticking out her tongue, she turned away from the mind reader and asked. "Anyone have any ideas how I find this party?"

"According to the dark web site that gives live updates about fights, fighters have to be invited in or nominated by someone who has been invited."

"So, I just need to track down someone shady who might have been invited. Supernatural central it is then."

Kenzie spun on her heels, ready to head out when Caitlyn said. "Wait a moment."

Pulling out her phone, Caitlyn started to speak in French before she switched to English. "Don't play coy with me, Chester. Have you or have you not been invited?"

Kenzie tried to hear what was going on, but Chester was muttering low. Caitlyn let go of an exasperated sigh. "I assure you that P.I.T has no quarrels with you and yes, I still appreciate what you did in assisting with the demise of Cain. All I ask is that you accept the invitation and perhaps suggest a fighter."

Caitlyn glanced in her direction. "I'm sending in Kenzie."

Chester's voice was loud enough they all heard his response. "You're sending in the slayer!"

Everyone looked at Kenzie, and she shrugged with a grin.

"Who else would we send, Chester? Even you have to agree she is well equipped to handle herself."

Chester response was low, and Caitlyn lifted a hand to her forehead. "I'll send her to you now."

She hung up, sliding the phone into her pocket.

"What did Chester say?" Sarge asked. "Did he object to sending Kenzie?"

"Quite the opposite actually," Caitlyn replied, much to everyone's surprise, including Kenzie. "He just wanted to know, since he's helping P.I.T out, would it be unethical to place money on Kenzie to win."

Sarge shook his head as the rest of them laughed. Once the laughter had died down, everyone looked grimly at Kenzie. Having been starved of affection from anyone but Cain for years, Kenzie felt awkward with goodbyes or see ya laters.

"Is he at his bar? Cool...I'm out of here."

Kenzie all but bolted out the door, pausing only to grab her scythe from her locker, and she made it pretty far, out into the darkness, before Caitlyn caught up with her. Kenzie looked at her great whatever aunt, and realized that she would have looked like Caitlyn if she had stayed with Cain much longer.

Caitlyn looked jaded, like life had kicked her in the ladynuts far too many times and she was just done.

"You will be careful." An order, not a request.

"I will."

Kenzie's heart went to her throat as Caitlyn came forward and embraced her, muttering something in French that Kenzie couldn't make out, cursing the little French she had picked up in her ten years in Paris. Then Caitlyn stepped back, giving Kenzie her back as she walked back to the station.

"Caitlyn?"

"Yes, Kenzie."

Kenzie swallowed hard, probably because she was bordering on inappropriate conversation with her relative when they barely knew each other. "Don't let him win. Cain, that is. You pushing Donnie away means he's winning, even when the bastard is dead. You suffered way more than I did. But what you are doing, closing yourself off, it's exactly what he wanted–to see you alone, having chased everyone away. Don't let him win, okay?"

Kenzie jogged away from the station, not sparing a glance back, and kept up the pace until she reached Supernatural Central. Striding into Chester's bar, earning growls and glares as she went down the stairs where she had not so long ago killed a few vamps, Kenzie lifted her head, a smug smile on her face.

Chester stood at the bar, one of those margarita or martini glasses in his hand as Kenzie strode up to him.

"Hey Chester, what's the story?"

"We must leave right now if we want to get you registered for the fight tomorrow night. We can only observe this evening and the man in charge wants to assess you first."

"Then let's blow this shithole and get going."

Chester spluttered in indignation as he followed Kenzie up the steps and out the front door, pausing at the waiting Mercedes before she ducked inside. They travelled mainly in silence, until they pulled up by a house just off Fota, on the outskirts of Cobh.

As Kenzie made to get out, Chester dropped a hand to her arm. "Remember that you are going in as my fighter. You keep quiet unless you are spoken to. The wrong word out of your mouth might end us both. This is not a place to act the fool."

Flashing him a grin, Kenzie showed her teeth as she said, "Dude, nice dropped the ole Luda on me. You're not so bad for a dead guy."

They made their way into what Kenzie assumed was an old abandoned house, but this place was fitted out! The downstairs had been gutted, an octagon ring complete with a cage sat in the middle of the ground floor. Hundreds of supernaturals gathered around the ring, roaring and shouting. Money exchanged hands as Kenzie slipped her hood up, following Chester like the good little minion she was supposed to be.

Sparing a glance up, Kenzie saw the more elite of the supe community were on the first floor, where the fighters readied themselves, giving the richest the chance to view the goods before they placed a bet.

Chester was led to a room just off the main area, and when they ducked inside, the hair on the back of Kenzie's neck prickled. Reclined in a chair, dressed in a blue suit the same colour as his hair, ears pointed and eyes almost catlike, was the person running the show.

"This is the fighter you want to enter into my ring, Chester? This child?"

"This child is blood kissed and trained by the first of my kind, Cain. This child is also the very girl who took Cain's head with her scythe."

The man's eyes flashed a bright blue as he inhaled. His body trembled as he spoke, and Kenzie felt dirty. "So much inner chaos in you, girl. How many have you killed for fun?"

"Not enough."

The games master laughed. "That is what I like to hear." To Chester. "The dance card is full for tonight. But go and mingle, Chester. Tomorrow your girl will fight. I have the perfect opponent for her."

"Thank you, Felix. I'm bringing some guests tomorrow night, if that is quite alright?"

"The more the merrier." Felix answered, his ears twitching as they exited.

Kenzie pulled out her phone, shot off a quick text to Caitlyn to tell her she was in, and that Chester had scored an in for them as well. Caitlyn messaged her back, telling her to keep her eyes open and look out for Erika.

Slipping the phone back into her pocket, she followed Chester up the stairs, leaning on the balcony to look down on the fight below. Chester turned to look at her.

"Are you ready, slayer?"

"I was born ready."

Tristan da Cunha, a remote volcanic island in the south Atlantic Ocean, lying two thousand kilometres from the nearest inhabited land, began to rumble, the waves from the surrounding water crashing against it, thunder and lightning ripping through the skies. The ground shook, dislodging rubble and rocks from the mountain.

The volcano that had been dormant for years threatened to erupt from the force shaking the island. Storms were a common occurrence on the secluded island, yet this storm was like no other. It had been almost a century since a storm of this magnitude had struck any place on earth.

Deep inside the mountain's cavern, lightning cracked through the rocks and illuminated the cave, which had been shrouded in darkness. The ground trembled under the weight of the magic, and the sound of ravens cawing mingled with the clashes of thunder.

As the mountain and the island trembled, a man with long white hair and beard lay on a slab of stone, a sword clasped in his hands as he lay unmoving on the cold stone. The thunder clapped harder and louder, and lightning continued to streak through the sky, a mirage of silver and gold.

A single finger twitched, and the ravens screeched in delight as slowly, testing, there came another twitch of fingers when the man gripped the sword tighter. The man's eye opened, his other eye long since perished from where his daughter had plunged a dagger into the socket, divesting him of sight in his left eye.

Stretching out his tired limbs, Odin, The All Father and god of gods, sat up inside the volcano and ran a hand through his beard. Huginn and Muninn flew over his head as Odin swung his legs off the side and asked the birds, "Where is my daughter?"

They cawed their response, and Odin sank his sword into the ground. Lightning cracked and hit the sword, filling his bones with power. Legs still weakened, he tentatively strode to the mouth of the cave, the ravens coming to perch on his shoulders.

At the foot of the mountain, a large grey steed pawed at the group, braying slightly at the sight of Odin, his monstrous teeth clamping together.

Odin was awake.

He was thirsty for blood.

And, he would make his daughter and all of her Valkyrie bend the knee for him.

CHAPTER
NINE

Erika

After a fitful sleep, Erika was up before the sun set, a quick shower and breakfast resulting in too much time on her hands until her fight. She could trace to her sisters, spar a little with Marya, but truth be told, all Erika wanted to do was spill blood. The need to punch something or slice something raged inside her, brewing like a storm until she almost lashed out at the walls just for something to do.

Throwing herself onto the bed stomach down, Erika pulled out a novel and began to read. Her eyes had barely skimmed over the words before she felt that undeniable aura that was Loki saturate the room. Ignoring him for a few minutes, unable to concentrate on the words, Erika kicked the heels of her feet, slightly hitting her behind as she moved. Flipping over an unread page, Erika's lips curved a little as Loki sighed.

"Are you going to ignore me all evening?"

"No," Erika replied after a few minutes. "But if you're gonna be rude and interrupt me while I'm reading, then you can at least wait while I finish the chapter."

Closing the book and setting it back on the bedside locker, Erika turned her head to glance at Loki. With his hair slicked back, Erika could see all the angles of his features, strong jaw, almost feminine cheekbones that gave his smile a more devil-ish, sinful turn and eyes that held all the possibilities of the nine realms in them. Her heart skipped in her chest. Loki was not typically handsome, yet this man, this god, had charm in abundance and a string of broken hearts to prove it.

He sat in the chair in a relaxed pose, the way he always appeared, but even a tiger looked relaxed before it ripped out your throat. One leg was draped over a denim-clad knee, a soft green knit jumper that looked so soft, Erika wanted to stroke it, covered his upper body, and a cup of coffee was perched in his grasp.

"That's just rude. Showing up to annoy me and not even bringing me coffee."

Loki smiled and clicked his fingers, a steaming hot takeaway cup popping into his free hand. "Of course I would bring you coffee. Come here and get it."

With an exaggerated sigh, Erika slipped off the bed, walking slowly over to where Loki was perched, electricity singeing her fingers as she took the coffee from him. Much like the other night, Erika sank down onto the chair next to him, but instead of putting her legs in his lap, she tucked them under her and slowly sipped her coffee. Once they settled into a comfortable silence, Erika looked out under her long lashes and chewed on her bottom lip.

"Have you nothing better to do than pester me?" she blurted out, unable to take the muted conversation any more.

Draining the last of his coffee, the cup vanished into thin air as Loki clasped his hands together. "I am simply making sure that you are unharmed."

"And I told you before that I can take care of myself."

Resting his chin in his entwined hands, Loki asked. "Is it so hard for you to let someone look after you, General? You injure yourself to protect Ever, but it puzzles you that I may care for your well-being?"

Erika ran her fingers through her hair, clearing her throat. "You don't understand. Since I was five years old, it's been drilled into me that my sole purpose in life is to keep Ever safe. My wants and needs are secondary to that. We are at war, Loki, and war is not kind to most who partake in it. You have lived your entire life as someone who was revered, worshipped, and coddled by most of the Vanir and Aesir.

"You wreaked havoc in Asgard and were welcomed back into the fold with open arms. I was beaten when Ever was hurt on missions, I was chained up and denied food and water when I gave a smart answer. While you had a warm and fuzzy relationship with your adoptive siblings, my sisters hated me for being better than them. The only person who has ever shown me any amount of kindness has been Ever."

"And if I said that I cared?"

Erika tilted her head slightly to the left. "I would find it hard to believe you."

"That is not any kind of life to live."

With a shrug, Erika sipped her coffee, taking time to try and keep her eyes from betraying her cool exterior. "It is what it is."

Loki dropped his smile, his face void of any emotion. "I have lived a thousand lifetimes. I both adore and despise Thor. I love Ever as much as one like me can. I have fathered children and lost them. I have frozen myself off and tried not to care. But what do I have to do to prove to you that I care for you?"

"And if I said I didn't want you to care?"

Loki leaned forward in his chair, took the coffee cup from her grasp and set it down. He slowly slid his right palm up her leg, his eyes locking onto her so that she could see home imbedded in them. "I would say that you do not get a choice. You cannot dictate who cares for you. I would assume that, much to your irritation, those people you work with care for you as well. If you do not let people in, then you become bitter and twisted, a shell of who you used to be."

Erika brushed off his hand, and sat up straight. "Look how well that worked out for Odin. He was fine for millennia, screwing anyone and everyone, adoring the children who were born. And then he fell in love with Frigg. When she died, he became bitter and twisted, using his grief to hunt and kill his only daughter. So, tell me, Loki, each has the same result. I'm better off as I am."

Loki leaned back into the seat, setting his arms down on the armrests. "If Ever survives this, she will be happily mated to the wolf. What will you do then, when the war is won and Ever settles down to have pups?"

Erika flicked her hair off her shoulder. "We are immortal creatures. Someone is bound to start a war, and I will be there to lead the warriors of Valhalla into battle, as it was meant to be. Ever might be a Valkyrie warrior, but she is also my queen. If she decides to retire and have pups, then so be it. She needs to be alive to do so. Let's stop with the hypothetical and just remember that as of now, Ever's future hangs in the balance."

Fingers tap dancing on the arm of the chair, Loki sighed. "But you can stop this mission of self-destruction and stop fighting. How can you protect Ever if we have buried your body?"

Angry with Loki's presumptions that he knew her, body and soul, his words attacked everything Erika thought she was and how she wanted the world to see her. Rising to her feet, she pulled off the tee she had thrown over her fighting shorts and bra and strode forward. Loki did not move from his seated position as Erika stood in front of him.

"You know what?" she asked and climbed into his lap, her knees grazing his hips, her hands snaking up to clasp him by the throat. "I'm sick of talking."

Succumbing to her hunger for him, Erika gave in to the wants her body had been building for centuries. Pressing her lips to Loki's full pout, she nipped lightly on his bottom lip, holding it between her teeth before he opened up and kissed her back.

The moment his tongue lapped against hers, Erika groaned low in her throat and lost herself to the pleasure. Loki slid his hands up to cup her butt in a possessive hold. Erika arched her hips forward, relishing in the harsh growl that rumbled in Loki's throat as she pressed the most feminine part of her against the hardness of his jean-clad erection.

Pulling back from the kiss, she leaned away and grinned at Loki's kiss swollen lips. Slipping her hands from around his neck, she reached under his jumper and traced her hands over the planes of his chest and down his stomach muscles until she cupped him through the fabric of his jeans.

"Do you know how many times I've fantasied about having you in my mouth, defenceless, as I licked and sucked like my very own lollipop? I'm going to indulge in that fantasy right now."

Erika snapped the top button of his jeans and reached inside, Loki's fingers snapping to her wrist just as she was about to slip her hand inside his jeans. She tried to yank her hand away, but Loki held her in place, with his grasp and with an invisible hand on her throat.

"Let me go!" she exclaimed, the emotions inside her threatening to derail her. "Either let me go, or fuck me. Just get it out of your system. Once you get what you want, I won't have to deal with you. Stop being so fucking calm and just fuck me already!"

Horrified as tears began to stream down her face, Loki looked at her with such pity she hated him and herself in that moment. This time, when she yanked her wrist away, Loki let her go. She fled from his lap and faced away from him. Silent tears continued to flow and her body trembled. Loki wrapped his arms around her from behind, a kiss pressed to the side of her throat.

"There is a storm raging inside you, Erika. This turmoil of who you really are and who you think you should be are in constant conflict. You will crash and burn until it is the destruction of you. I do care for you, and as we all know from Odin, it is rather dangerous to give someone as old and powerful as me someone to care about. When I do have you, and I will, I want to be with the Erika that only I get to see; the real Erika."

A fist pounded on the door twice. Before Erika could try to formulate a response, Felix opened the door and stuck his head around the corner.

"Valkyrie, I have a few investors here for an early meeting and they want to see some of my most prized fighters go at it. You up for a fight?"

Loki's hands tightened around her waist, but Erika knew he'd made himself invisible. Stepping out of his embrace, Erika rolled her shoulders and turned to grin at the chaos demon.

"Hell yeah. I'm bored off my tree sitting around waiting for tonight's party. Gimmie a second."

Felix's lips twisted into a smile. "Don't you even want to know who you are up against?"

With a snort, Erika shrugged. "Doesn't matter. I'mma beat their ass anyways. Tell Viv to play track four on my cd."

With a chuckle and his pointed ears twitching, Felix said, "That's what I like about you, Erika. You have no fear. A demon could get very aroused watching you fight."

"A demon better keep it in his pants because the Valkyrie isn't interested."

Felix's laughter echoed throughout the hall as he strode from the door, leaving it slightly ajar, telling Erika she had five minutes. She grabbed a hair tie from the locker and yanked her hair up into a ponytail, tucking the end into a makeshift bun.

Not bothering to tape up her wrists or feet, Erika wanted to feel the pain and fucking own it. She needed to bleed, to feel every punch and every strike and burn away Loki's rejection.

If your mother did not even want to keep you, then why should someone else?

Words are pretty when spoken by a man, but actions speak volumes.

Loki will toss you aside once he has had you, and it will leave you ruined.

"Erika, none of that is true."

Erika spun toward him, her fists clenched. "Stay out of my head, Loki."

Stalking from the room, she tried to reign in the sudden rage that heated her blood, surprised at the growl that rumbled in her chest. Wanting to scream in frustration and anger, Erika bounced on her feet as she came down the hall and paused at the balcony where Felix's investors gathered.

Upon catching sight of her, fingers were pointed in her direction as they exchanged whispers and murmurs about the Valkyrie. Most people never saw one, until the hour of their death that is. And by then, the dead did not care whether you were a mystical creature from legend or an angel to take them to Heaven, they simply wanted not to be dead.

Felix stood in the middle of the octagon, lifting a hand to beckon Erika down. Her music pumped from the speakers, Trapt's "Headstrong", as she climbed atop the railing, a hand on her calf halting her.

"Please do not do this, Erika. I will never ask anything of you again if you stop this foolish quest to hurt yourself."

"Fuck off, Loki."

Erika stepped off the ledge to a collective gasp, and made her customary entrance into the ring, hitting the mat and rolling into a crouch with a snarl. Rising slowly, the crowd clapped, smiles aplenty as they sipped their champagne and waited for the blood to be spilled.

Erika's music cut off abruptly, as Five Finger Death Punch's "White Knuckles" began to play. Not that you could hear it over the sound of the footsteps that thundered down the corridor before bursting into the arena with a roar. An enraged troll, chained at the ankles and wrists, came toward the octagon, its eyes crazed, salvia dripping from its maw.

Trolls were not the fabled creatures who hid under bridges and tended to have a taste for goats. They were seven-feet-tall creatures with skin as green as seaweed, legs as thick as an elephants, and skin as tough as leather. This particular one had hands bigger than Erika's body. Gigantic tusks, longer than Erika's arms, protruded from a flat, wide nose. The troll didn't wear a scrap of clothing, his thorny penis made Erika blink.

Swallowing hard, Erika spared a glance at Felix. "Dude, a troll?"

"I thought you liked a challenge?"

"I also like my head attached to my neck."

Felix quirked a brow. "Want to back out?"

Erika dismissed him. "I never back down."

The troll lumbered into the octagon, and the entire ring shook, groaning from the weight of the beast. The security who wrangled the troll, whipped away the chains, and Felix backed out of the ring.

Erika's mind flashed back to many a time while under the age of ten, she had faced Danae in a fight that often ended with bloodshed. Neither Erika nor Danae had wanted to submit to the other. Danae's brute strength was well matched to Erika's speed and precision. As she had grown, Erika had more than once gotten the better of Danae because the girl had been cocky, arrogant, and under the allusion that being bigger meant she was better.

Erika had enjoyed it every single time she made Danae bleed.

"Valkyrie." Felix's voice dragged her back to the present. "Catch."

Erika's short blades sailed through the air, and she caught them easily. As soon as her fingers wrapped around the hilt, energy sang in her veins. She might be good with a fist or kick, but with a blade in her hands, Erika was deadly.

"Let's go to war!" yelled Felix, and the troll took that as go time. As the troll charged her, Erika flashed behind him and grinned. This expedition was all about showcasing the fights and what went down, so Erika would use all the skills in her arsenal. She sensed Loki watching her and tried to block out his presence.

The troll swung his head wildly, looking for her, screaming so hard Erika had to cover her ears. He lumbered around, spotted her, and charged. Erika waited until the last possible minute, and then she ducked, swiping out with her right hand and then her left, catching the troll in the calf, making him bleed.

The troll shrieked in pain as Erika slid underneath him and backed up against the wire of the ring wall. Running forward, she used her speed to walk up the troll's back and slice one of her blades across his neck, but by the gods, his skin was thick and hard to cut.

As Erika dropped down from his back, the troll lashed out with a meaty palm and smacked her right in the ribs, sending her flying against the mesh wire. She heard the crack as she broke a rib or two. Lungs inhaling hard to compensate for the pain, they burned as she got to her feet, and the troll backhanded her as she tried to get her balance.

The sword in her left hand flew out of her grasp when he grabbed hold of her left arm and shattered the bones from wrist to shoulder with once clench. Erika bit her lip to stop from crying out, staggering back with her left arm dangling at her side. Her shoulder was dislocated, and Erika tried to pop it back into place. The troll came at her again and she thought she was going to die, just like Loki predicated.

A haze of white hot fury sparked in her veins, and she went on a rampage, slicing and lashing out at the troll as he tried to reach her again. Erika ducked and dived, ignoring the agony that burned in her arm. The troll lifted his leg and Erika dodged, but not before the troll stepped on her foot, crushing the bones in her right leg, leaving her unbalanced.

Her ass hit the ring and she scrambled back so that her back was to the wire. Twirling her wrist, Erika flung the blade in her right hand and found her mark, the centre of the troll's forehead, the softest place on its body. The blade went straight through and penetrated the brain, killing him.

He crashed to the ground, falling backward and taking most of the ring with him. The structure collapsed around Erika, and she was jerked along with the ring, her body screaming in pain.

Her vision swam, nausea swirling in her stomach. She heard Felix call her name, heard their footsteps as they tried to get to her, knowing by the time they got to her, by the time her Valkyrie blood kicked in and started to heal the damage, they would all be too late.

Loki's aura engulfed her as something warm trickled from her mouth. She heard Felix scream at Loki, who simply ignored the demon as he carefully scooped her into his arms. She could not understand what Loki was saying, and she lifted a hand to pat his cheek.

Then, darkness became a welcome friend.

CHAPTER TEN

Ricky

O h, he was jonesing. Jonesing bad, those two small pills Ricky had left were burning a hole in his pocket. He hadn't taken a single pill, not even a goddamn painkiller, since Zach had turned up on his doorstep. Ricky's sole focus had been on his son and only his son.

Like little lashes of fire against his skin the powder keg of magic that coiled inside his veins began to lick out. Clenching his fists to stop the tremble in his hands, Ricky leaned against the cold of the wall and watched his son sleeping on his bed.

Having exhausted himself playing with the team, Zach had fallen asleep in Caitlyn's arms and the vampire had carried him down to the underground sleeping area, sadness in those eerie gunmetal eyes of hers. Ricky, loathe to leave his son, had left the team to chase after Kenzie.

Now, as he sank down to the ground, knees bent so that his elbows rested on their edges, the silence frayed his nerves. Doubt plagued his mind, his eyes never wandering from Zach as he tried to figure out how in the hell he was going to parent the kid. It wasn't like Ricky himself was the epitome of responsibility. He tended to live his life on the fringe, and he had no idea how to look after himself, much less a child.

As Ricky scrubbed a hand down his face, sweat drenching the back of his neck and seeping into his hair, he cast his mind back to a time where he was the kind of person who could have raised a child, who had a woman he thought loved him, and he loved in return. Ricky had his whole future planned out, until Sadie had trampled on his heart. The night he proposed had been one of the best nights of his life.

Ricky leaned in the bedroom doorway, his eyes fixed on the woman who had just agreed to be his wife as she lay on her stomach, hand outstretched to admire the ring on her left hand, the sheets covering her from the waist down. It was a small ring, but Ricky did not make much on a young cop's salary and it had taken him twelve months to save up for the modest diamond. He'd known from the very first kiss that he wanted to marry Sadie.

With a smile tilting up the curve of her lips, Sadie cast a glance over her shoulder, the long tresses of her rich, dark hair tumbling off her neck with the movement. She looked at him with such love, it made his heart skip a beat.

"What are you looking at?" she asked him.

"My beautiful fiancée, that's who."

She shook her head as he strode into their bedroom and threw himself down on the bed beside her, lying on his stomach as well. He pressed a kiss to her bare shoulder, a silent thrill inside him as she shivered under his touch. He fucking loved that she still reacted to him like this. He hoped that she never stopped reacting that way.

Sadie ran her thumb over the small cut stone, and he suddenly felt self-conscious as he took hold of her hand and said, "I know it's not the biggest, but if you want to change..."

She lifted his knuckles to her lips. "Stop, I adore it. I was never one for statement jewellery. This is perfect. Stop stressing."

Ricky feathered kisses down her shoulder. With a sly smile on his lips, he glanced into the eyes of his future wife. "Fionn is going to have kittens when he finds out you said yes. I was told under no circumstances was the princess of the pride to marry a warlock."

Shaking her head, she said, "You're enjoying that far too much. Fionn will get over it once he becomes an uncle."

The image of Sadie, belly rounded and carrying his child, popped into his mind and revved his engine. Nuzzling her neck, letting his hands wander down her bare spine, he grinned and asked, "So how many little minions are we going to have? I think I'm going to enjoy trying to get you pregnant."

She flipped over onto her back, giving him better access to her body as she linked her arms around his neck and hooked a leg around the back of his thigh.

"I don't care how many cubs we have, as long as they are happy, healthy, and loved."

He pressed a kiss to her lips. "Our kids will never worry about being loved. No matter what, they will always feel that they are loved."

They made love, quickly and quietly, the only sound their panting and murmurings of love and adoration. When they were sated, they lay in each other's arms, discussing the future and what it might hold.

"Our kids will have normal names," he told her. "They don't need to be labelled with some weird ass name that gets them beat up in school."

"I take it Apple and King are out of the question." Sadie joked, her chuckle as much as a caress as her touch.

"Hell no!" he snorted. "Our boys will have normal names, like Zach, Matthew, or Daniel. For girls, I like Izzy, Zoe, or Caitlyn."

"No matter what they are called, they will be loved. You'll make such a good dad."

Ricky kissed her senseless, eager to start this stage in his life, and be a better man than his da expected him to become. With Sadie, he would have the family life he never had as a boy, raising his children with love.

"Hey."

Derek's whisper broke Ricky free of his memories, and he glanced up at his best friend. Getting up from the ground, he pulled the door of his bedroom closed, leaving it slightly ajar so he'd be aware if Zach woke and was scared.

Reaching for the coffee pot, Ricky's hands shook as he tried to pour himself a cup, all the while Derek studied him like he did any UNSUB who sat in an interrogation. Ricky inclined the cup toward Derek, who shook his head. Setting the pot down, Ricky sipped the lukewarm liquid, trying to avoid the inevitable lecture that only Derek would give him.

Ricky hoisted himself up on the kitchen countertop, leaving his legs hanging.

Derek leaned against the wall between their two sleeping quarters. His friend waited for a few minutes before he said, "So, Sadie was pregnant."

It was a statement rather than a question, and Ricky simply shrugged.

"He seems like a great kid."

"In spite of me, is it?"

Derek sighed and shook his head. "That's not what I meant and you know it. Don't get defensive on me because you are angry and confused and whatever else the hell is going on with you."

"Oh, thank you very much, Derek. Since you ran off without even a mention of where you were going, we had to deal with being short staffed. Caitlyn and Donnie fecking take off to Paris, and then the first goddamn vampire rocked up and tried to start a war with his little Caitlyn-lookalike assassin. It was down to me and Melanie to handle an entire team's worth of stuff."

"But you managed."

Anger rolled through him, like a fire raging through a forest. Ricky knew Derek hadn't said it to anger him, but to acknowledge Ricky's ability to handle things without him.

But Derek was wrong, terribly wrong.

Ricky had never been cut out to lead, that was Derek's jam. Ricky knew deep down he was a good agent. Feck that, he was excellent, but Derek... Derek had that alpha wolf quality, and he probably had when he'd been human, too. Now that he was a wolf, it leaked from his pores like it needed to be known.

When Ricky didn't answer, Derek gave an exasperated sigh, a sound Ricky had become used to since he started working with Derek. His best friend and teammate ran his fingers through his boyband perfect hair and asked, "If it had been Melanie, what would you have done?"

Ricky glanced down at his shoes. "We've been there, remember? I waited like a good little agent for *my team* to figure out where she was before I ran off half-cocked by myself to face God knows what. I went into that building with you to find her... you didn't see me running off by myself into a slaughter house without telling anyone."

"Point taken."

No apologies, just a simple acknowledgement that Ricky's thoughts were valid.

They sat there in a comfortable silence for a couple of heart-beats. Ricky felt his jaw tick as the magic inside his veins began to stir once again, this time with stronger lashes of fire against his flesh, and it took all of his stubbornness not to groan with the pain. It felt as if someone was lighting a dozen matches inside his skin and burning him from the inside out.

Ricky blew out a hiss, slid off the counter and went to the fridge that stood off the side. He took out a bottle of water and drained the whole thing before turning around to see if Derek was watching him, which of course he was.

"How bad is it?"

Ricky shrugged. "I think I could burn down the entire city of Cork and not care that my hometown was nothing more than cinder and ash, if it meant I was rid of it. I never wanted to manifest power like this. I spent my whole life avoiding it, content to use little magic to get the job done. I never wanted to be my father's son."

"That you will never be, Ricky." Derek affirmed. "I met your dad only a few times, mostly with you, and I disliked the way he spoke to you, not even as a son, but the way he disregarded the position you held within P.I.T. There are a lot of people who respected the hell out of you for all that you did, as a rookie and with P.I.T. If you had been my son, I would have shouted from the rafters about how capable and brave my son was."

"I'm not brave, D. I'm simply terrified of being mediocre."

Derek shook his head. "That you could never be. Everything you do, you excel at. Sarge may gripe and yell at you, but he's prouder of what you've accomplished than you can imagine.

Do you remember the first ever case we went out on for the council? Sarge was terrified that you would open your mouth and trouble would spill out...but that didn't happen, did it?"

Ricky leaned against the fridge and closed his eyes, remembering the first time he had laid eyes on his Da in three years.

After getting a massive warning from Sarge not to open his mouth and simply observe, Ricky stood beside his partner, the moody wolf who barely even cracked a smile, and let a mask slip onto his face. His heart beat like a bass drum, the thought of coming face to face with his Da wringing a knot in his stomach.

He swallowed hard as Derek glanced down at him, concern in his eyes. "You okay?"

Ricky just nodded as he stood in the centre of the very room he'd wanted to avoid his whole life—the supernatural council's meeting auditorium. Stepping inside had hit him like a battering ram, and his mouth ran dry. Then his father, Xavier Moore, and Chester Birmingham came out to shake hands with Sarge.

"Tom, it's good to see you again."

"And you, Xavier."

Great, just great. His Da and Sarge were friends; he might as well hand in his transfer papers here and now, because his Da would totally get him fired from the team he worked his ass off to get into.

Sarge introduced them, causing a smirk to curl his Da's lips. Ricky stood ramrod straight while Sarge roamed his eyes from Ricky to Xavier and back again.

"Do you two know each other?"

"You could say that, Tom." Xavier said with a cackle. "I see my son still does not like to tell people which family he belongs to."

As his boss and his partner stared at him, Ricky opened his mouth, surprised at how calm his voice was. "Oh forgive me, Da. I thought I was thrown out of the family for joining the guards? I didn't think you would like me admitting that I was the black sheep of the Moore family. My mistake; it will never happen again."

To Ricky's surprise, Sarge chuckled and clasped him on the back. "Damn, Xavier, I've been waiting for someone to put you in your place for years. Figures it would be your own kid that did it."

Xavier's face almost went purple in rage as Sarge walked around him and asked what they had been called about. Chester, the head of the Cork vampires, a creepy SOB in Ricky's opinion, told them about a theft of some rare spells from the vault where all the rare and valuable things were kept. They stood outside the massive iron door, and Ricky could feel the power the leaked from it.

Chester told them that no one but council members had been in the chamber the day the spells were stolen, and all of the council had passed the truth test with a Griffin. Ricky closed his eyes, his brain raking over all the information he stored, the countless nights he had stayed up reading books about supernaturals and learning every minute detail he could about them. Few creatures could bypass security cameras, magic wards, and fingerprint scanning for entry to the vault. Even less could do all three. That meant the thief had to be one of the council members, or someone posing as one.

"Ricky, son, I see the wheels in that big brain of yours turning. Tell us what you think."

Sarge's words hit him like a goddamn baseball bat. Ricky glanced at Derek, who stood, arms folded across his chest and just nodded. Sarge also gave a brief incline of his head for Ricky to continue.

Echoing the thoughts in his head, Ricky began to lay the crime out.

"The security in this place is top notch. I spied twelve hidden cameras and a few motion sensors, and I can feel the wards underneath the floorboards. The fingerprint scanner means no one but a council member can gain access to the vault. Some creatures could get into the vault with brute strength, yet, that would set off any alarms."

Ricky began to walk around, thoughts swirling in his head. He flipped through his mind catalogue until he found what he was looking for.

Turning to look at Sarge, Ricky grinned. "We're looking for a chameleon. But not just your average chameleon. Either one who can change his or her appearance by touching a photograph, or a chameleon who has been under the nose of the council, close enough to touch each council member and get an imprint of their physiology."

Derek returned Ricky's grin, and Sarge told the council to turn off the heating, lowering the temperature to freezing as chameleons cannot change shape in the cold. It would flush out their thief. Sarge also said that he would send some uniforms to patrol in plain clothes, in case the council needed any more assistance in solving their thief issue.

Derek strode across the floor and motioned for Ricky to follow. As Sarge came up behind him, Ricky spine stiffened as he heard.

"Boy, your mother misses you."

Boy, even now.

Ricky didn't even look back. "She knows where I live, if she misses me that badly."

Legs shaking like a newly born foal, Ricky made it outside before his stomach revolted, and he vomited into the bushes in front of the council headquarters. Wiping his mouth with the back of his hand, he gave a small smile to the two men who studied him.

"Sorry."

"Humph," grunted Sarge. "You have nothing to be sorry about. Never liked the man, like him even less now. Come on, Ricky, let's get out of here."

They'd never spoke of it again, and Ricky was glad for that. It was after that experience that Derek started asking him for a pint after work, involved him in trips to rugby matches with Donnie. Caitlyn also began to be less cold, providing small smiles when he tried to make her laugh. It was Derek who stopped him from drowning when Sadie had cheated. But could Derek help him to keep the demons in his mind at bay this time around?

"Ricky, you need to stop with the drugs." The words were spoken softly, but Ricky heard the order in Derek's voice.

Ricky glared at him. "Can you yank this fucking magic from me? You gonna turn me into a wolf in the hopes this curse in my veins is wiped out? How the hell am I supposed to raise a child when I'm fucked up inside?"

"You can beat it."

"I'm not sure I want to, Derek."

Derek growled at him. "What the fuck is that supposed to mean?"

Slipping his hand into his pocket, Ricky pulled out the small baggie with the two remaining pills and held it up for Derek to see. "When I take these, it's just me, Ricky, in my head. No magic, no dead Da, and no Sadie. There's no voice telling me that I will never be good enough for Melanie or that she's gonna find a nice handsome vamp to shack up with. There's no Xavier Moore telling me that I don't deserve Zach. I'm free from it all."

"Drugs aren't the answer, Ricky. Let Caitlyn or Donnie drain the drugs from your system and get help with your magic. No one wants to lose you like this."

Ricky laughed, and it sounded bitter in his ears. "You don't get it, D. These pills are all that is holding me together. Without them, I'm a ticking time bomb, and I could explode at any time. And this time, you might not get the chance to evacuate the area. I'll take you all with me. I don't want the magic, I never have."

Ricky stormed up the steps without another thought, taking them two at a time before he was out in the open, much needed air filling his lungs. He wanted to scream into the abyss, let go of everything banging around in his goddamn head. He pulled his car keys out of his pocket, barely noticing as drizzle landed on his arms.

Halfway to his chair, Ricky smacked himself in the face. He'd forgotten about Zach.

Yeah, some dad he was going to make.

CHAPTER
ELEVEN

Loki

The moment Erika had killed the troll, the ring imploding around the Valkyrie as the troll fell down dead, Loki had been in the ring, not caring who saw him. He'd gently scooped up Erika, careful not to injury her any further, and vanished with the unconscious Valkyrie in his arms. Now, the woman lay in his bed, above the covers, Loki having tended to her wounds, but still she did not wake.

Minutes had turned into hours as he sat by her bedside, awaiting the beautiful storm of a woman to wake. She looked almost fragile as she slept, though he would never admit it to her. From the very first day he laid eyes on her on the sands of Valhalla, Loki had been captivated by the fierce fire burning within her. He told himself she was far too young to be anything to him and had tried to keep away from the lure of this woman.

Yet, he found that he wanted to visit Valhalla more and more, the disappointment of arriving and finding Erika had gone out to retrieve souls still confused him. It had not been in Loki's makeup to long for something; he usually went and took what he wanted. But it felt different with Erika, as if she were his to protect.

Perhaps she had been right when she said that caring for someone other than yourself only brought heartache and misery. Loki had been born many, many decades before her, and he understood her cynicism, for he had been forced to watch his children persecuted because they were his. He had spent his youth mocked and ignored for being the son of Laufey. After Odin slayed him, Loki was raised in the court of Asgard. Hidden by his father who was ashamed that his son not a frost giant, Odin had taken the boy who looked like a normal Asgardian boy back home to be raised alongside Thor.

Frigg had been a wonderful mother, sitting for hours and hours reading to Loki when Odin took Thor away to be trained as a warrior. They had spoken of poetry and prose, and at night Frigg had kissed Loki on the forehead, just as she had done with Thor.

Loki had used the love Frigg had given him, tucking it amidst the cold and bitterness inside him that made him feel like he was different from the Asgardians he'd been raised with. He tried his hardest to be there for Ever, who had more responsibility on her small shoulders than Thor and him combined. He shared his love of books, and showered her with meaningful gifts.

When Frigg had died, Odin had lost all reason and focused on gaining back any semblance of power he felt he had lost. In the end, Odin had alienated the only family that remained. Even his son, Thor, was horrified at his actions.

Loki had spent his grief causing mischief and havoc wherever he went, sating his body and leaving a trail of heartbreak in his wake. He cared for nothing but his own self-gratification. His children despised him, his brother Thor was exasperated with his behaviour and his sister, Ever, had her own battles to fight.

It was only a mere few months before meeting Erika for the first time that Loki had come across a remote village and bedded the chieftain's daughter, incurring the wrath of her medicine woman mother. This had curbed Loki's appetite for mayhem a little as the medicine woman told him of the path he was heading down.

Loki slipped off the bearskin rug, the young woman rolled over and sighed, content with the vigorous sex they had just had, but Loki was not feeling at all sated. He didn't spare the woman a glance when he exited the hut. He froze when the woman's mother, a medicine woman revered by her people, who was almost as old as Loki, but not quite, confronted him. Skin so dark, she almost became one with the shadows, her eyes reminding Loki of an abyss, like a stairway to Hel. There was power in her stance, and the age she chose to portray had nothing on her true appearance, if the woman remembered her true face at all. Her walking stick rattled in the wind as she snarled at Loki.

"You have defiled my daughter. Now no man will marry her."

The woman's birth language, a smattering of clicks and grunts, sounded harsh, but Loki heard the words only in his mind, translating the language to one he understood. The beads in her hair seemed to move on their own like Medusa's snakes as Loki shrugged, uncaring about his nakedness.

"She should be thankful to have been bedded by a god. No man will ever compare."

The woman shrieked and lashed out her stick, but Loki moved fast enough to catch it in his fist. Her eyes, before a murky shade of blue, now went completely white as the woman cackled, the sound cracking in the air, like some sort of ancient magic clinging to his skin.

"You have always only cared for yourself, Loki, son of Laufey. You think you are a gift among men, and this will never change. But I see what is coming, Trickster, and she will be your unbecoming."

"What do you mean? Tell me, old woman, and tell me now!"

His own power snapped free of his control, whipping and clawing at the woman who laughed as gashes appeared along her bare arms.

"There is one who can set you free or bind you further. She will be all that you wanted and all that you could dream of possessing. A soulmate who will want nothing to do with you, and you will be helpless under her spell. You have power now, but she will be the one who will reveal your true power.

"She will be your end or your beginning. The future is not set, dear Loki. But I shall enjoy watching you suffer, should she decide that you are not for her. Because once you love, and love with all your heart, you will not come back from it."

The medicine woman sank her walking stick into the ground and it shuddered with magic. Loki felt the power of her words deep in his soul. He vanished from that place, never to return, but her words had always stuck by him, especially when he met a warrior with honey whisky hair who made his blood sing mere months later.

Loki had tried to stay away, afraid that Erika would be his downfall, but nothing but death itself could keep him away from her. She scowled far too much for such a beautiful woman, and Loki revelled in trying to get her to smile. His heart hitched the first time he had made her laugh. He'd brought her treats from Midgard, decadent chocolates, sweet smelling flowers, and even a blade or two made from the finest Asgardian steel.

Erika had been suspicious at first, as if she had never received a gift without an ulterior motive. But Loki had coaxed her, so much so that when he arrived on the shores of Valhalla, after a torturous period away, Erika's eyes had betrayed her excitement to see what he would arrive with next, all the while her face a blanket of emotionless expression.

A groan dragged him from his thoughts as Erika shifted in the bed, and Loki bolted upright. He summoned a glass of water, holding it to her lips as she drank, taking it back when she coughed, grabbing her ribs as she did.

"Gods, I feel like I've been hit by a bus."

"It was a troll, so possible same thing."

Erika, stubborn as ever, pulled herself into a sitting position and leaned her head against the wall. "Where am I?" she croaked, clearing her throat as she peered at Loki under tired eyes.

"My bed."

"Oh this is great. First you diss me and dismiss me, then you drag me to your bed while I'm out cold. Doesn't say much about you now, does it?"

"What can I say, when I imagined having you in my bed, you were very much awake and very athletic."

She groaned again, shifting as if to get out of the bed. "Wow, can we just pretend, for one second, that you're not a complete douchebag?"

Letting out a hiss, Erika tried to move the leg that was almost crushed by the troll, and Loki pinned her gently to the bed with his hands on her shoulders. "Damn woman, just stay where you are for a minute. Less than twenty-four hours ago, you were beaten to within an inch of your life. Let me look after you."

Blinking at the tone of his voice, she sighed and rested once more on the bed, not before glancing down at her clean wounds and the shirt she wore. She rolled her eyes as Loki grinned.

"*Up all night to get Loki*...could you not have put me in anything else?"

"Forgive me, Erika. It was the only clean thing in my wardrobe."

"Yeah, whatever you say."

Erika's long lashes brushed her cheeks as she closed her eyes, and for a second, he thought that she was asleep once more, yet her breathing did not change. Coming to the other side of the bed, which was big enough to fit more than a couple, Loki kicked off his shoes, and laid down on the bed, making sure that there was an acceptable distance between himself and her battered body.

He folded his arms behind his head, waiting for her to speak. When she opened her eyes, big, rich-coloured eyes the same shade as her hair, she looked at him and asked, "Did you stay up all night to make sure I was okay?"

"I find it hard to sleep. My mind has a terrifying capability of being dark and tormented. My dreams are rarely pleasant."

"Are you afraid of your dreams?" her voice was merely a breath, an intimate whisper, the unspoken words hidden behind her silence. *Just like me...*

"Yes," he replied quietly, wanting to be honest with her in a way he never was with other people. "More than I would like. I am too old not to be scared. I have seen more than you can imagine. War. Death. Murder. The world changes, but it doesn't."

Loki closed his eyes for a moment, loathe for Erika to see the conflict inside him. When several seconds had ticked by, he felt her tense next to him, clearing her throat as she said. "Loki."

He angled his body so he could look at her without her having to move over much. Her tongue flicked over her full lips to moisten them, and he instantly wanted to kiss her.

"Thank you for looking after me. If you hadn't been there, I'm not sure Felix would have kept me alive. A fighter half dead isn't of much use to him."

Loki reached out, brushed a strand of hair from her face. "I told you that I cared for you, Erika. I would never want to see you hurt."

She stretched out her limbs, and he heard bones crack, wincing as she flexed and moved her muscles. He wanted nothing more than to keep her here, protected from the harm she seemed so keen on inflicting on herself. An image popped into his head, of Erika running a hand over her stomach, smiling at him as she carried his child. It hit him like a battering ram, but not because it was an unpleasant thought. It made his heart swell.

"Why are you looking at me like that?"

"Like what?"

"Like you have sin on your mind."

"When it comes to you, that's where my mind goes."

"Ass." She snorted, a small smile curving her lips.

"I think I like you like this," he admitted.

She quirked her eyebrow. "What? Beat up and unable to flee from your bed?"

"In my bed, wearing my clothes, in my personal space where I have never brought anyone else."

"Yeah right."

Loki turned, sliding over the bed until there was no space between them, his elbows keeping his weight off her still sore body. He held her gaze, which widened as she saw the truth in his eyes. "I have never, in all my years, brought another woman into this loft, let alone this bed. This bed is for the woman I intend to make mine and mine alone. Look at my eyes and know the truth."

Erika sucked in a breath, her hand reaching out and grazing the side of his face. He found he could not restrain himself any longer. He leaned down so that his lips pressed against hers, gentle at first, Loki was fully aware that he had almost lost her mere hours before. That thought sent his instincts haywire and he deepened the kiss as soon as she opened her mouth and welcomed his tongue inside.

His erection strained against the seam of his jeans as Erika sucked on his lower lip. He felt his control slip, almost thankful when a new aura entered his home, stopping him before they were at the point of no going back.

"Oh my gods! My eyes.... I can never unsee that!"

Flopping over onto his back with a groan, Loki grinned at his sister. "Then perhaps you should knock before you barge into someone's private quarters. Another few minutes and you might have seen more of me than you ever wanted."

Erika had covered her face with her hands, causing Loki to grin wider at his woman's cheeks, flushed from their kiss. And, when had that changed, his claiming of her as his own? Perhaps she had been his from the first moment their eyes had met in Valhalla. It took until now to realize he never wanted to let her go.

"Because once you love, and love with all your heart, you will not come back from it."

The medicine woman's words clanged around in his head, but he ignored them. He was not sure if he could love, but if what he felt when Frigg kissed his forehead, read him stories, and listened to his tales, was love, then the same feeling punched his heart whenever he laid eyes on Erika.

"I felt that Erika was hurt and came to find her. I was not expecting to find her in your bed."

"It's not what you think," Erika whispered, and Loki could feel the progress he'd made with his general slipping from his fingers. It made him angry that she seemed ashamed of her feelings for him, because of her loyalty to Ever.

"It's exactly as you think. Erika was hurt, and I brought her here to watch over her. How was your little jaunt? Did you enjoy running away like a coward?"

Ever sucked in a breath, and Loki despised himself a little for putting the hurt look on his sister's face. But Erika needed to have someone fight for her, and he wanted to be man enough to do that.

She put a hand on his arm to stop him. Turning back to Ever, Erika's warrior mask now firmly in place, she said. "So you're back then?"

"I am."

Erika glanced at the clock and scrambled from the bed, letting out a slew of swear words as she put weight on her leg, healed thanks to her Valkyrie blood, but still tender. She put her hands on her hips and asked. "Loki, where are my clothes?"

He held her gaze, his blood heating. "I had to cut you out of them since your leg was crushed and your shoulder was dislocated. Keep the t-shirt. It looks good on you."

Her eyeroll should not be sexy, but to him, it was.

"I need to get back to the arena."

Loki jack-knifed off the bed. "You can't be serious. You almost died."

Erika shrugged, infuriating him. "We call that Tuesday in Valkyrie terms."

"Erika," Ever said. "Loki's right. You can stop with the fights now."

Erika snorted. "Oh thank you, your royal highness, for your permission not to fight. Did you ever consider I might like to fight? It makes me feel more useful than babysitting your ass and then having you run off."

Loki felt her summoning her ability to flash and said, "Erika." When she turned to him, he let his intentions show in his eyes. "To be continued."

"Dream on, babe."

She vanished from his sight, and he turned his attention to Ever, who stood looking at him, her arms folded across her chest. "She'll get herself killed."

"I do not think she would mind at this point in time."

"What are you doing with her, Loki?"

Loki perched on the edge of the bed. "I'm trying to convince her that she can have a life beyond this blinkered idea she has that her life is only designed to shield you. Do you even know her? Or have you spent all of your lives only thinking of what she can do to aid you?"

Ever blinked, surprised at the venom in his words. Truthfully, he was taken aback also, as he had never spoken to Ever like that before. Realization flashed in Ever's eyes and she gasped. "Oh wow, you love her, don't you?"

He made to deny it, deny the emotions that he'd felt for a millennia. But if he was to pursue Erika and pursue her in truth, he had to be honest with everyone, especially himself.

"Is it that obvious?"

"Not before," Ever said with a shake of her head. "Before I thought you wanted her because she said no. But now, now I see it. Your eyes soften when you speak of her."

Loki sighed, resigned to his fate. He needed Erika like his next breath. All he had to do was prove that he was worthy of her, and that this blind devotion to Ever was not all that Erika was.

Piece of cake, right?

———

PUNCHING his fist into the wall, the berserker raged at the missed opportunity to slay the Valkyrie, her body broken and ready for the pickings. That interfering bastard, Loki, had appeared and taken his spoils.

Had he known that Loki, forgotten son of Jötunheimr, had a special interest in the little bitch general, then he would have sated his blood-lust many times over, not waiting for permission to rip her apart.

Now he would wait for his chance. Felix told him he could have her after her next fight and do with her as he pleased, as long as he did it in front of a packed house.

He would rip her limb from limb while that bastard watched, powerless to do anything else.

And he would avenge his master once and for all.

CHAPTER
TWELVE

Donnie

D onnie felt it the moment Caitlyn slipped from their bed, listening as his mate softly made her way across the wooden floor, the pad of her feet barely audible in the silence of the day. Caitlyn didn't even close the door fully, in case the sound would alert him and cause another awkward conversation.

Ever since Kenzie had taken the head of the monster who made her, Caitlyn fell back into old habits, putting an impenetrable wall between her and any emotion that terrified her. The bond between them, the fragile thread that tied them together through blood and spirit, it made him want to touch her constantly. Hell, he'd wanted to do that before. Yet now, when he reached out to tease a curl between her fingers, he goddamn hesitated.

Nightmares still tormented her, and they leaked inside his mind through the bond, but the dreams had shifted, bringing Cain back from the ashes and ripping apart Caitlyn's new family. Even though the bastard was dead, his presence still lingered, at least in her mind.

Donnie had studied Caitlyn as she observed Kenzie. The girl easily smiled and had injected herself into their lives as if she always had been a part of them. The way the former vampire hunter and Melanie had befriended each other was impressive, but then again, Melanie had a way of making everyone at ease.

Pillowing his hands behind his head, Donnie let out a frustrated sigh, trying to stop himself from following Caitlyn and blurting out his frustration. He was not such an insensitive ass that he wouldn't allow the woman he loved her time to adjust, he just wished Cait would let him help her.

Closing his eyes, he cast his mind back to the night they were meant to leave for their little honeymoon, but she refused to go.

"What do you mean you don't want to go?"

Donnie tried to mask the anger in his voice, but hell, his trigger seemed to be minimal right now, which according to anyone he asked was another symptom of his new bond.

With an exasperated sigh, Caitlyn schooled her features before replying. "I did not say that I did not want to go, Donald. I simply stated perhaps it would be best to wait until Kenzie is more settled, and the team is more stable."

He clenched and unclenched his fists, unable to stop the growl in his throat. "Our team has never been stable. That's why we work. Goddamn it, Cait. We deserve this. We earned it."

He took a step toward her, and she took one back, and white rage enveloped him. "You really think I would hit you? Because you turned me down? You really don't know me at all, do you?"

Caitlyn blinked in surprise, seemingly unaware of what she had just done. He closed his eyes and began to count to ten in his mind. He could smell her scent, and it lashed at all of his vampire tendencies. He sensed her coming to stand by him, felt her fingers tentatively touch his chest, and he shuddered.

"*I am sorry.*"

Her other hand came to rest on his bicep, and Donnie's eyes sprang open, red blurring his vision, his fangs elongating at her proximity. A snarl loosened from his lips, but he clamped his mouth shut mid snarl.

He couldn't think when she was near. It was like the resolve he'd built up for the last twenty years had gone up in a puff of smoke, and he was a randy new-born vampire again, dry humping her in the dirt.

"*When I asked you to delay, it was not because I did not want to go. I simply did not want to leave Kenzie so soon, when she has just come home. And perhaps leaving Ricky to his own devices is not such a good idea. We will have time together, I promise.*"

Donnie heard the sincerity in her voice, yet that niggling doubt held firm in his gut. Had she only mated with him to have an out with Cain? Would she have done anything to be free of Cain?

Suddenly, he stepped out of her grasp, and her gunmetal eyes opened wide. Turning away from her, his shoulders hunched while he struggled to remain in control.

"*I need to go,*" *he all but growled, yet made no move to do so.*

Caitlyn's hand pressed against his back, and he shuddered. "*Don't,*" *he croaked out.*

"*Pardon?*"

"*Please don't touch me, Cait. I'm barely holding on here. You touch me, and I'm gonna be inside you, and we can't sort through this. If you are not going to be with me, if you need to break this bond, and me with it, then please don't touch me. Because when I mated with you, I told you I wanted all of you. I can't go back to having bits of you. I can't.*"

He had forced his feet to move, shuffling from the bedroom. He bypassed his own room, knowing that she would not go back to sleeping in her own bedroom, waiting until their new home was complete. Donnie went into one of the spare rooms, furthest away from anyone. He'd made it two steps into the room before his fist punched the wall, cracking the skin on his knuckles, blood seeping from the wound.

Time seemed to stand still as he took his frustration out on the bedroom, smashing furniture and ripping shit apart. He tossed the bed against the wall, heard the wood splinter. Pictures were dislodged from the walls, glass shattered. When he stopped his rage, he peered around at the destruction and groaned.

Sliding down the wall, he sat staring at the blood staining his hands. Heartbeats seemed to pass before a small rap came at the door, and his little sister popped her head in the door.

"You done hulking out?"

Donnie scowled and shrugged his shoulders. Melanie came inside and closed the door behind her, before coming to sit down beside him, resting her head against his shoulder. They remained silent for a good while before he felt her tense.

"I shouldn't be sitting with you like this, should I?"

"Why not?" Donnie asked.

"Don't newly mated vampires get territorial over their mates?"

He let loose a snort. "Cait wouldn't care. Besides, it's only you."

Melanie nudged his shoulder. "Gee, thanks. You really know how to make a girl feel special."

"Yeah, I'm a pro at that these days."

"Will you guys be okay?" He heard the quiver in her voice, and he wanted so much to reassure her, to tell her that they would be fine, but any words he spoke now would be a lie. Because right now, he wasn't sure.

She heard the answer in his silence; however, she chose not to press him. "When I first started working with you guys, when I was terribly human, I was totally in awe of you two. No one told me just how tragic Caitlyn's story was, but you stood by her, like a pillar of strength. You remember that case where young supes were being trafficked into Cork?"

Donnie nodded as Melanie went on. "I had never seen Caitlyn lose her shit like that; she ripped that guys arm off without batting an eye. I watched the whole video, and do you know what I saw? Nobody could calm her down. Not Sarge, not Ricky, not even Derek, but you, the instant you said her name, she stilled. She was blinded by rage because of what was done to her, what she had gone through, and you said her name and that was it."

He could sense Caitlyn listening by the door, but Melanie continued. "I knew then that you guys would make it happen. For a brief second on that video, Caitlyn heard your voice and she got this look. It's the way Derek looks at Ever, the way Sarge looks at Anna."

"The way Ricky looks at you... I still wanna break his legs for that."

"Anyways... moving on. It's an adjustment. Things have changed dramatically in such a small amount of time. Hulk out all you want, but remember how far you've come. This—whatever it is—will pass."

He wrapped an arm around her shoulder and pulled her into a hug. "When did you get so wise, little sister?"

"I was always wise; you guys just listen to me more now that I'm dead."

Donnie had laughed at Melanie's joke and felt Caitlyn stride away from the door. She'd barely touched him since that night, so sleeping beside her was agony. But he supposed that he had asked that of her, and she had only complied. She still responded to his touch when he could not fight the desire to graze her cheek with his knuckles or twirl a curl in his fingers. They slept beside each other every night, but they might as well be sleeping alone.

Throwing off the covers, Donnie pulled on some pyjama pants in case any of the girls happened to wander through the halls. Walking barefooted, he followed the pull of the bond that led him to Caitlyn. He felt her sadness when he paused in the doorway leading into the living room. His mate stood by the patio door looking out at the sunset.

Wanting to stride over, wrap his arms around her waist from behind, and press his lips to the side of her throat, Donnie folded his arms across his chest to hold off the compulsion. The sun was a deep shade of orange as it finalized its decent, the glow shimmering across the darkened sky as night began to take hold. The light caught the fairness of Caitlyn's complexion, her grey eyes almost ethereal in the reflection.

"Did I wake you?"

Caitlyn's words were a low murmur, the first words she had spoken to him directly in a few days. Donnie needed to be blunt and find out how to fix this broken link between them.

"I've never slept well when you're not beside me, even before we mated."

Turning her face in his direction, she gave him a small smile. "You always had a way with words, Donnie."

Donnie shook his head, taking a step into the room. "Nah, never been good with words, but the truth, I'm good at that."

He crossed the room and plonked down on the sofa, resting his arms on the back, feeling a smug sense of satisfaction as her eyes lingered on his bare chest. His fingers gripped the ends of the sofa hard. Thoughts of Caitlyn being very naked crept into his mind, and he cleared his throat, trying to remember that he had things to say.

"Hey, can we talk?"

She instantly stiffened, but came to perch on the end of the sofa beside him. Slipping an arm around her waist, he yanked her into his lap. She let loose a squeal of surprise. He rested a hand on her hip, another on the small of her back. Instantly, her hands went to his chest and he shivered. Her fingers danced over the plains of his chest, a small grin playing with her full lips.

He opened his mouth to speak, but Caitlyn silenced him by pressing her lips against his. She nipped on his bottom lip, and Donnie's hand snaked around her neck as they lost themselves in the kiss, a frenzied clash of teeth and tongue. The objectives fogged from his mind as she slid her delicate little fingers inside the waistband of his pyjama pants and wrapped her hand around him.

He jerked at the sensation of it, and his mouth latched onto Caitlyn's shoulder, his fangs pressing softly against her flesh. At the sound of her gasp, he knew he needed to intervene. If she continued to stroke him like she was, then another day would go by and they would slip back into a tension-filled relationship.

"Cait, stop, we need to talk. I can't think with your fingers on my cock."

She instantly halted her movements, but the devil woman left her hand where it was. He kissed the side of her throat and then said, "I've been doing some research. There's this agency in America that deals with supernatural couples who can't have kids. I think we should go talk to them."

Caitlyn jerked back in surprise. She removed her hand from his pants and tried to shift off his lap. Subtle as a sledgehammer, he was.

"What are you talking about?"

"I see how you are with Zach. I watched pure joy light up your features as you played with him. I supposed it's not something we talked about before... kids. Things are different than they were years ago. We could adopt a child who grew up like me and give him or her a good home. What do you think?"

Caitlyn was up and out of his lap in breakneck speed. "Are you fucking insane? What makes you think I want to adopt a child? You think I can replace the ones I lost that easily? How dare you! How fucking dare you?

She rarely swore, and he couldn't figure out what he had done to make her so mad. "I wasn't suggesting you replace anyone, Caitlyn. Those are your words. I'm trying to figure out what will make you happy. I'm drowning here and looking for a lifeline. Seeing how happy you were with Zach, I wanted to make you that happy again, because you certainly aren't happy with *me*."

Caitlyn's features turned vicious, but before she could speak, a blood-curdling scream ripped through the house from Melanie's room.

Donnie was on his feet and down the hall between one second and the next, Caitlyn hot on his heels. He nearly ripped the door off the hinges as he stormed into Melanie's room ready to make someone bloody.

His eyes fell on Melanie, standing on her bed, clutching at her stomach, her clothing ripped from her, leaving her in nothing but her briefs. Clawing at her stomach, she screamed again. Donnie made to reach for her, but Caitlyn's hand on his arm halted him.

"She is lost in her nightmare, unaware what is real and what is not. Grabbing her may only make it worse," Caitlyn whispered, a haunted look in her own eyes.

Donnie inched closer as Melanie began to beg. "Please, please don't kill me. You don't have to do this. *Please,* Stephen. *Please.*"

Melanie screamed again and sank to her knees, tears streaming down her face. Donnie looked at Caitlyn, helpless to assist his sister. Caitlyn crouched on the bed, her eyes bleeding to red, and spoke in a tone that nearly brought him to his knees also.

"Melanie, hear my voice, listen to me."

When Melanie continued to scream, Caitlyn said in a very stern voice, "Melanie."

A whimper escaped the young vampire's lips, but she stilled.

"Open your eyes."

Melanie's eyes snapped wide at the command. Realizing she was naked, she yelped and pulled the blanket to cover herself. Caitlyn patted her knee under the blanket.

"Are you alright?"

Melanie swallowed hard as Donnie sat at the edge of the bed. "Ya, I think so. They haven't been that vivid before."

"Before?" Donnie said with a raised eyebrow. "How long have you been having these nightmares?"

Having the good grace to look sheepish, Melanie looked at her fingernails. "A while."

"And you did not say a word?"

Melanie glanced at Donnie then back at Caitlyn. "You guys have your own things to deal with. Adding my PTSD to the mix isn't going to help."

If Donnie could have kicked himself, he sure as hell would have. Melanie was suffering in silence and didn't want to disturb them with her own night terrors. They'd let her down, big time.

Caitlyn brushed Melanie's hair from her face. "No matter what is going on, you can always come to us. You should not have to deal with this by yourself."

"I didn't want to burden ye."

Wiping a tear from Melanie's face, Caitlyn replied with a sigh. "You will never be a burden. We did not expect this. You took to your second life as if you were born to be undead. Out of all of us, you seemed in the most control, we did not see this coming."

Melanie pulled the blanket to her chin. "I hid it pretty well, huh?"

"Yes, you did. But, we need to find out why now? And you need to talk to someone about it. You never did tell anyone what happened that night."

Melanie's eyes flashed red. "What's to tell? I was kidnapped, stabbed, touched ...I mean, I died and then I didn't stay that way. There's not much to tell."

Donnie growled at the implications in Melanie's words. "He touched you?"

"Not in the way you're thinking, doofus. Donnelly just implied that he would. I'm fine. I'll be fine."

Her eyes darted to Caitlyn, and Donnie sighed. They'd made a mess of this. Instead of looking after Melanie, they were consumed with their own problems. That stopped now.

"OMG, I can't believe you've seen me naked!" Even now, Melanie was trying to diffuse the situation.

Donnie gave her a big grin. "Ricky's gonna be so jealous."

Caitlyn chuckled and got up. "I think we could all do with some hot chocolate. None of us will sleep any more today. Shall we watch a movie before Donnie and I head off to the fights?"

Caitlyn strode out without waiting for an answer, as Donnie tossed Melanie a tee, turning away from her. "Haven't you two got more interesting things to do than babysit me? I'm solid now."

He let loose a strangled laugh. "Interesting no...stupid, probably."

"What's going on?"

"Not right now. I'll tell you later."

"Tell me now, distract me." Melanie pursed her lips.

He put his head in his hands. "I asked Caitlyn if she would be happier if we had kids."

Silence greeted him, causing Donnie to groan as Melanie slapped the back of his head.

"You idiot! And you said it like that, right? Didn't give her a hint or nothing, just blurted out about kids."

"Yeah, yeah I know. I blew it."

"Dude, you didn't just blow it, you freakin' nuked it!"

He stood, holding out his hand to help her off her bed. "I know. I just don't know how to reach her."

"Caitlyn's entire undead life has been dedicated to avenging her family's murder. Job done. What will she do now, when she is free to do as she wants? You guys have been together all of five minutes, and there you are dropping the kid bomb into the mix. I thought you were smarter than that?"

"Obviously not."

She patted his cheek, her eyes still full of horror. "Grovel. That's all that you can do. Besides, the fact she hasn't ripped you a new one is a good sign. Just learn to use that brain of yours before you activate your mouth."

He tugged her into him, engulfing her into a hug, even as the little vampire began to cry again. He said nothing, simply held her until the tears had run dry and anchored her to the present. Caitlyn came to stand in the doorway, holding his gaze as he mouthed *I'm sorry* over the top of Melanie's head.

Caitlyn gave him a strained smile before she went back the way she had come, leaving him with the feeling that he had stepped back and fallen off the cliff.

CHAPTER THIRTEEN

Erika

"Are you absolutely off your rocker? You almost got killed two nights ago and now you want to take your damaged body and subject it to more trauma? You're immortal, not invincible."

Ever stood in her dressing room at the arena, hands on her hips, her blonde hair pulled back into a ponytail, looking very much like the warrior queen Erika knew and loved. She waved a hand in the air, dismissing Ever's concerns as she stretched out her tired limbs. Truth be told, she *ached*. While most of her wounds had healed, Erika tried to deny the way her legs trembled as she stood. Or the way her stomach revolted as she moved. Even her head pounded like a drum. It was as if she was experiencing the world's worst hangover without drinking a drop.

"I could order you, you know."

At Ever's words, Erika snarled, jumping to her feet and wincing as her bones groaned. "You could. Ever my friend would never dare to order me to do something. But Ever my queen, she's just the bitch to do it. So, are you Ever or are you my queen?"

Erika bowed, sweeping her hand out to the side. It was Ever's turn to growl.

"We are friends, Erika. I don't want to see you hurt. Stop this foolish errand that Freya has set you on."

"In case you have forgotten, I was bred to fight. I was forged on the sands of Valhalla and the blood of the battlefield. I have looked upon the faces of soldiers at their death and felt nothing. I was beaten by warriors for being small until I learned to use it against them. This, fighting, is what I am good at. If it brings us closer to finding Odin's place of sleep, then I will gladly take a beating for the cause, like the good little soldier I am."

Ever rubbed her forehead and Erika went back to stretching. "There is just no talking to you, is there?"

Erika shrugged. "Nope. Besides, now that you have all your memories back, you should remember we had this conversation many times before. Do you recall what happened when I turned ten and Danae wanted to make an example of me on my birthday?"

"You almost died then, too. Of course, I remember." Ever closed her eyes.

Erika thought back to that day on the sun-drenched sands of Valhalla.

"There is just no talking to you, is there?"

Ever stood beside her while Erika waited to face the challenge that had been set down upon her. Grinning up at her best friend and future queen, Erika removed her sandals, the grains of silky sand sliding between her toes. She had dressed simply in a loose pair of pants and cropped top, exposing ab muscles that should not be so defined on a child of her age.

Danae, five years her senior, hated the fact that Ever had chosen Erika to be her general, the one who would lead the Valkyrie army into war at their queen's command. Danae thought that she would be chosen. Her brute strength and capabilities meant that she was the one who most assumed would hold the coveted rank, not some petite girl of unknown origin.

Danae came out of the trees accompanied by Freya, and Erika felt Ever bristle beside her.

"We could stop this now. Simply go off and enjoy your birthday. I'm sure, if we call loud enough, we could try and convince Heimdall to send us to Midgard, and we can walk among the humans. We can have ice cream and soda and perhaps watch a movie. Don't do this, Erika."

Erika turned to face Ever and with a wink said, "You know I never back down from a challenge. Danae needs to respect me, if she is to follow my lead."

Strange words to come from a ten-year-old, yet Erika had not been a child since her mother dumped her on the shores of Valhalla and left Freya to rid the girl of any fond childhood memories. Even now, Erika struggled to remember exactly what her mother looked like, what she smelled like, or even the sound of her voice.

Freya patted Danae on the shoulder before beckoning Erika closer. Danae tried to give Erika a menacing grin, but she ignored her. When Erika stopped shy of Freya, the goddess turned to her. "Are you sure you wish to do this?"

"I am."

"Then so be it. Fight until one of you submits or is knocked out. If I deem it necessary to end the match, for fear one of you may be damaged beyond repair, I will end it. My word is to be obeyed. Do you both understand?"

"I do." They replied in unison.

"Weapons or none?"

"Give the little girl a weapon. Make it a fair fight." Danae taunted Erika, but she was having none of it.

"If it was a fair fight, Danae, you wouldn't have tattled to Freya and would have just faced me on the battle field. But sure, my blades are thirsty. They might as well feast on your blood."

Danae growled, reaching for the axe that Rebekah handed to her. Erika held out her hand and felt Ever press Erika's own sword into her hand. It was a handy blade that split in two in battle. Rotating her wrist, Erika drew a line in the sand and closed her eyes.

Danae lunged for her, but Erika was quicker off the mark, side stepping the blow so that Danae's ax cut only the sand at her feet. Erika continued to keep her eyes closed, despite Ever's shouts to open her eyes.

Erika had to show Danae that she could beat her, even with her eyes closed. Danae came at her again, and Erika dropped to the sand, pressing the hilt so that the blades split apart. As Danae stumbled over her, Erika held the blades out to the side, the sharp edges angled so as not to injure Danae too gravely.

The brutish Valkyrie crashed to the ground with a howl and Freya let out a sigh, obviously hoping her star pupil could best Erika. Yet she had not.

Freya clapped her hands once to signal the end of the fight, having seen enough. When Erika cast her attention in Ever's direction, an angry Danae lifted her axe and lashed out.

Erika ducked on instinct, yet Danae managed to clip her across the head with the wooden handle of the ax. Ears ringing, Erika sank to the ground, nausea rolling her stomach. A second later, she got back up.

Danae dropped the ax when she realized the gravity of her actions. Legs wavering, Erika launched at Danae, her fists punching until a strong arm pulled her off her fellow Valkyrie.

Freya deposited Erika into the sand and pulled Danae up by the neck.

"And that is why you will never be general. You cannot take defeat. Erika could have hurt you far worse. Now get out of my sight before I teach you a lesson in restraint."

Danae scrambled away from the beach. Erika spat out her blood on the sand, her ears still ringing. In the height of her slight confusion, Erika almost thought she heard Freya mutter, "Like father, like daughter" as she strode away without even acknowledging her own daughter.

When Erika opened her eyes, Ever had taken a seat in front of her, legs crossed and hands resting in her lap. Erika grinned. "I was a badass, even back then."

Ever burst out laughing. "Oh, how I have missed you."

"I missed you too."

Before Ever could respond, Erika leaned in, cupped Ever's cheek, and pressed her lips to Ever's. For a brief moment, Erika thought Ever would kiss her back. That Ever would respond in a way that Erika had dreamed of, but her best friend pulled back. Ever's look of pure dismay sent Erika's heart into tatters.

She bolted to her feet, her cheeks flaming in embarrassment. She tried to scramble from the room as fast as inhumanly possible, yet Ever barred her way.

"Hey, what was that?"

"That was a kiss, Ever. Perhaps I should have a word with your boyband since he's not doing it right."

"But you kissed me? Why?"

"Because I'm in love with you, stupid!" Erika yelled, her voice carrying over the silence.

Ever clasped a hand over her mouth, her eyes widening, and Erika could almost taste her best friend's revulsion. Refusing to let Ever see her cry, Erika turned away to face the door, tears pricking her eyes.

"You aren't in love with me, Erika. You love me. There's a difference."

Erika spun around and got right up in Ever's face, jamming a finger into her chest. "Thank you for telling me how I feel, Ever. Damn, it must be a goddamn family trait, along with dissing and dismissing me. I'm not surprised Loki beat you to it, though. Who'd have thought that the manslut could refuse anyone? Well fuck you, Ever. Go fuck off!"

Going into a fight angry was never a good idea, but Erika bull-dozed her way out the door, ignoring Ever's pleas to wait. Erika didn't even bother stripping and simply waited for her music to play. She jumped over the edge of the balcony and landed in a crouch as Felix announced who and what she was.

"And, introducing her opponent, I give you the infamous vampire slayer of Paris, forged in the depths of The Catacombs by the very first of his kind. She comes to us with something to prove, but can she take out our reigning queen of the ring?"

Cheers erupted around the arena, like hounds baying for blood. Meek Mills', "I'm A Boss" pounded from the speakers. Erika did a double take at the young girl of about seventeen sauntering down to the ring with Chester Birmingham, the creepy head of the Cork vampires, at her side.

Stepping into the octagon, the girl didn't even flinch as the gate slammed shut and the crowd began to chant. With her hair pulled back off her face, Erika thought of how much she looked like Caitlyn and remembered that the vampire had also been remade by the monster of Paris. This girl was an obvious imitation of Caitlyn, right down to the almost black of her eyes, yet this girl's heart still beat, because her face was flush.

Erika cracked the bones in her neck and grinned at her opponent. She could sense someone's eyes on her and looked up to see Ever watching from a spot on the balcony.

The girl was talking to her, but Erika blocked out her words. The holler went up to go to war, and Erika did just that. She speared the girl, taking her to the ground in one move, trapping her in an arm lock, and then yanking back. The girl let out a scream of pain before pulling her knees to her chest and rolling out of it.

Erika crouched low, a snarl twisting her lips. The raven-haired girl crouched to face her.

"Damn you're pretty. It's almost going to be a shame to break your face," Erika said, grinning as the girl flinched.

"Erika, I'm Kenzie... your team sent me to find you."

Lost in the fight, Erika grabbed the girl, who got in a few kicks to Erika's ribs. They each got in a punch or three, and a few hard kicks to the stomach. When the girl landed a hit to Erika's still fragile knee, pain singed the bones. She lost the thin hold she had on her rage and decided not to play nice anymore. She was sick and tired of being every immortal's punchbag. Her blood pulsed in her veins as she caught the girl by her neck and flung her against the wall of the cage.

The crowd around her cheered, and Erika held out her hands. Her opponent rose, and Erika applauded the girl's resolve. She bounced on her feet and feigned to move to the right, but Erika saw the movement in her mind. As the girl came at her, Erika clotheslined her with such force, she was surprised that she didn't decapitate the kid.

The girl hit the ground with a thud, and Erika dropped into a straddle. She put all of her anger, all of her embarrassment, and every bit of wavering strength that she had and laced into the girl. Erika felt bone shatter under the force of her punches, felt the blood splash against her face, and heard her name being shouted over and over again.

The girl had tears in her eyes as Erika coiled her fist to punch, but that did little to stop her. Erika slid off the girl and grappled her into a headlock, poised to snap her neck, bloodlust over taking her senses. The girl's breathing was ragged–probably a few broken ribs–when Erika caught sight of Caitlyn clutching the mesh fence, anguish on her face.

"She's my niece, Erika! Please don't kill her!"

Caitlyn's niece?

With a startled gasp, Erika dropped the girl, and Caitlyn rushed in to tend to her. Erika sank down to the ground, blood dripping from her hands. Oh gods, what had she nearly done? She had lost control and nearly killed a teammate's family. She was a monster. She was just as bad as the ones she hunted and unworthy of the title of Valkyrie.

Donnie crouched down in front of her, and she jerked back.

"Hush, little Valkyrie. I'm not going to hurt you. We don't hurt our own."

Erika couldn't stop her gaze from wandering over to the bloody body of the girl she'd almost killed. Seeing where her gaze went, Donnie simply said, "You didn't know who she was. No worries."

Ever stepped into the octagon at that moment, and Erika held her gaze for a few seconds before she willed herself away from the arena, away from anyone else before she could hurt them.

Erika flashed to nowhere specific, shuddering as she found herself in Loki's loft. Standing in his living room, blood dripping on his Persian rug, Erika let out a sob that had Loki rushing from the kitchen. At the sight of her, he dropped the tumbler he was holding and came to her.

"Erika, where are you hurt? What happened?"

"It's not my blood."

Those eyes filled with galaxies held her gaze, a small smile tugging at the corners of his mouth. "I should hope not. Come now, love, let's get you cleaned up."

Erika allowed herself to be steered toward the bathroom, stood dripping blood on the porcelain floor while Loki filled the giant bathtub. Erika barely moved as Loki stripped the bloodstained clothes from her and nudged her into the bathtub.

The warm water nearly wrung a groan from her, but Erika's body began to rebel, trembling. She had never felt as vulnerable as she did right then, but it saddened her that she had nowhere else to go.

He began to run a cloth over her skin, having somehow rolled up the sleeves on his shirt. She shivered, but she wasn't sure if it was the shock or his touch.

As he sat on the edge of the bathtub and began to wash the blood stains from her face, she lowered her lashes.

"I'm sorry for dripping blood on your expensive rug."

He chuckled in response. "No need for apologies, love. But you scared me half to death appearing like a modern-day Carrie on my doorstep."

"Sorry."

Cool fingers tipped up her chin. "No more apologies. I mean it. Or I might get cross."

She sighed, but kept her mouth closed.

"Are you going to tell me whose blood you swam in?"

She peered up at him and said, "I got angry. I kissed Ever and she rejected me. So, I beat a girl almost to death. Turns out, she's Caitlyn's niece. Turns out, I don't take rejection well."

"I see."

Erik's brows kicked up. "I see? That's all you have to say."

Loki leaned away from her. "I'm partially to blame for your rage. I have no right to offer any reproach. Did it make you feel better? Beating the girl within an inch of her life?"

"No," she said with a shake of her head.

"And how did you feel when you kissed Ever? Were you angry because it wasn't what you imagined or angry that she rejected you?"

Erika sank lower into the water. "I didn't exactly have time to consider my motives."

"I see."

She threw some bubbles at him, but he only chuckled.

"And if I might pry, how did you feel when I said no?"

She blinked at his bluntness. "Why do you want to know that?"

He folded a knee onto the edge of the bathtub. "I do not understand human emotion fully. I take what I want, what gives me pleasure. I want to know if your reaction to Ever's rejection differs from when I did it. Then I might understand you more."

She hesitated with her answer, her heart hitching slightly as this beautiful man tried to figure her out. Hell, she wasn't sure she could figure herself out, let alone have him figure her out. Thinking on it now, she had felt little when her lips met Ever's, yet her entire body heated whenever Loki was near.

Did that mean she was really in love with Loki?

"The rejection hurt more because I expected it. But, I think I was angry that I felt nothing when I kissed Ever. Not like I do with you."

A smug smile tugged at his lips. "I see."

Erika pointed a finger at him. "If you say 'I see' one more time, I'm gonna snap."

Loki touched his finger to her nose. "You are just so cute when you are angry."

"Oh, you think I'm cute when I'm angry? Well get ready, I'm about to be fucking gorgeous."

He burst into a fit of laughter, as she growled. She pulled him down into the water, and he landed on top of her in the bath. She kissed the hell out of him, her lips hungrily taking in as much of him as she could, fire igniting her entire being.

Just as he reached for her, she flashed from the tub, standing naked on the tiles as she winked and blew him a kiss. The heat in his eyes almost melted her bones.

Perhaps everyone had been right. She loved Ever, but could she let herself love an immortal who might grow bored of her and leave, breaking her heart in the process? This thing with her and Loki, it was dangerous. If she loved him and he went elsewhere, then another person she had opened her heart to would have deserted her.

Erika needed time to gather herself. "Thanks for the rub down, babes. I'll see you soon."

"Don't you dare, Erika. We have something to finish."

She shivered under the promise in his words. She winked again, grinning as she flashed from Loki's home, unaware that the god knew so many swear words.

CHAPTER
FOURTEEN

Melanie

Melanie waited until the sun had barely set before she escaped the confines of Caitlyn's home, having been told sternly to take the evening off after Caitlyn and Donnie bore witness to the nightmares that had begun to creep into her dreams whenever she tried to sleep. The worry in the two vampires' eyes made her feel utterly guilty, considering they had their own issues at the moment.

Since becoming a vampire, Melanie had been totally absorbed in learning to control her lust for blood, adjusting to her new lie detector abilities, and becoming a fully-fledged member of P.I.T. It left her with little time to think about what had happened to her. Which, Melanie thought, was perfectly fine with her.

Walking through the suburbs of Cork City, the crisp evening air against her skin, Melanie adjusted the collar of her denim jacket, simply for something to do. At this time in the evening, people, finished with work, were strolling around, taking in a nice evening stroll before the weather became too Irish. Melanie came to a halt at the traffic lights in Togher, where if she went right, it would take her down to the station.

Since she'd been effectively banned from work for the night, she veered left instead and headed down the road. At first, when the nightmares began to seep in, she had been able to stop herself from reacting. However, over the last few weeks, the dreams had become more vivid, resulting in her outburst today. What she found hard to comprehend was why the dreams scared her. She was fine with what happened to her. Well, not fine, cause she like legit died, but becoming a vampire... it had been everything she wanted in life, to be special, to be supernatural.

Somehow, despite her acceptance of her new vampire status, Stephen Donnelly had managed to creep into her subconscious and remind her of the things that had happened while they were alone.

Her entire body ached and Melanie groaned, coming back to consciousness slowly. Fire ignited her arms when she tried to move, and she cried out. What was happening? Where was she?

Blinking her eyes a couple of times, she felt a warm liquid trickle down her face. The fogginess in her mind began to clear. Stephen Donnelly had blind-sided her in the hospital carpark and hit her on the head. Taking in her surroundings, she glanced around as much as she could, realizing that she was suspended from the ceiling, her bare feet atop an old desk chair. Oh, and she was naked as the day she was born.

The room holding her was in an old telecommunications building, long ago burnt down in an arson attack. The wooden floor was rotten with numerous holes. It didn't look very stable to walk on, so Melanie was unsure how Donnelly had managed to drag her across the floor and hoist her up from the ceiling. The desks and chairs were nothing more than charred remains. When Melanie took in a breath, she could almost smell the burn in the air.

The door to the room opened, and Melanie struggled in earnest as Stephen Donnelly came into view. The moment she began to struggle, panic lodged a wedge in her chest, agony ripped through her body, and she cried out again.

Eyes widened in terror, she watched the inhuman smile creep over his lips. In Donnelly's eyes, she saw her death.

"It is futile to struggle, Miss Newton. There is no way anyone so human could escape those binds."

"Please, let me go. I'm nothing special. You can let me go."

Donnelly came farther into the room, the glint of the knife in his hand catching her eyes. She swallowed hard, her throat burning at the dryness.

"But you are special, Melanie." Donnelly began, his eyes darkening. "You are very special. Those with powerful abilities consider you theirs. She will come for you, and then I will become special, too."

Melanie didn't have a clue who the woman was that he was referring to, but he was wrong, oh so very wrong. The team would mourn her, or she hoped anyway. Yet, they would move on... until she was a distant memory of the tech girl they used to know.

As if she accepted her death, she couldn't help but wonder if her parents would come to her funeral. Would her brothers take time out of their lives of crime to say goodbye to the sister they barely acknowledged when they all had lived under the same roof?

A tear slipped down her cheek, and Donnelly reached out to wipe it away before plunging the knife into her stomach.

Melanie screamed and continued to scream as he slowly pulled the knife out, only to slide it back in at another location on her stomach. She screamed until her throat ripped, and it came out a hoarse croak.

Blood seeped from the wounds, and she glanced down and began to cry in earnest.

"Please, please don't kill me. You don't have to do this. Please, Stephen. Please."

Melanie had never begged for anything in her life, but she sure as hell wasn't proud enough to not beg for her life. She wanted time; she wanted to live.

"Oh, you are going to die, Melanie. For that I am truly sorry. But we all die in the end, us humans, just some sooner than others. I do hope your warlock gets to say goodbye before you are dead."

He drove the knife in again, and Melanie heard it slide through her flesh, felt when the blade scraped against the bones of her ribs. Then, the pain made her black out.

Opening her eyes, Melanie heard herself growling and noticed people avoiding her as much as possible. She was planted in the middle of the footpath. Obviously, people didn't want to walk around a pissed off vampire.

Seeing a mother usher her child into their car, eyes weighed down with fear, Melanie muttered a quick apology before picking up the pace with her head down. Only when she had walked a few steps away did she pick up a familiar scent. It lured her into the amenity park.

The park was nearly empty at this time in the evening; the swings and slides abandoned for a warmer climate. But Ricky balanced himself on the back of a bench, his son scrambling over the bars with the grace of a cat. Standing in the gateway leading into the park, she watched Ricky scrub a hand down his face. He looked exhausted, but now Melanie knew he was using drugs to suppress his magic and things had taken a sinister turn in the road.

As if sensing eyes on him, he glanced in her direction and smiled, the light filling his eyes for a split second before they darkened again. Melanie strode into the park, taking a seat on the bench next to him. They sat in comfortable silence for a few minutes before he spoke.

"You been benched as well, vampire girl? Or have you been sent to keep an eye on me?"

Melanie shook her head. "I've been benched as well. Went for a walk to clear my head. Purely coincidental that I came across you two."

Ricky ran a hand through his hair. "I know why I got benched, but why did they bench you?"

She shrugged. "It's not important."

"Humour me."

She ground her teeth together. "I've been having nightmares reliving the night Stephen Donnelly killed me. Caitlyn and Donnie found out that I've been keeping it a secret and said I needed a night off."

"How long?" he growled.

"Couple of weeks," she admitted, unable to hide the guilt in her tone.

"Damn it, Melanie. Why did you not tell someone? Out of the lot of us, you were the one we didn't need to worry about!"

She raised a brow. "Oh, and while you were off experimenting with ways to cull your magic, did you bother to share that with the class?"

He flinched, yet held his tongue. She sighed, more out of habit then necessity.

"I'm sorry. I shouldn't have said that."

He nudged her shoulder with his own. "Nah, we good. I was being a prick."

Turning his attention back to Zach, Melanie followed Ricky's gaze. The little boy swung around on the monkey bar, and almost dropped. Ricky was out of his sitting position in a heart-beat, but the cat managed to land on his feet. Zack looked in their direction with an amused look on his face, and then gave a tiny wave to Melanie before he proceeded to climb back up the bars.

Slumping down on the bench beside her, Ricky scrubbed a hand down his face. "I'm not sure I can do this," he said in a hushed whisper.

"Do what?" Melanie asked.

"Be his dad. Have this responsibility. I can barely look after myself, let alone a kid. I walked out of the bunker earlier on when he was sleeping and forgot him. I got angry at Derek and stormed off, and I forgot about my son."

Melanie's heart ached for him. "You got in a fight with your best friend and stormed off, but you didn't leave him alone. Derek was in there with him. Derek would lay down his life for you and your son. In the back of your mind, you knew Zach was safe or you'd never have left."

"Like I thought you were safe and left you?"

She pivoted her body so her knee rested on the bench as she faced him. "What happened to me was not your fault. I stormed off to have a pity party because you were right. I wandered off because you said that I could get hurt, and guess what? I did. If you hadn't begged Caitlyn to make me a vampire, then I'd have spent the last few months rotting in a grave."

Ricky shuddered, but Melanie continued. "You will be a brilliant dad because, like me, you know what it's like to have a crap parent. You will do everything, and I mean everything, in your power to be there for him. You won't be perfect, but that's okay. Because Zach needs to know it's okay not to be perfect, and that you will still love him. Got it?"

"Yes Ma'am." He saluted her and smiled.

"If only you were this agreeable all the time," she replied with a grin.

Ricky's face went serious as he said, "I need to go somewhere... will you come with me?"

"Sure."

With a nod, he stood, reaching out his hand to help her up. He whistled for Zach, who bounded over to where they stood.

"Hey Zach, we need to make a little house call before we head home. Melanie's gonna come with us, if that's okay?"

"Sure," the little boy said with a shrug and began to make his way over to Ricky's car. Without so much as a word, Zach slipped into the backseat. Melanie got into the passenger side, and they drove in silence. Melanie looked out of the window, watching the world go by.

They drove towards the airport, zipping past Caitlyn's house, before Ricky veered off to the right and Melanie's jaw almost hit the ground. In front of her was a sprawling estate that resembled her own childhood home. It was lavishly kept, the lawn mowed and the house in pristine condition. Ricky rubbed the back of his neck as he came to a stop, his skin flushing.

In order to save him any more embarrassment, Melanie glanced at him and smiled. "Be thankful that your mom hasn't a taste for gold. We had a golden fountain in our front garden."

She got out of the car and waited until Zach exited before closing the door. Ricky stood with his back to them, inhaling a deep breath and exhaling it. The door to the house opened, bathing them in light as an older woman stepped out onto the gravel.

"Richard?"

Ricky dropped his head as the woman came closer, and another figure stood in the doorframe. Melanie clasped a hand over her mouth as Ricky began to sob, the woman wrapping her arms around him and holding his head against her shoulder.

"Shh, it's okay, son. You're okay."

His mom? Now that she could see the woman's face, she saw some resemblance, especially around the eyes. Hair brandished with a few strands of grey, the woman had the typical mom look about her, a proper mom that is. Her eyes were heavy and puffy as if she'd been crying, and Melanie could smell a sadness in her scent. The woman lifted her head and gave Melanie a smile that was all Ricky.

"It's cold out here, my dear. Why don't you take the child in out of this night air, and we will follow you inside?"

Ricky stepped out of his mother's embrace and beckoned Zach over, leaving Melanie to stand there feeling left out. As soon as Ricky scooped Zach into his arms, Ricky's mom gasped and reached for the boy, who quickly ducked his head, hiding behind Ricky's hair.

"It's okay, Zach. This lady here is my mom. Your grandmother."
To his mother, he smiled. "Mom, this is Zach. We've only just
met, but I thought he could make you smile, like he has me."

Gathering her composure, Ricky's mom patted Zach on the
shoulder. "Hello, Zach. Let's go inside by the fire where it's
warm."

Ricky's mom ushered them inside, Melanie hesitating as she
felt that her presence might be interrupting a family moment.
Kicking at the gravel, Melanie made to leave, giving them the
space they need.

"Lanie? You coming?"

The tone in his voice. Fear and a little bit of uncertainly.
Melanie did the only thing she could; she followed them in. A
sullen looking man stood at the end of the stairs, his lips
pressed together in a firm scowl.

"Killian, put the kettle on. That poor girl must be frozen."

"She's a vampire, Ma. She's dead and doesn't feel the cold."

Melanie flinched at the man's words, and Ricky growled.
"You're lucky that I'm holding your nephew, Killian, or I swear
to god, I'd punch you."

They continued into the sitting room, where Zach proceeded to
burst into an array of shimmering lights and a black cat clambered out of Ricky's arms and straight into Melanie's lap as she
sat down. Melanie rubbed the cat behind the ears and he
purred.

"I'm sorry for Killian, my dear, he has taken his father's death
hard. It's a pleasure to meet you."

"And you, Mrs. Moore."

"Call me Diane."

Ricky stood in front of the fire, his hands clasped behind his back, facing away from them. Diane chatted away to Melanie, as if she understood that her son needed a few minutes to compose himself before they spoke.

Killian came in, his features so similar to Ricky's, yet his eyes held no warmth in them, and set a tray on the table with a teapot and a few mugs. When Diane went to fill a cup for her, Melanie's stomach sank even as Killian began to smirk.

"Mom, Melanie's a new vampire ...she's more likely to take a bite from the kid than drink your tea."

Melanie hissed in a breath as Ricky spun round, Killian vanishing out the door with his brother striding across the floor to go after him.

"Leave him, Richard."

"Little upstart needs to learn some goddamn manners." He looked at Melanie. "You okay for a sec?"

"Sure. But there's no need to defend my honour. It's not the 1950's."

Ricky snorted, but he was smiling as he walked out. When Melanie looked back at Diane, the other woman had a broad smile on her face. Melanie smiled back.

"It does my heart good to see him with such a strong woman."

"Oh, um...we..." Melanie stuttered, before clearing her throat and starting again. "We're not together."

"You will be. A mother knows when someone is right for her son. He needs someone who will argue with him. Someone who doesn't let him get away with retreating into himself. I think you wouldn't let him get away with much."

Melanie really didn't know how to answer that, so she said, "I'm sorry for your loss."

"Thank you dear."

They lapsed into silence. Zach fell asleep in her lap, and Melanie continued to slowly trace her thumb along his ears.

"I've always wanted to be a grandmother," Diane said softly as she watched Zach sleep, before lifting her head to meet Melanie's gaze. "Can you handle the fact that Richard has a child? Can you accept that the boy is not yours, and if you and Richard become an item, can you be there for them both? I need to know."

Melanie considered her words, but didn't have to think much on it. "The fact that Ricky has a kid has nothing to do with how I might feel about him. I've known him since I was alive, and I'm only here today because of what he did to ensure I would be around. Ricky is smart, funny, and a pain in the ass sometimes, but he is loyal and dedicated. If only he would take his head out of his ass and realize he doesn't have to carry this weight by himself, then I'd like him a whole lot more."

Diane laughed and nodded. "You'll do, my dear. You'll do."

A commotion sounded in the kitchen, and they both peered at the door, when a mighty crash sounded. Melanie set Zach on the couch cautiously and raced out of the room, following the sounds of a scuffle.

Ricky had Killian pinned to the fridge, his right hand engulfed in blue flames that he kept slightly away from Killian's face. Killian tried to lift an arm, obviously wanting to use his own magic to defend himself.

"Boys, you stop this right now!" Diane screamed, but the two idiots ignored her.

Melanie was aware of Zach creeping in and standing beside Diane, now in human form. In order to prevent a family crisis, Melanie strode over and put a hand on Ricky's arm, ignoring the flames that licked up and down, and leaned into his ear.

"You need to back off, Ricky. Your son is watching you. Killian might be a dick, but he is your brother. Don't use me as an excuse for your grief and anger. C'mon, be a good boy and let the dickhead go."

As soon as Melanie stepped back, Ricky dropped Killian, strode over to his mom, and kissed her forehead.

"You'll stay here tonight, all of you."

Zach slipped his hand into Diane's, and the woman nearly melted. She lifted the naked boy into her arms as he yawned, and told them she was going to put him to sleep in Ricky's old room. Killian followed her out with a grumble, leaving Melanie alone with Ricky.

She saw it in his eyes when he was about to lose it. When the weight of everything crashed over him and he wanted to run. He walked over to her, kissed her forehead like he'd done his mother, and said, "Tell her I'll be back in the morning."

And then, before she could reply, Ricky was gone and Melanie had her phone out, urging Derek to pick up.

"Derek," Melanie said, her words rushed. "I think Ricky's about to do something very, very stupid. Can you come get me? I'm at his mam's."

FREYA STOOD on the shores of Valhalla, barking orders and in a terrible humour. Word arrived that Ever had returned to Cork, but she had yet to come and speak with Freya. Neither had the general. It irked Freya that people were not following orders. The remaining Valkyrie in Valhalla were good little soldiers for the time being, more under her influence than her own daughter and the meddlesome girl who was her daughter's closest friend.

Freya had known that Erika was trouble the moment her mother had brought her to Valhalla, yet Freya was loath to cast away a perfectly good warrior. It was harder and harder to recruit those to the cause, most feared the wrath of Odin.

The sky suddenly darkened, thunder rumbling so loud it was all Freya could hear. It ripped through the sky as a cloaked figure landed in the sands, his aura almost as strong as his father's was.

Hair the colour of a fox's pelt and a face so stern it made Freya's knees tremble, Thor Odinson rose from his crouched position, his red cloak flapping in the wind. Muscular and broad in build, Thor held thunderstorms in the blue of his eyes. His body was coated in the finest Asgardian metal, impenetrable and durable, the emblem on his chest marking him of the Royal house of Odin.

He gripped his hammer, the mighty Mjölnir, its strength, along with Thor's, was legendary. Looming over her, the god of thunder stretched to his almost seven-foot height.

"Tell me where my sister is, woman," he demanded, his voice almost as loud as the thunder that boomed around her.

Freya hissed at the demand, never comfortable with the way the Aesir looked down upon the Vanir. "Your sister—my daughter—is in Ireland in the county of Cork with that nuisance you call a brother. Go and lord over them, Thor, be gone from my island."

"Father is awake and will soon wreak havoc on the world. We do not have time for niceties, Shieldmaiden."

Thor lifted Mjölnir in the air, summoning the lightning into his hammer. He flew through the air and was lifted off the sand a second later. The sky cleared and the sun returned, leaving Freya standing in the sand, little Marya coming to stand beside her.

"Was that who I think it was?" she asked, amazement in her voice.

"That was a bad omen, child. A very bad omen."

CHAPTER
FIFTEEN

Erika

E rika had returned to her home, the little apartment above Ever's garage, and dressed in combats, a vest and sturdy boots, considering her next action. She wanted to go and see if the girl was all right. Guilt weighed heavily on her. Avoiding Ever was also a high priority while Erika came to terms with the implications, or lack thereof, of the kiss they shared. It was strange that she felt mortified over her actions, and that her heart did not skip, her blood did not heat, when their lips had met.

Quite the opposite of when Loki had kissed her. Gods, while he tended to her–not once, but twice–Erika had felt more in those encounters than with any lover before. And, they hadn't even done anything interesting yet.

Perhaps, all this time, the love she shared for Ever, the protectiveness she felt toward her best friend, was simply that–the love a person had for family. Erika had never experienced that, and the bond between her and her mother was a distant memory. Freya wasn't exactly the warm and fuzzy type, either. Had Erika really mistaken the fact that she loved Ever, as a sister and a friend, and warped that into thinking she was in love with Ever? It was easier than considering that Erika had little else in her life.

Loki had never lied about his desire to bed her. He'd even indicated that she was the only woman to sleep in his bed, to visit his loft. He cared for her without expecting anything in return. Was it that simple? The answer to that scared the freakin' hell out of her.

She knew she was stalling, not wanting to face the consequence of her actions. Flashing to Caitlyn's home minutes later, Erika traipsed back and forth outside the door, lifting her fist to knock numerous times, but hesitating. What if they hated her? They weren't exactly fond of her before, but now she'd almost killed a family member. Pulling out a packet of gum, she popped the apple flavour treat into her mouth as she paced.

Blowing a bubble, she cursed herself for her stupidity, because there wasn't a hot hope in Hel that Caitlyn would welcome Erika inside their home after what she had done. She understood that her actions had consequences and considered that if Caitlyn had not broken through Erika's haze of rage, then that girl would be dead. Adding the fact that she had lied to them for months about who and what she really was, almost killing a family member would have been the icing on the cake.

"If you keep pacing, you'll wear a hole in my driveway."

Erika spun around and faced the vampire. Absolutely stunning, Caitlyn had a regal air about her, a woman who didn't understand just how beautiful she was. But those eyes, slate grey, almost black in colour, held a sadness that leaked into her aura. Erika felt it the moment she had met the vampire. Yet, she admired Caitlyn's ability to carry on, despite the obvious trauma the woman had been through.

Caitlyn was a warrior who any Valkyrie would be honoured to have fight beside them.

Erika kicked at the gravel. "Is the girl okay?"

Caitlyn stepped back and beckoned Erika inside. Walking slowly down the hall, she spotted Donnie leaning against the kitchen counter. He nodded in greeting. Erika returned the gesture, her cheeks heating with embarrassment.

Caitlyn opened the door to a bedroom, and Erika stepped in, wincing as she laid eyes on the girl in the bed. Bruises littered her face, and her breathing was laboured with a wheeze that indicated a broken rib or two. Her eyes were closed, and her skin was a sickly shade of white.

"If she had not been blood kissed, then she would not have survived the fight."

"Isn't that illegal?"

Caitlyn gave Erika a weary smile. "My sire was not one for following rules, even those he had dictated."

"Ya, I know a prick like that too. Makes all the rules but doesn't follow them."

"At least my prick is dead. Hopefully we can kill yours too."

Erika chuckled softly, and then one look at the girl sobered her. Perching on the edge of the bed, Erika peered up at Caitlyn. "I'm sorry."

Caitlyn waved a hand in the air. "What is done, is done. She is alive. Perhaps, had we tried harder to find you, this could have been avoided."

"Or if I hadn't run off to solve things by myself like I normally do, then this could have been avoided."

Donnie, who had come into the room, snorted. "Seems you two have more in common than we thought."

Caitlyn tsked, but a small smile crept onto her face. Erika studied them, their auras intrinsically linked, maybe beyond their recognition. Erika wondered if they knew that when they were in the room together, they angled their bodies toward each other, postures relaxing and expressions changing. Even the darkness in Caitlyn's aura brightened whenever Donnie was around.

Erika tilted her head and gave them a small smile. "You mind if I try and help her out?"

"How?" asked Caitlyn.

"Us Valkyrie," Erika started, placing her hand on the girl's leg. "We aren't just soul stealers. Some of us have other talents. One of my sisters can speak to animals. Another can detect poisons in someone's bloodstream. Along with my fighting skills, and flashing ability, which Freya says are traits from the sperm donor I never knew, I have my mother's power to kick start the body's natural healing ability. Works better in humans, so it might not help much with a blood kissed, but I can't do her much more harm, can I?"

She closed her eyes, exhaled a breath, and concentrated. The power that came from her mother's bloodline flared, searching the battered girl's body until it located the root of her most intense injuries. Ignoring the guilt growing in her chest, Erika willed her power to repair the damage done to the girl's ribs. Erika winced as the pain slid from the girl's body and into her own. The cost for using her powers always came back on her.

As the girl's breathing started to improve, Erika removed her hand and coughed, covering her mouth and sneaking a peek down to see blood. Clearing her throat, she stood, dizziness causing her to stumble. She only avoided hitting the ground because Donnie grabbed her. Waiting until most of the dizziness passed, she moved out of his hold and peered back at Caitlyn.

"I've repaired the broken rib, but it's still bruised. She's still going to be in a lot of pain, but after a few pints of blood, and a few days' rest, she should be fine. She is a fierce warrior, like her aunt, one I would proudly have within my ranks."

Erika stumbled to the doorway, stopping only when Caitlyn called her name.

"Thank you, Erika."

Erika braced herself against the wall, her strength beginning to come back as she said, "Why are you thanking me? I caused this. I'm the reason she's in that bed. If you hadn't broken through my haze, then I'd have snapped her neck. I wanted to, I wanted to feel powerful and strong and superior."

Caitlyn watched her for a second before she spoke. "We have all done things that we regret, especially in the heat of the moment. But you have shown remorse for your actions. That is what matters."

Erika schooled her expression. "I'm not sure how to respond to that."

Donnie chuckled and clasped her on the shoulder. "It means that you're family. We make stupid mistakes, but we do it together. There's no more lone wolfing it, Erika. You are ours, and we are yours. Today, tomorrow, and always."

"I... I mean..." Erika stuttered, clearing her throat before she started again. "I'm a stranger to you guys. I haven't exactly given off the warm and fuzzy vibe since I arrived. Why would you do that? Claim me as family?"

Caitlyn sat down on the edge of the bed. "When I arrived in Cork, I was dealing with some things that happened to me. Even after joining P.I.T, I was not warm and fuzzy. Derek was the first person to crack through my walls, and then Ricky. Then I came across this oaf dying in the streets, and I finally began to let people in again. We are not meant to walk this world alone, Erika, despite what we might have conceived in our own minds."

Donnie winked at her. "I take offense to being called an oaf."

"Stubborn headed mule."

Donnie grinned at Caitlyn, and Erika's chest ached. That was what she wanted. A bond with another person who knew her, and she knew them. Erika knew everything about Ever, yet, Erika was quite certain that Ever knew little about the secrets Erika held inside herself like armour.

"Erika," Caitlyn said softly, dragging Erika's gaze to eyes of gunmetal grey. "What happened to Kenzie was not of your doing. Yes, you hurt her, but she has been hurt far worse than this before. I guarantee that once the pain and embarrassment of losing runs its course, Kenzie will be knocking on your door, looking to train, so that she might best a Valkyrie warrior next time round. She would not hold this against you, and neither do any of us."

Tears pricked her eyes as Erika flashed away from the emotional scene threatening to unravel her. She had never had a family, besides Ever that is, so having people who were willing to stand by her, even after all she had done, pulled the rug out from under her.

Reforming on an isolated cove within the shores of Valhalla, Erika sat down on the sand, and rested her chin in her hands. Emotions in turmoil, she didn't know what to make of Caitlyn.

Her own sisters, those blood sworn to follow her and protect Ever, had spent most of their long existence excluding her and making her feel isolated. All she had ever tried to do was to show them that she was worthy of their respect.

They respected her as a leader, perhaps out of fear, yet she doubted that they followed her out of love. Erika had proven time and time again just how capable a warrior she was. Still, her sisters never included her in gatherings.

She thought on the relationship that Donnie and Caitlyn had, the way they gravitated toward each other despite some obvious issues between them. Oh, how Erika longed for someone to care for her, to wish only the best for her.

Hasn't Loki taken care of you twice now? Has he not been open and honest with you?

The thoughts formulated in her mind, and Erika flashed herself to Loki's loft without another thought. Appearing in his sitting room, her heart raced at the sight of the trickster god. Relaxed into the couch, he had one lean leg braced on the edge of the coffee table, strands of raven black hair freed from his loose ponytail. His shoulders held no tension, but a frown marred his beautiful face.

She wanted to crawl into his lap and kiss that scowl away.

"Go away. I'm training my mind for battle."

Erika snorted, her eyes wandering from the controller in his hand, to the screen of the widescreen TV. "You're playing video games."

He didn't so much as glance in her direction as he replied, his tone clipped and void of emotion. "Exactly. Training. Now go away. You're distracting me."

She strode in front of the screen with a grin on her face. "And what if I want to distract you?"

"Little girl, I do not like the games you are playing."

She peeled off her vest and tossed it aside. "I'm not playing games, Loki. And you well know I'm not a little girl."

His eyes flickered in her direction and held her gaze. She knew he was testing her, pushing to see if she would run. She had run away from things her entire life. She was done running.

Tracing a hand up her bare stomach, her thumb grazed her nipple through her bra. Loki's mouth gaped a little, tightening his grip on the controller and causing a crack. As Erika moved, she kicked off her boots and came to stand in front of him.

"Erika…" he began, but she shook her head.

"I want you. I want you more than I have ever wanted anything in my life. I think, from our very first meeting, I wanted you. Maybe as a girl wants a cute boy, not as a woman wants a man. Now, I'm a woman who knows what she wants, and I want you."

He set aside the broken controller as she climbed into his lap, bracing her legs on either side, her hands resting on his shoulders. His hands tightly gripped her hips.

She leaned in, pressing her lips to his jaw, smiling when he shuddered. She feathered kisses along his jawline, nipping slightly on his ear, relishing in the groan that escaped his mouth.

Leaning back, she held his gaze. "I can stop if you want."

He captured her mouth in response, his hands roaming up and down her spine, before cupping her butt with strong possession. She licked and sucked and took until she had to pull back, breathless and chest heaving. His lips kicked up into a satisfied smile.

"I had all these plans in my mind for the first time I took you. I wanted you on your back, legs spread wide, your core wet and ready for me. I wanted to take you slowly, waiting until you were about to come, and then bring you to the edge, over and over, my name on your lips."

He clicked his fingers, and she was naked in his lap. When she grinned back at him, he slid his hand along her thigh, his fingers ghosting over her core.

"But," he said, "I think I like the idea of being taken by you. I have never been taken by anyone before."

The idea of it thrilled her, that Loki would allow her to take the reins and have control. She leaned in and pressed an open-mouthed kiss to the side of his throat.

"You are wearing far too many clothes," she muttered against his skin, her entire body aching for his touch.

With a very sexy chuckle, he nipped at her jaw. "We can't have that now, can we?"

Faster than she could blink, he was naked as well, and her mouth watered. Later, later she would lick every inch of him until she was addicted to his taste, but right now, she didn't care. She held his gaze as she reached out, wrapping her hand around his cock and stroking.

Loki closed his eyes for a brief moment, and when he opened them, Erika gasped. His eyes came alive, like all the stars in the sky had been captured there and were twinkling. They captivated her, halting her movements for a moment until he jerked his hips to urge her.

Not wanting to waste any more time, she rose up slightly, positioning his thick arousal at her opening, and slowly eased herself down. He wasn't small by any means, and he stretched her inner walls to an almost painful pleasure, but she needed it.

When she moved too slowly for his liking, he gripped her hips and bucked his own up, filling her completely. They both let loose a moan. They began to move slowly, gathering pace, neither of them uttering a word, the only sound in the room their breathing and the slap of flesh against skin as Erika leaned back, Loki latching onto her breast with his mouth.

She slid her fingers into his hair and dragged his head up, kissing the grin off his face. She felt like she was flying, her entire body feeling weightless as she continued to rotate her hips, her release building and building until all she wanted to do was scream.

"Look at me, Erika."

Normally, she would have bucked at the command, but she held once she looked back into Loki's eyes. Her orgasm ripped through her, Loki capturing her scream with his mouth as he continued to lift up his hips, sliding in and out of her core until his own release claimed him. He kiss her repeatedly, his hands stroking down her hair and face as she sat back.

"That was..." she began, unable to find the words.

"It was," he replied, a satisfied grin on his lips.

She made to slip off his lap, usually a leave-um-and-weep kinda lover, but he gripped her hips and rose off the couch, still inside her. She wrapped her arms around his neck. He placed a quick peck to her lips before sliding out so slowly that she almost came again as he set her on her feet.

"Did you think we were done, little Valkyrie?"

"Pretty much."

He kissed her hard, his cock stirring again against stomach. When he pulled back, she looked down and grinned. "Again?"

"I plan on making you come many more times, Erika. Many, many more until you scream my name. I have learned many tricks over the years," Loki said as his hands cupped her cheeks and his magic touched more intimate places. "I'm eager to show you."

Erika laughed, kissing the thumb that traced over her lips. "You'll have to catch me first."

She slipped out of his grasp, racing toward the bedroom, glancing behind her only to slam into a muscular chest. She slipped under his arm and into the bedroom before she was tackled and pinned to the bed, her hands over her head, a gorgeous god playing games with her.

"Things have changed now, Erika. You are mine. I do not share."

She rolled her eyes. "Just shut up and kiss me, Loki."

"As my lady commands."

She burst out laughing, as he began to kiss down her body, his hands slipping from the grip on her hands over her head, his magic holding them in place. Erika's eyes closed as he lavished her body with licks, kisses and well-placed grazes of teeth. As she wiggled, wanting and needing more than the teasing from Loki, the handsome man lifted his head and with a grin so wicked it was sinful, licked his lips.

The next time he kissed her, Erika swore she saw stars.

CHAPTER
SIXTEEN

Caitlyn

Caitlyn sat in the dark, her fingers intertwined on her lap, gaze never wavering from the girl who remained unconscious on the bed. Caitlyn rested on a fireside chair. Donnie had lifted it into Kenzie's bedroom, pressing a kiss to the top of Caitlyn's head before striding out of the room. She hated that Donnie felt that he could not touch her like he had done before they had mated, and she was entirely responsible for that. She was simply doing what he had asked of her, to not touch him if she wasn't sure she could stay mated to him.

The very thought that she would not be with Donnie made her stomach revolt. Yet, she still found that she could not tell him the truth about her feelings and why she was being so distant.

Caitlyn herself was uncertain why she was being like this. Should she not be overjoyed that Cain was dead, and she was free to be with the man she adored? Donnie had been patient and loyal, embracing the memories of her fallen family as if they had also belonged to him, and offered nothing but support.

How did she tell him that she felt guilty for seeing a future with him? How did she explain to him that every time he made her smile, every time her body came to life at his touch, this horrible voice inside her mind told her that she did not deserve happiness?

And, by the gods, when Donnie had blurted out that he had looked into adopting a child, Caitlyn had been so taken aback that she had freaked out. Children was something that they had not discussed. She had found a spark of joy when she held Ricky's cub in her arms, along with an abundance of fear. The last child she had held in her arms had been her own, and Caitlyn was not sure that she could bring herself to form an attachment to any child again because of the risk that came with who and what she was.

Kenzie sucked in a breath, still wheezing slightly, yet not as bad as she had before Erika had come to visit. It had surprised Caitlyn that despite being raised differently–Caitlyn with love and family, and Erika seemingly with not much–they had quite a lot in common. The Valkyrie, who Caitlyn assumed was far older than either her or Derek, had questioned Caitlyn's reaction to the fight and her willingness to still welcome Erika into her home.

It would seem that the Valkyrie happened to be as afraid of her emotions as Caitlyn was.

A slight tap came at the door, and Derek peered around the opening.

"How is she?" he asked, coming in to sit cross-legged on the floor.

"She is breathing easier, thanks to Erika."

With a quirked brow, he waited for her to continue.

"Apparently," she said with a sigh. "There is much that we do not know about Valkyrie powers."

"You can say that again," Derek huffed, scrubbing a hand down his face. He looked exhausted, as if he had not slept in days. She supposed he had not, considering his own mate had only returned after running off. Caitlyn remembered Donnie's ragged appearance when he had shown up at her apartment in Paris. He had known what perils Caitlyn might encounter in the country of her birth, yet Derek hadn't had those clues when Ever left, or even confidence he would find her.

"What brings you to my door this evening?" Caitlyn asked, running a hand through her hair.

"I'm going to collect Melanie from Ricky's mom's house and said I'd stop in. I wanted to see how the girl was. I kinda feel responsible for getting her hurt."

She leaned forward and patted him on the head. "It is not your fault, *mon ami*. Kenzie will be the first to tell you that she was fully aware of the risks. It was not our intention that she come face to face with an angry Valkyrie."

Derek responded with a shrug. "Still."

"You cannot take it upon yourself when others suffer misfortunes."

"Ha. Look who's talking," he said pointedly.

She chuckled. "That is why you and I get on so well. We like to make everyone else's problems our own."

He patted her calf with a grin, his face sobering. "Wanna tell me what's up with you and the big man? You two should be walking around with the biggest smiles on your faces. Cain is dead, and there is nothing standing between you and happiness."

She sank back into the chair, tapping her fingers on her knee. "I am the reason for the unhappiness, not Donnie. I...I...I cannot tell you, especially when I cannot tell him."

Derek cocked his head in a very wolf-like manner. "I'm sure Donnie would prefer that you talk to anyone about what's up with you."

Caitlyn glared at Derek, who smiled at her innocently.

"He asked you to talk to me, did he not?"

"His exact words were," Derek stated, his grin widening. "'Dude, I'm royally fucking this up. Come help me out.' He knows that you'll talk to me, that I won't bullshit you, and you appreciate that. He also knows that we have leaned on each other with our little therapy sessions, and you tell me things you might not ever want to speak about with him. I don't know, if you were my girl, if I'd have the stones to ask another man to help his woman out. Think about that."

He stood, his gaze wandering over to Kenzie before he turned his attention back to Caitlyn. "Talk to him, Cait. If the guy hung around for twenty years with slim hope of being with you, then you won't scare him away with a few truths. You guys have the chance to be happy. Don't deny yourself the opportunity because of some misconceived notion that you don't deserve it."

Derek slipped silently from the room, the door closing with a snick. Caitlyn knew that he was right, that she was sabotaging any chance at happiness by pushing Donnie away.

"That damn wolf talks too loud."

Caitlyn leapt to her feet and was at Kenzie's side in an instant. "Kenzie, *mon dieu*. I am glad you are awake. How do you feel?"

"Like I got run over by a truck. Twice." Her niece tried to sit up, a hiss escaping her lips, and Caitlyn carefully put her hands on Kenzie's shoulders, grabbed some pillows that she must have thrown on the floor, placed them against the headboard, and gently lifted Kenzie so that she was sitting up.

When she seemed settled, she looked at Caitlyn, a sheepish expression on her face. Kenzie began to speak, but a coughing fit wracked her body. Caitlyn gingerly lifted a glass to Kenzie's lips so she could have a sip.

"Thanks," she croaked. "So how bad did I screw up?"

"You did not screw up, Kenzie," replied Caitlyn, her tone soft. "You were faced with an angry Valkyrie who wanted to prove a point. Take from it that you survived a battle against the general of a mythical army. Your pride is safe."

Tears began to drip from Kenzie's eyes. Caitlyn shushed her, lying down on the bed next to her. "All I wanted to do was prove I was useful to the team. I can't even get that right."

Kenzie burst into tears, but she allowed Caitlyn to hold her close until the tears ran dry. Caitlyn began to sing in French, a lullaby that she had once sang to Jessamine, only realizing she had begun when she heard her words. When she finished, Kenzie rubbed her eyes and sat up straighter, moaning as the movement tugged at her sore ribs.

"I'm sorry I scared you."

Caitlyn was about to deny that she had been frightened, yet Kenzie must have remembered the absolute panic and terror that had ripped through Caitlyn the moment Erika went for the kill. It had taken all she could do not to lash out at Erika, but common sense had prevailed, Caitlyn scooping Kenzie into her arms and not letting her go until they were in the safety of the compound.

"It has been a long time since I have been afraid of losing someone. I may have panicked a little. I apologise if it distressed you."

"It's okay. It's been a while since I had someone look after me like that. I think we both have things we need to adjust to."

Kenzie yawned, and Caitlyn detangled herself, slipping off the bed. "I will let you get some rest. Erika managed to kick start your healing, and you drank a pint of my blood, but you still need to rest."

"Yes, boss."

Caitlyn made for the door.

"Caitlyn?" Kenzie said, and Caitlyn paused, glancing over her shoulder.

"Yes?"

"Did I really fight a Valkyrie?"

Caitlyn shook her head. "Yes."

"She had some sweet moves. Think she'll show me?"

Caitlyn made an exasperated sound. "Erika has already stated she is more than happy to train with you once you recover."

"Sweet!" Kenzie said around a yawn, drifting off to sleep a moment later.

Caitlyn waited until Kenzie's breathing deepened. As soon as Caitlyn was certain the girl had fallen into a deep sleep, she left her to her rest, safe in the knowledge that she would be alright.

Caitlyn moved down the hall, making her way toward the living room where she could feel Donnie's presence. It was like déjà vu, but with him staring out the window and her watching from the doorway. He would have known when she entered the room; the bond gave them the ability to know where the other person was.

However, he continued his observation of the world outside, a bottle of beer hanging from his fingers, as if she was not there at all. His entire body stiffened upon her walking into the room, which should not be a mate's reaction to their mate entering a room.

Caitlyn thought back on Derek's words, *"You guys have the chance to be happy. Don't deny yourself the opportunity because of some misconceived notion that you don't deserve it,"* and decided she had to come clean about her fears to Donnie if they had any chance to survive as a couple.

Wetting her lips with her tongue, Caitlyn took a step into the room before she whispered, "I don't deserve it."

Donnie tensed, yet kept his eyes on the world outside, his fingers tightening around the mouth of his beer. "Excuse me?"

She took in an unnecessary breath. "I do not deserve to be happy. The way you make me feel does not sit well with me. The happiness I feel when I am near you, I feel I do not deserve it. I know I am being irrational. I understand my feelings are not valid, yet I cannot help to think that after all I have done, I do not deserve the life I want with you."

He turned in her direction, walked over to the sofa and sat down, setting the bottle of beer down on the table. He leaned back, stretching his arms out on the back of the chair. "Of course your feelings are valid, Cait. But I'm a little on the stupid side, I blame the numerous concussions. Come sit down and explain it to me again."

She walked over to the table, lifted Donnie's beer and took a slug. It tasted bitter and not at all to her taste. "That is awful. How can you drink it?"

He took the beer from her fingers and drained the rest of the bottle. "It's an acquired taste. Come on, babe. Sit down." He patted the couch beside him and waited until she took a seat, curling her legs underneath herself.

"Derek said that I think that I do not deserve to be happy, and that is why I am giving you a hard time."

Reaching out, he took a wisp of her hair and wrapped it around his fingers. Caitlyn almost sighed at his touch and realized it must be hell for him also.

"I feel this guilt inside me. After all I have done, I still have the opportunity to live my life with you. I do not think, having buried my family in the ground, that happiness is what I deserve, and when I am with you, I tend to forget them for a moment and smile. I should not forget them even for a moment."

He continued to twist her hair in his fingers. "Caitlyn, being with me does not mean that you forget them. Have I even once asked you to do that for me? You've told me a little about Sebastian. He sounded like a good man, Cait. Do you honestly think Sebastian would hold it against you for being happy? For finding something to smile about? I understand where you're coming from, I really do. And I'm not exactly helping, am I? I'm sorry for saying stupid shit and upsetting you. That was far from my intention. I'd blame the stupid on the multiple concussions again, but I open my mouth and stupid comes out."

She shifted so that she faced him and rested a hand on his knee. "We are both guilty of saying stupid stuff. I think we have had little chance to discuss the future due to Cain and Kenzie. Perhaps, we should talk now."

Donnie tucked her hair behind her ear. "I'm down with that. You wanna go first?"

Caitlyn shook her head rapidly, so he rolled his shoulders. "I only brought up about us having kids because I wanted to see you happy, and I have never seen such unbridled joy as when Zach was cradled in your arms. I wanted to do that for you, because all I want is to make you happy."

She squeezed his thigh. "It had been an age since I held such an innocent in my arms, and it unnerved me. It felt wrong, to hold a child when I cannot hold my own. I am afraid to even contemplate becoming a parent with you, because I still have enemies out in the world. I could not bear it, if I were to love someone as a mother loves a child and they were taken away from me. I do not think I could survive it."

"Okay."

Caitlyn lifted her brow. "Okay?"

He gave her a small smile. "Yes, okay. I can't imagine what it's like to suffer that loss, and I accept your feelings. I'm not going to lose the rag when you make a valid point. We can shelf it, talk again another day if you change your mind."

"You are being very reasonable."

"I try."

She leaned in and pressed her lips against the curve of his jaw, the stubble on his chin tickling. "I promise to try and communicate more. It is an adjustment for me, *oui*?"

"Can I ask you a question?"

Looking up into those oceanic eyes, Caitlyn replied, "You can ask me anything."

"Do you love me?"

That was not the question she had expected, but she answered him anyway, "Can you not see the answer in my mind?"

He grinned. "I can. But I want to hear you say it. Words spoken out loud become more real. I can read your mind, when you let me. Yet, there is power in words, Caitlyn Hardi. I love you, and I have loved you for too many years. Hear the strength in my words and understand that I am here for the long haul."

Caitlyn reached out and cupped his cheek, her answer the surest thing she had thought for a while. "*Je t'aime*, Donnie. All that I am, is yours. I will try and use my words more."

"Make me a promise, Cait. Here and now. That no matter how mad I make you, no matter what stupid shit I say, or territorial vampire crap I pull, you will talk to me rather than pull the ice queen act on me. These last few weeks, I was afraid to touch you, terrified that I was going to fuck this up before it even began. It has been torture. Thinking you did not want me almost killed me. Not when I'd had a taste of you."

Oh, how her chest ached. She had been so consumed with her own feelings, she did not consider his. Slowly she climbed into his lap and pressed her lips to his, realizing how much she had missed him, even when he had been close to her.

Resting her hands on the sides of his thick neck, Caitlyn gave him a small smile. "And if I turn ice queen again, feel free to call me on it. I know I am not easy to deal with, but I promise to try and be better."

Donnie pulled her in close and whispered. "You do not have to be anyone else, but Caitlyn. My Caitlyn. Frost n'all."

This man made her wish that her heart still beat, for she longed to feel the sensation of it skipping at this man, who was patient, who was kind, and most of all, who loved her. Maybe, she considered, she had been consumed with who she had been when she was alive, not the Caitlyn that Donnie knew and loved.

Caitlyn pressed another kiss to Donnie's jaw. "Do you think we can be quiet?" As she scraped her fangs along his jaw, he growled and rose, taking her with him. She laughed as he strode toward his bedroom.

Kicking the door closed, he sat down on the bed with her in his lap. "Remind me to tell the contractor that we need noise resistant walls in the new place. Really thick, noise resistant walls."

Kissing him with a fierceness she hadn't been aware she possessed, she pulled back with a smile.

"I love you, Donnie."

"Love you too, Cait. Now kiss me again."

And, she could not deny his request.

CHAPTER
SEVENTEEN

Erika

After spending the rest of the night and most of the morning in Loki's bed, Erika left before Loki woke, the implications of what she had done too much for her to deal with. Now that they'd sated the curiosity of what it would be like to be together, she was certain he would lose interest, much like he had done with so many other lovers.

But the way Loki kissed and caressed her, making her feel as if she were a queen before he possessed her utterly, made Erika's heart hurt in ways she never imagined. Now as she sat on the floor in her room in the arena, she knew that even if he tossed her aside, there would be no one else for her. One taste had not been enough; she was addicted.

Closing her eyes, she inhaled a breath, exhaled, and tried to clear her mind. She was so used to handling things by herself and having limited support that the past few days had been maddeningly confusing. Caitlyn could have killed Erika for what she had done to Kenzie, yet the vampire had offered support rather than reproach. That definitely was a new one for Erika.

Her phone began to ring, and she opened her eyes, glancing down to see Ever blowing up her phone. Erika pressed ignore and closed her eyes again, thinking back to the first time she realized her feelings for Ever might not have been strictly platonic.

Erika had barely slept the night before, the ceremony that would bond the seven Valkyrie together as Ever's chosen sisters was the most exciting thing to happen to Erika since she had been chosen to be Ever's general, the head of the Valkyrie army. It would be Erika they took orders from in Ever's absence, Erika who determined what battles warriors could be harvested from, and Erika who held Ever's confidence.

There was no grander compliment than to be the queen's chosen number two, and Erika had never been chosen for anything in her entire life.

Erika bounded out of bed before the sun had even inclined to rise that morning, dressing in her new warrior clothing, the finest of Asgardian steal on her breastplate, embossed with the Valkyrie crest. The same steel clasped her knee-high boots, and her skirt was formed from a thick animal hide, doused in the blood of the sacrificial creature.

Glancing in the mirror, Erika pulled her hair back, slipping the headdress on. Sticking three fingers into the blood colouring on her vanity table, she smeared the blood from left to right, down her face. When she lifted her eyes, she saw not the abandoned child of some Vanir healer. The woman staring back at her was confident, assured, and fierce. She was a warrior yet to face defeat on the battlefield. The warrior holding her gaze was a tactician who knew where and when to strike an opponent.

This woman was strong, resilient and present.

I wonder, will my mother be here today?

The thought popped into her head before she could dispel it, yet Erika wasn't certain that she would even recognise the woman who gave birth to her if they crossed paths. The sweet-as-honey voice that used to sing Erika to sleep had dissipated over time in her mind. Having spent the last twenty years training and working towards her goal, the child Erika had been when her mother dropped her on the shores of Valhalla had died, and Erika the Valkyrie had been born.

A knock came at her hut's door and Ever walked in, dressed in similar attire. The headdress that adorned Ever's blonde hair was entirely regal, decorated with gemstones befitting a future queen.

Ever gave a bark of laughter at Erika and pointed a finger at her face. "Being a little over dramatic, aren't we?"

Erika grinned back at her best friend. "This is the first time those in the Aesir will lay their eyes on me. Once they do, I never want them to forget who and what I am."

"Come on." Ever sighed, holding out her elbow to Erika. "Let us get this over with. My father does not tolerate tardiness."

Erika took Ever's outstretched arm, and they left Erika's hut and made their way down through the shade of the trees and onto the shoreline where the ceremony would take place. Erika gasped at the sheer volume of immortals who had come to witness the blood bonding, but it was the ones who lounged in the section dedicated to the royal family that caught Erika's attention.

Thor sat with his wife, Lady Sif, and Odin, Ever's father, sat with his new wife, Frigg. Balder, Hod, and Hermod were sitting beside their mother. Erika's gaze skipped over them all until her eyes landed on the most infuriating person on the planet.

Loki reclined in his chair, dressed in a striking suit of black and green, peeling an apple with a penknife. As if he felt her eyes on him, the god of mischief cast his gaze in her direction, and Erika felt her cheeks redden. Loki, arrogant ass that he was, simply chuckled, lifting his apple in salute.

"Your crush on my brother is very nauseating."

Erika nudged Ever with her shoulder, reluctantly removing her eyes from Loki's, as Freya beckoned them over. They stood in formation, in accordance of rank, in front of the most powerful gods in the world, hands clasped behind their backs, feet set apart and heads held high.

Ever stood beside Freya, with Erika by her side, Danae stood beside Erika, and then came Rebekah, Joslyn, Ilnala, Almira, and then the youngest of them, Marya, each dressed in similar clothing, energy buzzing as the seven new Valkyrie were to be introduced to the world.

"Gods and goddesses, I welcome you to Valhalla to witness the birth of the most impressive Valkyrie class to ever watch over the world. Today, they bond themselves to one another, sisters in every sense. Blood spilled and shared. Warriors from now until Ragnarok."

Freya's words ignited the excitement in Erika's veins, and she had to use all of her discipline not to bounce on her feet. Freya took a blade from her waist and handed it to Ever, bowing her head slightly to her daughter in a show of rank that must have irked Freya so.

"Share your blood with your sister and become as one."

Ever took the blade and moved down to the end of the row, slicing her palm open, then doing the same to Marya. Ever clasped her hand in Marya's, and the young Valkyrie trembled as power saturated the air. Ever repeated the action, making her way along the line until she stood in front of Erika, and paused.

"As future Queen of the Valkyrie, Ever has chosen Erika, warrior of unknown origin, to be her general. She will be the one to lay down her life for her queen, even before that of her sister. Erika will lead the armies of Valhalla into battle, upon orders from her queen."

Ever, who had her back to the audience, grinned at Erika as she slashed her already healing palm again before taking Erik's hand and slicing through her flesh. Erika didn't so much as flinch at the sting, simply lifted her gaze to meet Ever's

"May your blades be sharp and your arrows find their way." Ever whispered and clasped her hand to Erika's. Power almost made Erika's knees buckle. The wind whipped her hair into her face, but she did not let go of Ever's grasp. As the magic of the bond settled into place, Ever slipped her hand out from Erika's, the biggest grin on her face.

Erika stared at her best friend, saw the love Ever had for her, and her heart twisted. The thoughts that had plagued her for some time, when Erika happened to think about how beautiful Ever looked today, or how much she wanted to kiss her, all came rushing over her as the crowd erupted into thunderous applause.

And as Thor lifted his hammer, exclaiming that now was the time for mead, Ever turned away from Erika, and she wondered if this was what it was like to fall in love.

Erika opened her eyes, sighing long and hard. It wasn't wrong for her to have feelings for Ever, but over time, maybe her feeling for Ever had warped into something that went above love and loyalty. It wasn't like Erika hadn't been attracted to a woman before. She believed a person should be attracted to both men and women.

Ever looked at "Boyband" the way Erika had seen Caitlyn and Donnie look at each other. Their story went back for generations. Soulmates, if there was even such a thing. They were meant to be together, and Ever and Erika were simply meant to be best friends.

As if the epiphany suddenly struck her with lightening, Erika bolted up from the ground and made for the door, coming face to face with the chaos demon who had left her for dead.

"Erika! How wonderful to see that you are well!"

"Cut the bullshit, Felix." Erika snorted. "What do you want?"

The demon's ears twitched as he stroked the little tuft of hair he thought was a beard. "I have a fight for you."

"Not interested. Bye bye." Erika went to pass him by when Felix said three words that stopped her in her tracks.

"It's the berserker."

Erika froze, her fingers clenching into fists. This was what she was waiting for, the chance to beat Odin's location out of his rage monsters. Midgard had somehow dampened the full fury inside the berserker. This was her chance, and she couldn't back down from it.

"When?"

Felix gave her a slow, sleazy smile. "Right now. I have a packed house waiting to see the woman who defeated a troll and took apart the Slayer of Paris."

"Let's go."

Erika strode out, dressed in her usual clothing of combats, boots and a vest, as Felix prattled on about having a full house. Pulling her hair into a ponytail, Erika thought back to her memory of the warrior in the mirror who was fierce and feared.

"Gimmie a knife."

"Pardon?"

Erika sighed and held out her hand. "I'm not gonna stab you, Felix. Just give me a knife."

He nodded at one of his bodyguards, Erika taking the blade and slicing her left palm open. Felix studied her as she dipped three fingers into the blood and smeared it on her face. Erika flashed away for a moment, reappeared with her twin blades, and rotated her wrists.

"They forget that I am not a mere mortal. Let me remind them of what I am."

"And tell me, Erika," Felix began, ushering her out into the roar of the crowd. "What are you?"

She turned her head to stare at Felix, a smirk curling her lips, and she was almost certain she saw fear in his eyes. "War."

Blood pumping in her veins, she took a running jump, somersaulting in the air and landed in the octagon, the berserker ripping off his muscle shirt on sight of her.

"Calm down, Hulk Hogan. You might as well die with your clothes on."

The berserker roared in anger. "I will enjoy beating you to death, little one. And then I will fuck your corpse."

Erika threw back her head and laughed. "Aww, is that the only way you can get a girl, rager? I'm sure they have websites to help with that."

"I will crush your tiny bones to marrow."

"Bring it on, bitch."

Erika backed up against the fence, glancing over her shoulder when she heard her name. Her eyes connected with Ever, and she felt nothing as her friend mouthed. "May your blades be sharp, General."

Erika let her gaze fleet over the man sitting beside Ever. His relaxed pose, right leg folded over his other knee and hands clasped together was familiar, and her heart skipped a beat. There it was. The truth in the confusion of her mind. She was in love with Loki.

Those eyes of a thousand universes watched her, until the god winked at her, flashing a confident smile in her direction. Erika nodded her head, facing her opponent once again.

"I will give you one last chance to walk away alive. Tell me where Odin sleeps and you can keep your head."

The berserker smashed his fists together. "I could, little Valkyrie. But the Allfather no longer sleeps. I will lay your body at his feet in tribute."

Erika scratched her chin with the hilt of her blade. "First, I'm not little, I'm fun sized. Second, thanks for the spoiler alert. Third, I will be happy to present your head to my queen in tribute. Fourth, stuff an apple in your mouth like a good little piggy. Oink, oink."

He charged her, but Erika flashed to the other side of the ring, avoiding the berserker who skidded to a halt before colliding with the railing. He pivoted, beating a fist to his chest, as Erika taunted him some more.

"Here, piggy, piggy."

This time, when the berserker came at her, she bent back for a second and struck out with the hilt of her blade across his back, sending him stumbling. War sang in her veins, acceptance of who she was, what she was, for probably the first time in her life. It bled new life into her tired lungs.

The berserker kept coming at her, Erika avoiding each blow without batting an eye. Each move was on instinct, and the berserker's eyes widened in surprise as Erika dodged another blow. When she brought the hilt of the blade up to his throat, taking him to his knees, she stood in the centre of the ring with her arms outstretched, and the crowd went wild.

Flashing to stand behind the berserker, Erika crossed her blades against his throat, a foot pressed to the berserker's back. He made to get up, but she dug the blades deeper into his flesh.

"Any last words before I send you to Hel?"

"I look forward to the day Odin crushes your skull."

"Pity you won't be around to witness his demise. I'll see you in Hel."

Erika uncrossed the blades, taking the berserker's head clean off in one action. It bounced on the mat while she sheathed her blades across her back. Ever and Loki entered the octagon, and Erika picked up the berserker's head and held it up to the crowd. When Ever came within reach, Erika dropped to her knees, placing the severed head at Ever's feet, head bowed as the entire room went silent.

"I lay a tribute at your feet, my queen."

A collective gasp rang out as Ever hissed, "Get off the ground, you idiot. You've just outed me to the goddamn world."

Erika rose, not caring that Ever wanted to keep herself hidden. The time for hiding had long passed. "You are their queen. They should all bow before you. Your father is awake and coming for us. We can no longer keep silent."

"It is not your place to decide that."

"Then start acting like the queen you were destined to be."

Erika flashed away from the arena, flashing to the highest point of the city and looking out onto the array of lights that shimmered in the darkness. She felt euphoric after her fight, finally feeling for the first time in her life that she was her own person. Loki's aura penetrated the air, and she laughed loudly as Loki and Ever materialized next to her.

"Look at all these people. Oblivious to what is happening around them. All of those people are alive right now–because of her. They owe their lives to her. To all of us." She turned to face Ever. "I thought I was in love with you, but I'm not. I shouldn't have kissed you. I crossed a line that got blurry. It won't happen again. But Odin is awake and we cannot pretend like this isn't almost the end."

Walking over, Erika placed her hands on Ever's shoulders, repeating her message, "Odin is awake. We are out of time. I cannot lose my best friend. I cannot lose my sister. I have been by your side each and every death, and I refuse to witness that again. We must hold strong. It is time for this to end."

Ever reached up and put her hands over Erika's on her shoulder. "And what do you suggest we do, General?"

"We use everything we have in our arsenal. Before, it was us Valkyrie who bore the cost, and we went it alone. We have your champion, we have warriors that will fight with us. We bring them in on this, and Odin will not see us coming. He will expect us to close rank, fight him by ourselves. We do all that we can to finish this once and for all."

They held each other's gaze for a second before Ever nodded. "I will follow you, Erika. We do this for our futures."

"And we do this for all those we lost in battle."

Removing her hands from Ever's shoulders, Erika glanced over at Loki, who watched her with a bemused smile on his face.

"How about you, mischief maker? You wanna say screw the rules with us and possibly incur the wrath of Thor?"

Loki folded his arms across his chest. "I've never been fond of rules, anyways. I will follow you, Erika. Even if it's just to watch your pretty ass."

Ever smacked herself in the face. "I think I'm going to be sick."

"Then turn away now, sister dear." He swooped in like a hurricane, wild and furious, as he kissed Erika. She kissed him back, ignoring the doubt that lurked in her mind that this could not, and would not, last.

If she was going to die soon anyway, Erika wanted to die with a smile on her face, rather than regret in her mind. When she pulled back from Loki, he cupped her cheek and she held her breath. The end of the world was coming, but she would go down swinging with those she was proud to call her friends by her side.

Peering over at Ever, Erika tugged up her lips. "I guess this means you need to have a conversation with 'Boyband'."

As her friend groaned, Erika laughed, and a weight lifted from her shoulders.

CHAPTER
EIGHTEEN

Loki

Odin's rage and despair could be heard in the skies above Asgard, thunder and lightning ripping through the city, striking out at buildings and monuments, the ground beneath the city trembling against the anguish that sent the Allfather into a tailspin.

For it was on this night that Odin lost his beloved Frigg, and Thor and Loki lost the only mother they had known. The very moment Frigg took her last breath, those born of her had wept openly, pressing kisses to their mother's cheeks before being escorted from the room, leaving Odin to his grief. Thor had tried to offer some comfort to his father, yet Odin had dismissed his favoured son with the swipe of his hand. Thor brushed his knuckles over his mother's cheek even as Lady Sif led him from the room.

He had paused at the doorway, his eyes meeting Loki's, and then he was gone from sight, leaving Loki to deal with Odin. It was strange to him, to feel compassion for a man who had in all essence murdered his entire tribe and then spared Loki because he looked like an Asgardian on the outside.

As Odin stood beside the bed where Frigg lay, Loki bent down and pressed a kiss to the woman's cheek. She had been one of the only people besides Thor to treat Loki with any affection after Odin had brought him back from Jotunheim. Almost immediately, Frigg had bundled Loki into her arms and insisted that he become family instead of a prisoner of war.

When, as a child, Loki had been responsible for the death of Baldur, Frigg and Odin's handsomest son, she had not banished Loki like he suspected she would. Instead, the goddess kept Loki so busy that he had little time for mischief. She shared with him a love for books, the ability to slip between the pages, escape to another world, and experience the magic within the pressed pages. They sat for hours listening to music, neither of them speaking.

What Loki held dearest in his heart were the times when he could not sleep after seeing his parents' deaths in his dreams, frost licking his skin and the pale cream colour turning blue. Frigg ignored the sharp burn of the frost to cradle him in her arms and hum a lullaby until he had calmed down enough to stop the tears from falling. She had never spoken of Loki's night terrors, for Odin was not one for weakness.

The goddess Eir had lain a hand on Odin's arm and said that Frigg could not be healed, for there was no cure for a broken heart. Having lost two sons, Frigg found it hard to deal with the sorrow. She had fallen into the deep sleep of immortals, until her heart simply stopped beating.

What no one, not even Thor, knew was that a day before Frigg had fallen into her slumber, she and Loki had been seated in the helm of the keep, in the great library that held all of Asgardian history and those of the nine realms. Loki had been engrossed in a novel, one of his favourites, The Bacchae, a Greek tragedy by Euripide, when Frigg had set down her book and risen.

"Out of all of my children," she sighed, glancing out the glass window at the kingdom before her. "It is you that I worry much over, son."

Loki smiled, that rush to his heart whenever the beautiful goddess called him son. "Fear for me, mother? Why would you do such a silly thing?"

Frigg turned to face him, and the smile that tugged on her lips did not quite reach her eyes of golden brown. "I worry that should something happen to me, you would be alone. You guard your heart more than you should, Loki. You cannot spend eternity by yourself."

Loki closed the book, set it down on the seat beside him, and rose. "Mother, I am quite content to spend eternity alone. I see what humanity has done in the name of love and I do not want it. Besides, I should rather spend eternity reading good books, and listening to prose and poetry with you, while still finding time to get up to mischief with Thor. Please do not speak of such melancholy."

Walking over to stand in front of him, Frigg took his face in her hands, and he blinked in surprise. "I want for you, dearest child, to find that all-consuming love, the one that comes out of nowhere and holds you captive. Find that one person who you think of constantly, who makes you want to be more, be better. It is a wonderful thing to find someone who sees you as you are and loves you terribly. Every night with a different lover tires after time. Coming home to someone who knows your wants and needs, that is what happiness feels like."

"Mother..." Loki began, before Frigg shushed him.

"Promise me that you will not close your heart off. I want for you to find someone who will challenge you, who will not be afraid to argue with you, but will also show you that you are loved by them. Do not settle for someone who will not have you seeing the best of you. Love, my dearest Loki, love with all that you are and make me proud. Promise me."

Loki had studied the desperation in the eyes of the only woman he had called mother and promised her that he would try. She had kissed him, asking him to read for her while she rested her eyes, as she was just a little tired. Loki had spent twenty minutes reading before he realized that something was utterly wrong and alerted Odin.

A mere forty-eight hours later, and Frigg had been gone.

Loki pushed aside the memory, along with his own grief, and came to stand beside Odin.

"Asgard has lost one of its treasures. We must hold strong for the people. Show them that we stand strong."

Thunder snapped outside and Loki could hear the sound of glass crashing as Odin spun on him and snarled. "I have lost my only love! I do not care whether or not the people of Asgard mourn, or what you, son of frost, have to say. Be gone from my sight before I do what I should have done when I first laid eyes on you and dashed your brains out against the concrete."

Loki shuddered at the venom in Odin's voice, watched as darkness seeped into the man who craved knowledge more than power once, and saw that the road ahead would not be a pleasant one.

He spared one last look at his mother and flashed from the keep, unsure of where he would go. His feet settled on the shores of Valhalla, in search of the one person who Loki could not get out of his mind, even if she were too young for him, barely into her second decade of life.

Erika sat in the sand, her toes kissed by the crest of the waves, her long whiskey-kissed hair hanging loose down her back. The moonlight glinted against the bronze of her skin, giving off the appearance that it almost glittered. Her palms were planted on the sand, and she looked entirely peaceful, the only sound in the darkness of night was the crashing of the waves and the lull of her breathing.

Since he had first laid eyes on Erika, he had felt this deep connection with the Valkyrie, had found himself wanting to be near her, if only to hear her barbs against him.

Was this what Frigg had spoken of when she spoke of love and finding someone who challenged him? If love caused someone to forget who they were, was it even worth it?

Erika did not give any indication that she knew he was there, yet she always knew, much like he knew when she arrived at the keep with Ever in tow. Flicking out his long cloak, Loki plonked down beside her, but refrained from speaking. They sat for a time, watching the waves roll in and out of the shore.

"I was sorry to hear about your mother."

Loki turned his head to peer at her, the stunning profile of a woman who did not know how breath-taking she was. Erika tilted her head to look at him, a small sad smile on her full lips.

"Thank you."

"It's hard to say goodbye to someone you love."

"It is."

He felt that he had no other words for her, however she placed her hand on top of his knee before saying, "The world is full of beautiful things that we take for granted. But, how can we have beauty without seeing the ugly too? Life must have balance, and that is death. I have seen many deaths in my short life, yet I have not experienced the loss of a loved one. It would seem that even we immortals are to be kissed by death also."

Loki blinked in surprise. Erika, the usually upbeat if not snarky best friend of the sister he had chosen for himself, was lulled into the same melancholy that Loki tended to find himself in.

"You are far too young and beautiful to be this cynical."

Erika snorted, yet Loki saw a faint hint of a blush creep into her cheeks. Oh, by the gods, he wanted to kiss her. He wanted nothing more than to lower her into the sand and hear her moan his name. Yet, he refrained. Not because he had the self-control, but because he could not offer her an eternity of faithfulness. He could not promise that he would be hers and hers alone, and she deserved that. He thought this even as she leaned in to press her lips against his.

He pulled back, and a deep shade of red coloured her cheeks.

"I'm sorry...I don't...I mean..." she stuttered, scrambling off the sand as Loki ruined the peace of the night. He should not have come. He should have stayed in Asgard and away from the Valkyrie that tempted him so.

As she fled from the beach without sparing him a second glance, Loki could not erase the weight in his chest that he had not lost one person he cared for this night, but two. And perhaps, it was for the best.

Loki bolted upright in his bed, the memories of the night Frigg had died playing out like his worst nightmare. After losing Frigg, Loki had covered his heart in a cage of ice, trying to block out sadness and grief, and especially love, which was a foreign emotion for him. The people he loved could be counted on one finger. Yet, coming to the realization that he was *in love* with Erika caused ice to formulate in his veins, because his actions over the years, as well as the life she had lived, had hardened her so that she expected the worst from him.

The realization had occurred shortly after the night when Loki slept with the chieftain's daughter and invoked the curse upon him. The medicine woman had been right. The moment his heart began to feel something for Erika, long before the curse, Loki had felt his end coming.

After a night with Erika in his bed, Loki did not want to spend another alone. In fact, he was quite resigned to his fate, and if he spent his last days with the woman who melted his heart of ice, then so be it.

He clicked his fingers, dressing in jeans and a tee, and willed himself to find Erika. He found himself standing in the little apartment above Ever's garage. The one bedroom was Erika to a tee. It held no material possessions, and the walls were blank apart from some décor that Ever had placed there. The bed was unmade, a trunk of weapons lying open at its base. She would not be wooed by flowers and clothing; his woman was a warrior true and true.

Leaning against the wall, he heard her stomp up the steps, laughing at something Ever called after her. Erika flung open the bedroom door, spinning round when she sensed his aura in the room, the warrior in her reaching for the dagger at her waist. He reached out his arm and pushed the door closed. She stared at him for a moment, her expression unreadable, yet he could hear the quickening of her heartbeat.

"Don't you realize it's creepy to turn up in a girl's bedroom unannounced?"

"I was trying to be romantic. Had I more time, then I would have lit some candles and made the bed."

Erika barked out a laugh, and then she sobered, her expression going grim. "Why are you here, Loki?"

He shoved his hands into his pockets, but held her gaze. "I came to assure myself that you knew that things between us have changed. I won't allow you to take another man or woman into your bed, unless we are having some fun time. And I would never take another to my bed unless you wanted to watch."

Lust flashed in her eyes as she chewed on her bottom lip. Her hands planted on her hips, she watched him, as if she dared him to go on.

"I don't share, Erika. You kissed me in front of Ever. You indicated that things between us had ventured outside of being platonic."

"Things between us have never been platonic." Erika snorted.

Loki took a step toward her, his lips curving into a sly, seductive smile. "I agree. I tried to get you out of my mind, but you were never far from my thoughts. Dirty, delicious thoughts. I want to make it perfectly clear, Erika. I want to be yours... I want to be a part of your life. This is not just about sex, this is about finally realizing that everything I have been searching for, been waiting for, was right in front of my eyes all along."

She swallowed hard, and he could hear the conflict in her mind, the fears and the facts bouncing off one another. He inched closer, standing a breath away from her. "Frigg told me the day before she died that she wanted me to find the one person who I would think of constantly, who made me want to be more, be better. She asked me to allow my heart to find the person who challenges me, and who does not let me get away with the mischief and mayhem I bring with me. I ran from you that night on the beach, but I am done running."

Erika took a step back. Her fear, as cold as the ice that ran in his veins, rained down over him. She continued to back up until her back hit the farthest wall.

"I'm sorry, Loki. I really am. But I've told you before, Ever has to be my priority. When I am with you, I can't think about anything else or anyone else. Goddamn it, even when you're not here, I eventually begin to think of you. I cannot afford that. Yes, I kissed you in front of Ever, but I was riding high on adrenaline. I can't promise forever, because even immortals are kissed by death."

Her words, the same she had spoken the night Frigg had died, came back to haunt him. Loki felt Erika slipping through his fingers, and he was not about to let that happen.

Striding over to where she stood, he fisted his hand in her hair, giving it a little tug so that she looked up at him. Bending down, he captured her full lips with his. When he swiped his tongue across her lips, she gasped, opening her mouth for him. He kissed her hard, tasting and sucking her tongue until they were both breathless.

Pulling away just a tad, he took a step back and lied to her, "Do not promise me forever. I have to have you, even if it is only for one more night. I beg you."

She swallowed hard, looking like she was going to say no. He knew his actions over the years had been too much for her to believe a word he had spoken, especially since his last sentence had been complete lies. Still, he did not intend to let her go.

He turned away before she could read him, her voice sounding like the most beautiful of poetry or the most exquisite melody as she whispered, "Just one more night."

Loki was in front of her a second later, his own heart feeling like it would explode from his chest. He tore her clothing from her, as she popped open the button to his jeans and shoved them down. Not bothering to kick them off, he lifted her into his arms and leaned her back against the wall. Her body heated at his touch, his cock rock hard.

"I should have known you'd go commando," she mused with a chuckle.

He answered by angling her body and sliding into her tight sheath to the hilt. She swore, causing him to laugh. They both froze as music started to play loudly downstairs. The surprise of it causing them to both laugh, and Erika latched her arms around Loki's neck.

He began to move, slowly at first, sliding in and out as she held on tightly to his neck. When she kissed her way down his jaw, his body caught fire, and he let go of his control and pounded into her, her back slamming against the wall hard enough that the walls shook. Loki kept the frantic pace, capturing Erika's mouth to stifle her screams of climax, even as he emptied himself inside her.

With Erika still clinging to him, Loki kicked off his jeans and strode to the bed. His cock was still inside her, hardening again as the tiny aftershocks of her orgasm gripped him tightly. Lying her on the edge of the bed, he began to move once more. He forgot about the curse, forgot about Odin, and even forgot about Frigg.

Concentrating on having his way with the gorgeous Valkyrie writhing beneath him, Loki vowed to make her his, no matter the cost.

CHAPTER
NINETEEN

Ricky

"What's it feel like to fuck the dead, brother? Do you find yourself wishing you'd had a piece of that ass when she'd been alive with blood in her veins? And now you can compare what it's like to have fucked an animal and a dead girl."

Ricky tossed back the shot of tequila in front of him, slamming the empty glass down on the counter before he called Emily, one of the bar staff at Josephine's, to get him another. Having left Zach in his mother's capable hands, Ricky had spent most of the evening trying to consume as much alcohol as possible. His goal was to black out. So far, he wasn't having much luck, but the night was still young. He also felt like a massive dickhead for abandoning Melanie, but if he'd stayed under the same roof as Killian, Ricky might have killed the little shit.

Emily set down the shot in front of him, letting go a long sigh of annoyance as Ricky downed the shot without a second thought.

"If Josie was here, she'd have kicked your ass out already."

Ricky snorted and grasped his neglected whisky and lifted it in a mock toast. "Then let's be grateful it's her night off, and you have the pleasure of my company."

His lips were numb, and he was pretty sure he was slurring his words, but he just didn't care. He'd flushed the last few white rabbit tablets and was coming down real hard. His magic had begun to bubble inside him while arguing with Killian, willing him to burn his brother to ash. Only Melanie's voice brought him back to himself.

The last time Ricky had gone on a bender of this magnitude was right after he'd come home to find Sadie in bed with another man. Now, Sadie was dead, and he had to deal with trying to be a dad to Zach, who probably hated him.

Slugging down another burn of whiskey, Ricky thought back to the last time he'd gone self-destructive. He'd been kicked out of bars that night too, ended up being tossed out of Josephine's for picking a fight, because he wanted to hurt on the outside as much as he'd been hurting on the inside. Derek had appeared, hauled Ricky up off the ground, and as he swayed drunk, Derek looked at him sternly.

Ricky dropped his head on the bar and closed his eyes, remembering.

Ricky swung wildly at the idiot on the bar, his punch going wild considering he was three sheets to the wind and had the coordination of Bambi on ice. A punch to the gut sent him reeling, until security broke them apart. Things would have ended there if Ricky hadn't decided to lash out at the security guy, earning him a free pass to getting his ass thrown out of the bar. They literally tossed him out, Ricky hitting the ground with a thud as he groaned before he laughed to himself like an idiot.

Face pressed to the cold ground, Ricky groaned as he opened his eyes, his body screaming after the fifth fight of the night. Nausea rolled his stomach, the copious amount of alcohol he'd chugged coming back to bite him in the ass. A booted foot came into view as he rolled onto his back, cursing the throb in his head.

"Dude, I'd move away if I was you. I'm about to upchuck all over your Timberlands."

Hearing the slur in his words, he was surprised that he'd been able to utter even an understandable syllable after gods knows how many beers, whiskey and shots.

"You get sick on my shoes, mate, and you're forking out for a new pair."

Ricky shaded his eyes and looked up at Derek, the werewolf staring down at him with an impenetrable mask. He held out his hand, and Ricky had no choice but to grasp it as Derek pulled him up, his hand on Ricky's shoulder the only thing stopping him from listing over.

"D! Let's go inside and get another pint."

Derek frowned. "They only thing we are going to get is a coffee and something to eat."

Ricky backed away from his friend. "That doesn't sound like fun at all."

"Neither will the bitch of a hangover you're gonna have in the morning. Sarge is going to rip you a new one if you show up hungover again."

Too goddamn late for that... Ricky thought to himself as he stumbled away from Derek and sat down on the bench in the smoking area. Derek stepped up and sat down on the table itself, his legs resting on the seat. Ricky scrubbed a hand down his face.

"I was supposed to get married today."

"I know."

That was all Derek replied, knowing full well that Ricky was freefalling. Today should have been the happiest day of his life, the day Sadie walked down the aisle and they became husband and wife. Instead Ricky stuck a for sale sign on their three-bedroom dream home and tried to find solace at the bottom of a bottle of Jack.

"I want to strangle her. I want to shake her and ask her why she fucking did it. If she'd said she didn't want to marry me, I probably could have deal with that. I want to rip her apart the fucking way she ripped me apart. I wish she was fucking dead, D."

He felt Derek's hand on his shoulder, and the gesture was strangely comforting as if it anchored him to this world, instead of leaving him adrift like he'd felt for the last two weeks.

"You don't mean that, Ricky. I get you're hurting right now, but just remember, there are two things in life you just can't take back, words and bullets. So, make sure you mean what you say, and you hit what you aim for. It hurts now, and it's gonna fucking hurt for a good while. But, you can't continue down this path. I can't bury another friend."

Coming out of his reminiscing, Ricky felt someone sit down beside him and lifted his head to see it was Derek. The wolf gave a nod to Emily, who immediately brought over two coffees. Derek thanked the Fae while Ricky pushed the coffee away and reached for the remains of his whiskey. Derek took the glass and flung it at the wall.

"Goddamn it, Ricky. Don't be an asshole. I don't have time to coddle you, so I'm going to cut the bullshit and give it to you straight. You keep using drugs and drink to self-medicate, and not even I can protect you from what's coming. You will lose the job you love. Melanie will see through those rose-tinted glasses and realize what a mess you are. Your mom won't want to deal with a junkie for a son, and if social services gets wind of what the fuck you are up to, they will take your son from you."

"He'll be better off without me." The words slipped from Ricky's lips, and the next thing he knew, Derek had him by the collar of his shirt, his toes the only things touching the ground. Derek shook him once, and Ricky almost heard his bones rattle.

With a growl, Derek snarled right in his face. "They will take Zach from you, and he will go into the system. Do you want that? Do you want strangers raising your kid, because when the going gets tough, you hit the bottle? Don't fuck up the best thing to happen to you by running at the first sign of trouble."

Derek let him go, and Ricky stood on solid ground again. "What do you want me to do, Derek? The kid hates me. I can't be his dad. I'm not a good person. I'm not a good person."

Derek folded his arms across his chest. "You are one of the best people I know. You might be a sarcastic pain-in-my-ass, but you are a good person, Rick."

Ricky turned away from him, water welling in his eyes. "I'm a fucking junkie."

The words came out in a hushed whisper, but Ricky knew that Derek had heard him.

"Yeah, you are. But what are you gonna do about it?"

Derek was right; damn he was always right. Rickey didn't want to lose Zach. The little boy deserved so much more than him as a father, but Ricky wanted to be the best he could possibly be, and he needed to be drug free for that.

Reaching across the bar, Ricky took the mug of coffee and slugged it down. It did little to clear the fog in his mind, but he looked back at Derek. "I need to get clean. I need to learn how to control my magic, and I need to have done it yesterday."

Derek clapped him on the shoulder. "Do you trust me?"

"With my life."

"Good, then come with me."

Ricky followed Derek out to his car, his feet not moving very swiftly or with great co-ordination. Derek's BMW sat outside the main door, and as Ricky got into the passenger seat, he glanced over at Derek.

"I lost my phone three bars back. Could you text my mom to see if Zach's okay?"

Derek started the engine and moved away from the curb as he answered. "I picked Melanie up at your mom's before I got the call from Emily. Zach was asleep, curled up in your old room. Diane tried to get him to sleep in one of the guest rooms, but your little cat went straight for your room, looked around and said cool, before curling up on the bed to sleep. He's good."

"Cheers."

Ricky leaned his head back, closing his eyes, and only came back to consciousness when Derek stopped the car. He must have fallen asleep. Rubbing his eyes, Ricky looked around and saw they had come to Caitlyn's house.

"Why are we here, D?"

"Just trust me."

Derek's voice held a slight waver, and Ricky turned to his best friend. "Tell me what the fuck we are doing here, Derek, or I ain't getting out of the fucking car!"

"We are getting you clean."

They want to take away your will.

They want to let the magic free to hurt everyone again.

They don't want to make you better, they want to make you worse.

Alarm bells rang like a chorus in his mind, and Ricky flung open the car door, ready to make a bolt for it. As soon as he was in an upright position, Donnie blocked his escape route. The vampire was like a tree; Ricky knew he couldn't escape.

"Hey, Donnie, buddy. Let me by, and I promise, no more happy pills for me. I swear. Just let me go, come on. I thought we were friends."

Donnie looked uncomfortable. "We are friends, Ricky. That's why we have to do this."

Ricky kicked out at Donnie's knee, the vampire was taken by surprise as Ricky bolted down the drive, skidding to a stop when Caitlyn blocked his path. There was no way he would hurt Caitlyn, but flames of blue gathered in his palms.

"Don't make me do this, Caitlyn. Please don't do this to me."

The gravel behind him crunched as strong arms went around his waist, and he felt himself hoisted over a shoulder. Donnie's shoulder dug into Ricky's stomach as he beat a fist against the broad frame of his friend. Caitlyn and Derek followed after, closing the front door and locking it with a click. Donnie strode into the living room, depositing Ricky on the couch.

As soon as his butt hit the cushion, he darted upright, retreating into the corner of Caitlyn's living room like a trapped animal. Concern creased the faces of his friends, and deep down, Ricky knew he was being irrational. The only thing keeping him sane right now was the remnants of white rabbit that lingered in his blood.

He needed to convince them that he was grand.

"C'mon guys, it's me. I do stupid, reckless things and I bounce back. There's no need for this Dr. Phil intervention. I'm grand. I haven't taken anything since Zach showed up on my doorstep. I promise I won't take anymore. You guys just need to back off."

Ricky heard the lies in his pathetic voice even as a voice as sweet as music said. "That's a lie and you know it."

Melanie stepped around Caitlyn, who tried to bar her way. Melanie held Caitlyn's gaze for a second before she removed her arm. This he could work with.

"Lanie, babe," he said with a grin. "You have to tell them I'm good. C'mon Lanie, this is me, Ricky. You know me. Let's get out of here, you and me. *Please*."

Melanie shook her head, and Ricky knew he had lost. "Yeah, I do know you. And so do they, even better than I do. Let us help you, Ricky. Let us save you."

"I wouldn't be in this fucking mess if I hadn't tapped into my magic to try and find you when you got yourself kidnapped." Ricky clasped a hand over his mouth, horrified at the vile words he had just spoken. Sliding down the wall, he cradled his head in his hands.

"I know you didn't mean those words, Ricky. I can taste the lies in your words."

Ricky was disgusted with himself, and he clenched his hands into fists and began to beat them against his temples, wanting to feel the pain, needing to feel it. Fingers grazed his wrist and halted his actions. Lifting his head, Ricky looked into Melanie's eyes and wanted nothing more than to take the sadness away.

"I'm sorry."

"I know."

Melanie rose, stepping away from him, as Donnie came to haul him up. A coldness washed over Ricky and he began to shake, even as he tried to stop himself. Ricky glanced over at Derek as he said. "What do you want me to do?"

"We need to get you clean."

"Well duh, but it will take a few days to get the drugs from my system. I haven't exactly been a one-a-day kinda guy."

Caitlyn strode over to him. "We are going to get the toxins out of your system right now, and then we can deal with everything else."

"Short of locking me up for a few days until my blood burns through it, how the hell are you gonna get the drugs out of my system?"

Donnie grinned, using his best count Dracula voice. "We are going to drink your blood."

"Or more accurately, I am," confirmed Caitlyn, as Ricky shrank back.

"Oh, no way in hell. Caitlyn, my blood's toxic. You can't do that."

Caitlyn placed her hand on his arm. "Donnie is too young to deal with the blow back of the drugs. I am not. This is happening."

"C'mon lads, there has to be another way. I can go cold turkey, not a bother."

Melanie sat down on the couch and called him over. Ricky went, simply to get away from Caitlyn. His palms were sweaty when Melanie took his hand in hers and said, "You'll be okay. I won't let anything happen to you. Close your eyes for me."

Ricky glanced around at the faces of his friends, doing as Melanie asked so he could avoid the pity in their eyes. He felt Caitlyn sweep the hair from the nape of his neck, and he shivered, waiting for the feel of fangs on his neck.

Caitlyn's fangs pierced his skin a second later, causing Ricky to jerk. Caitlyn drinking from him was different than the time Donnie had done it. Ricky felt the blood being sucked, felt his head begin to clear as the drugs trickled away.

Ricky felt himself weaken, his body held up by someone's steadying hands. He wondered if he could die like this. Even as his strength left him, Ricky felt his body harden, mortified that he had no control. Melanie continued to grip his hand, and he willed Donnie not to say a bloody word.

Donnie chuckled. "I won't say a thing, mate."

Ricky felt the moment the drugs left his system and his magic came flooding back. The dam built up by the drugs was gone, the firepower inside him building quickly, looking for release. He jerked away from Caitlyn, ripping his throat in the process, so he would not harm her.

He fell to his knees and vomited. Muscles locked and back arched and flames erupted on his skin, a blue lightning dancing up his arms. It sparked deep inside him, and he screamed, as if his insides were being ripped apart.

Ricky vaguely heard Melanie scream for help, and Donnie curse, stating they hadn't thought things through. A ball of magic exploded in his stomach, and Ricky wanted nothing more than to die at that moment. Then all he could hear was the blood rushing to his head as an arm locked him in a choke-hold, stopping his ability to breathe.

The fire lashed out, striking at his assailant, while spots flashed in his vision. His hands grasped the arm at his throat, and when Ricky tried to speak, his words came out in a croaked strangle of sounds. His legs kicked out, sending the coffee table flying, and he was helpless to stop his evitable tumble into the abyss.

I don't wanna die...

It was the last thought he was able to project, and he hoped Donnie heard his plea.

Right before he fell into darkness, Ricky was sure he heard someone crying.

FELIX SAT behind his desk at the arena, trying to match up fights for the coming evening, livid that the berserker had failed to kill the Valkyrie and had left Felix without one of his best fighters. Now that Erika had chosen to abscond also, his investors were screaming for blood, and the blood they wanted was his.

"How hard is it to keep hold of good staff these days?" Felix muttered to himself.

"I understand utterly, my friend. People have trouble following orders these days. Where have the good old days gone?"

Felix leapt out of his seat. The speaker was a man with a snow-white beard and matching hair, an eyepatch covering one eye, and a golden spear in one of his hands. Chaos swirled around the man in dangerous levels, and Felix knew he was in the presence of something other.

"What do you want?" the chaos demon asked, but the man moved faster than the blink of an eye, his hands twisting Felix's neck before the demon had the chance to hear a response.

Odin dropped Felix's body to the ground, morphing his own body into that of the games master. With a tap of his staff on the ground, the dead body disappeared, just as one of the security guards popped his head inside.

"Everything okay, boss?"

"Everything is fine. Someone summon the Valkyrie for me. Tell her I have an offer that she cannot refuse."

The security nodded, leaving Odin alone in his guise as the games master. Glancing in the mirror, Odin smiled. It was time that he rid the world of the Valkyrie general. With her gone, he would have a clear path at Ever, and not only the keys to Valhalla, but the keys to Ragnorok as well.

The world would become anew, and when the world was reborn, his beloved Frigg would come back to him, and he would never let her go again.

CHAPTER
TWENTY

Erika

T he arena was eerily quiet when Erika flashed to the abandoned building, the usual hum of noise and cheers gone. Perhaps that should have been her first clue that not all was right in the world when she left Loki in her bed to answer the games master's summons. She could still feel Loki's touch on her skin, and she still wanted him. Despite the murmured promises that he had whispered while their bodies were intertwined, she found it hard to believe that he would not grow bored of her and leave her in shattered pieces when he was done sating himself.

Packing up the few bits of clothing and weapons she had at her room at the arena, she felt a strange awareness prick her senses. Abandoning her belongings, she grabbed her blades and strode out of the room, sauntering down the hall, blades out in front of her.

The hall was abandoned, as was the viewing area. Every instinct in Erika's body told her to flee, but curiosity got the better of her. Glancing down at the octagon, Erika could see Felix draped over a high-backed chair in the centre of the ring. The blue-skinned chaos demon lounged in the chair as if it were a throne, and the arena was his kingdom.

"Come, Valkyrie, I have need of you."

Felix's voice held a sharp edge to it, and Erika slowly made her way down the battered staircase to stride down the long ramp toward the cage. The door had been flung open, and when Felix lifted his gaze to meet hers, she saw her death in his eyes.

"What's with the summons, Felix?" she said and walked into the octagon, swivelling her blades in her wrists, her voice not wavering once.

Felix tilted his head and assessed her, before a grin replaced the scowl on his lips. "You are just as beautiful as your mother was. Those eyes, those lips, even down to the sun-kissed skin of yours. It is like seeing a ghost."

Erika's heart plummeted at the spoken words. *Was?*

A comfortable distance away from him, she rested the tip of her blades on the mat and leaned against them as if she had not sensed what lurked behind the guise of Felix. Had he forgotten in the hundred years that he had slept, that Erika was alive and honing her skills?

"I wasn't aware you knew my mother, Felix. Perhaps you can tell me about her, since I have little or no memories of the woman who gave birth to me."

Felix tapped the goatee on his chin and made to stroke down a beard that was not there before he frowned and began to speak. "Your mother was a disciple of Eir, a goddess famed for her medical skill. A tremendous beauty, Livana was courted by many a god, yet she only wanted to be of us to the warriors in battle. Had she lived beyond her return to Vanaheim, having deposited her bastard child in Valhalla, then Livana could have become one of the Vanir. Had her life not be snuffed out by an assassin."

Her mother was dead, and that was why she did not come back for Erika. All the years of wondering summed up in one collection of words. Oh, Erika would mourn the mother she now had a name for once the beast was slain, but for now, she held firm. He would not see her waver.

The mirage of Felix tapped his chin again. "Did you know, dear Valkyrie, that even the great Odin courted your mother, but another god had already tempted her? Freya had already given birth to Ever, yet Odin, he wanted to recreate the Valkyrie race with a horde of daughters. Alas, his beloved Frigg birthed only sons."

"Perhaps the cosmos was trying to tell Odin that you cannot fight nature. We are born Valkyrie or we are not. That has been how it has been since the first star twinkled in the sky. Why should it be any different?"

Fake Felix curved his lips into a sadistic smile. "Even on Midgard, the humans are obsessed about creating the perfect soldier. Ones that will be the last men standing on the battlefield. But they discount the women. Women who are as blood thirsty as the men, but who fight for many different reasons. The closest I came to seeing the perfect soldier was when I laid eyes on you, Valkyrie."

Erika balanced the weight evenly, giving the man her biggest smile. "I assume there is an insult in that complement somewhere. I am a Valkyrie. I was born to wield a sword. I was born to carry the souls of the worthy to Valhalla for the final battle the world will face. I am not perfect. A perfect soldier does not love, does not care, does not think of things other than war, and blood, and glory."

"I blame that on your mother. For your father never once strayed from his path until he laid eyes on Livana."

Erika's heart raced. *Her father*...she needed a name.

"Come now, Allfather. Drop the guise and we shall continue this as Asgardians."

Waving his hands over his face, the face of Felix disappeared only to be replaced by Odin, Ever's father. Odin smoothed his hair and clasped his hands together in his lap. An eye patch still covered the appendage Ever had sunk a knife into upon her first death. Erika knew that Odin had the power to fix the wound, if he chose to, but for some reason, the mighty god decided not to. Dressed in golden robes and bare feet, he was the Odin Erika remembered from his visits to Valhalla, the dark aura of grief like a noose around his neck.

"Is that better, my dear?"

Erika snorted, the ghost of a smile on her lips. "I'm not sure if it's better. I prefer my men less old man-ish. I'm sure you were a handsome devil in your day, like Sean Connery, but, no offense, you just ain't my type."

To her surprise, Odin chuckled. Cracking the muscles in his neck, he studied her for a moment before he said, "No offense taken. From what I have heard from my spies, you lust after my daughter like a puppy, and my son has finally lured you to become another notch on his bedpost."

"Yadda, yadda, yadda. Erika's made some poor choices. Nothing new there, Odin. Now why have you brought me all the way here? If you want me to summon Ever, then you came to the wrong Valkyrie."

"I want to cripple my daughter with your death and send her your head in a box. I want to smell her fear in the air and watch as I take away those around her until she has nothing but me left in the world."

Erika laughed, incensing the god before her. He growled in anger. "I will tear you limb from limb, and when your soul flees your corpse, on its journey to Folkvangr, I will snatch it in my grasp. Your soul will scream for mercy, and you will have none."

Erika lifted a hand to stifle a mock yawn. "Dude, you're boring me now."

"Do you not understand, little girl," Odin snarled, rising from his chair, which instantly vanished, and his staff appeared in his grasp. "That it was I who created the first Valkyrie. And it is I who can destroy every last one until none of you exist."

"As I said, old man. We are born Valkyrie because it is our destiny, it is in our blood, written in the stars so that not even you, the mighty Odin, can stop a Valkyrie from being born. You may be the first of all Asgardians, but you were also created by beings more powerful than you are. I do not bow down to a man who has killed his own flesh and blood many times over. My blood and my loyalty stands with the queen who has earned it, not demanded it. If I am to go to my death on this day, then I go knowing my queen knows of my love and loyalty toward her. So let us stop with all the chatter, Odin, and see if death awaits me or you."

Erika did not hesitate a moment more before she lunged for Odin, the god vanishing before her eyes. She felt the hair on her neck stand to attention, whirled around, and managed to strike the god as he reformed at her back. He lifted his staff and plunged it into the mat, sending a shockwave rippling across the foundations, and Erika flying across the ring. Her back smacked against the wire, but she ignored the burst of fire along her spine as she sprang to her feet again, her blades criss-crossed and ready to strike. Erika disappeared in the blur of movement, every move instinctive and practiced until perfect on the moonlight beaches of Valhalla.

Odin lifted his staff to unsettle the earth once more, yet Erika slid across the mat, crossed her blades and halted the action, gritting her teeth at the sheer power in Odin's strike. She heard the clash of lightening outside, and she kicked out her legs in a scissor movement, sending Odin down to the mat, the god trembling with anger at being bested by her.

He cautiously got back on his feet, leaving her puzzled by the look of pride in his eyes. "When I created the Valkyrie, you are exactly what I envisioned. Pledge your loyalty to me, Erika. Stand by my side, become my new queen. I will only offer this to you once, and once only. Become my equal and we shall rebuild the world anew."

Erika rolled into a crouch and blew a stray strand of hair from her face. "I have no desire to be a queen. I am the general of Queen Ever's army. I am content with my lot. Why can you not be?"

Odin smiled wider, his eyes shifting as lightning struck the octagon. Ever appeared smack in the middle of Odin and Erika. Ever's eyes widened at the sight of her father, and Odin twisted his staff, ready to strike. Time seemed to stand still as Erika cast her blades aside and dove for Ever, knowing that when Odin drove the staff into Erika, she would die. But, if it came down to a choice between her and Ever, then Erika was happy to die for the cause.

I wish I had more time with her, with Loki, even the team.

Just as Ever screamed, and Erika wrapped her arms around her best friend's waist, the mirage evaporated. Erika sank to the ground, cursing herself for falling for Odin's trick. She lifted her head, peering through her lashes to hold Odin's gaze, the tip of Odin's staff morphing into a sharp edge that she had no doubt would pierce her flesh easily.

"Do you have any last words, Valkyrie?"

"I'll see you in Hel, Odin. I'm sure Hela will have a throne of ash and bone awaiting you."

Without so much as blinking, Erika waited as Odin recoiled his arm, gave her a smug, satisfied smile that said, I have won, and went to strike. She waited for the blow that would end her life.

But it never came. A burst of frost to Odin's chest sent him backwards, his staff sliding off in the opposite direction. Erika clambered to her feet to see Loki marching down the ramp. He looked like an avenging angel, his long cloak fluttering in the wind, his face full of anger, his skin flickering a shade of blue as ice shards crystalized on his fingertips.

Odin clapped, mocking Loki who held out a hand to help her rise. "I should have drowned you, boy, when you were a baby."

"Perhaps, Odin. But you did not. And I will not stand by while you kill another person I care for."

Odin's laugh thundered around the empty arena. "Care for? You, Loki, care for no one but yourself. Has it come to be that the god of trickery, whose own children despise him, whose lovers have been left heartbroken, miserable, and sometimes tethering on the edge of death, has finally weakened like the Midgardians he used to scoff at?"

Loki's skin returned to its natural pale shading. "Maybe, Odin, I have finally found the person my mother had always wanted for me to love. Do you forget what it is like to love and be loved?"

"I do this because I know what it is to love, boy."

"If that was true, then you would not have made a deal to kill the only daughter you have in an attempt to regain the love you lost. Do you think mother could love you, knowing she was reborn, and Ever's life was forfeit in the process?"

Odin said nothing, so Loki patted Erika on her cheek and said. "Are you alright?"

"I am."

With a nod, he turned back to Odin. "Do you know why I suggested that blasted curse? I wanted to give you time to get over your grief and remember that you had people who cared for you. But do you know what happened? Because of your actions, because you forgot who you once were, the people who cared for you stopped doing so. You can only do so much evil before the world forgets that you may have once been good and just."

Odin held out his hand, his staff floating across the room until it once more was grasped in his hand. "And your little plan backfired, as most of them do. I will kill the daughter who only lives because I chose to lay with her mother. Then I will usher in the new world, rid the world of those Midgard ants and create the world as it should have been."

Loki shook his head. "Do you forget in your old age that it was you and your brother who created the humans? You are the architect of your own misfortune. Come now, lay down your staff, and we can try and broker peace."

"Peace? Peace!" Odin scoffed, running a hand down his white beard. "There will be no peace. The time for peace has long since passed. I will not sleep, I will not bend until my task is complete. Stand not in my way, Loki, and you can spend the rest of your life carrying on in a similar fashion as you have done for centuries. The Valkyrie matters little."

"The Valkyrie matters much."

"Then there is nothing more to say."

Odin shot a bolt of lightning at Loki, and Erika reacted, shoving him out of the way, taking the bolt right in the shoulder. Letting loose a scream of agony, she went to the ground, clamping a hand over the gushing wound. Mere inches south, and the bolt would have gone to the heart, killing her in an instant. She may be a Valkyrie, made to ride the storms, but Odin was still a god. Her ears rang, and her head spun as Loki sank down to his knees, gently cradling her in his arms.

"Silly general. That bolt could not have killed me."

Erika winced as Loki lifted her hand to assess the damage. "Something you could have said before I got struck by lightning."

"Hush now. Argue with me later. You will need time for this to heal."

Odin chuckled behind them. "She might not need that much time to heal. Has she told you who her mother is, Loki? Or did Erika speak the truth when she said she could not remember her own mother's name."

Loki peered down at Erika, who tried to shrug, puzzled at why that was important to Odin. "My mother's name was Livana."

Loki's eyes widened, and for a moment Erika thought she was going to be sick. "Please don't tell me you slept with my mother... please don't say it."

Leaning in to brush his lips over her forehead, Loki whispered, "No, I did not sleep with Livana, but I know who did."

Thunder rumbled, the entire building shaking as the ceiling came down around them, an angry god and his hammer coming to stand between them and Odin. Thor, god of Thunder, protector of Midgard and all its inhabitants, lifted his head and glared at his father, Mjölnir planted on the ground. Thor rose to his full height, almost seven feet tall, his mane of reddish blonde hair whipping in the wind, thunder in his eyes.

"Father, stop this foolish errand. Ragnarok is not what the world needs. It is not your place to try and recreate the world. Let it be and return to Asgard."

Odin stepped forward, but Thor did not even flinch. Growing up, Erika had been terrified of Ever's brother. And now she understood why. The power that coiled in Thor's body, the unbridled strength, might be the only thing to save them this day.

"My son, it is good to see you after all this time." Odin held out his arms. "Have you no embrace for your father?"

Thor made no attempt to step into Odin's open arms, and Erika watched amazed, her senses overworked dealing with the power in the room, her shoulder screaming in agony.

"If the father I loved was in front of me, then I would welcome his embrace."

Odin dismissed his son with the wave of his hand. "Never mind. When the world is created anew, I will bring you back, my son, with no memories of this unfortunate stage of our lives."

"And Ever, my sister, do you plan to bring her back?"

Odin shook his head. "Ever should never have been born. I must right that wrong."

Lifting his staff in the air, he brought it down to rip the ground apart. It trembled as Odin grinned, dodging a blast of ice from Loki before he said, "I will take my leave. Sons, make sure to tell the general why she was chosen to be a Valkyrie. If you survive my berserkers, that is."

Loki let loose a yell of anger, sending a cool blast of ice toward Odin, who was unable to move in time to prevent the icicle from catching him on the arm. As he vanished, the god roared in pain.

"Did you get him?" Thor asked, his voice booming.

"I think I did."

Erika glanced upward, spotting five berserkers watching them from the balcony above. "Um guys...we got company." She got to her feet as Loki handed her one of her blades. He said nothing more, but cast a grin in Thor's direction.

"It has been an age, brother, since we have caused any mischief together."

"Then let us right that wrong. Valkyrie, are you ready for this?"

"I was born ready." Erika snorted as the berserkers clambered over the railings.

I was born for this.

CHAPTER
TWENTY-ONE

Erika

E rika had been at many a battleground. She had walked across scorched earth, watched as brave men and women fought until their deaths, and then ferried their souls onward. Blood and gore had stained her skin and hands, yet she always considered the battlefield something of great beauty. But she had never seen a more beautiful sight than watching the man who captured her heart fight.

Loki moved with a grace that was simply him, just Loki. The smile never left his face as he slashed and sliced, letting his frost giant powers free to take down the berserkers Odin had sicced on them. Erika couldn't help but grin as Loki winked over his shoulder at her.

She had one arm against her stomach and used her uninjured arm to keep the berserkers at bay. Thor worked his way through the two that came at him, using his trusty hammer to smash in their skulls with one monstrous thud. Erika managed to gut her own berserker from navel to neck before Thor and Loki dispatched their opponents.

Then and only then, when all the berserkers were dead, did she drop her blade, sink down to the ground, and let out an array of swear words at the pain in her shoulder. The gash, ripped open more by the fighting, had her collapsing to her knees.

Loki rushed to her side. She looked up and demanded. "Tell me who my father is."

Loki glanced over his shoulder at Thor, who was cleaning his hammer of the berserker's clothing. "It seems we solved the mystery that kept us awake for many a century. She was under our nose the entire time. Thor, let me introduce you to Erika, the long-lost daughter of Livana."

Thor's eyes widened, his bushy eyebrows rising to meet his hairline. Loki waved his hand over Erika's wound, and it was cleaned and bandaged. She sat up straighter, as Thor began to speak.

"You, dearest Erika, we have searched for, having promised our dear friend that we would not rest until you were found. He will be pleased that we have found you, even if it has taken us some time. And it appears Odin knew who you were all this time."

Erika almost couldn't breathe as tears filled her eyes. "My father is alive? And he knows of me?"

Loki caressed her cheek with his knuckles. "He does. When he learned that Livana, with whom he had fallen deeply in love with, had given birth to a Valkyrie, he was filled with immense pride. Upon returning from a battle with his army, he sought out Livana, only to find that she had died, and the little girl seemingly vanished from Asgard."

"Freya," she gasped. "Freya knew all this time. And she said nothing."

"It seems so." Thor said grimly.

She gingerly got to her feet, pointed a finger and pressed it against Loki's chest. "You, you tell me right now who my father is, or so help me, I will beat it from you."

Erika expected Loki to be at least a little outraged, yet he chuckled, the sound caressing her as she glared at him.

"What the hell is so funny?"

Thor clasped Loki on the back. "How did you not know, brother? She even sounds like him when his temper wavers. I shudder to think what he will think once he finds out that you have claimed the Valkyrie as your own."

Loki, with eyes of universes and galaxies, held her gaze as he said, "I claimed her before I knew who she was. I claimed her because she and I are one in the same. If only I can convince her my words are the truth."

She stomped her foot, anger turning to rage. "Oh, for fuck sake! Stop with the cryptic B.S and just tell it to me straight."

Thor nudged Loki aside, his big hand clasping her uninjured shoulder. "You, Erika, are the daughter of Livana, and of our friend and fierce warrior, who I have had the honour of fighting alongside, as I have done with you today. You are no mere Valkyrie, you are the daughter of the god of war, my friend, Tyr."

Erika blinked. She was the daughter of a god? But that meant? She was... she was?

Loki grinned at her. "That means that you, my darling, are a goddess. The goddess of war, in fact.

Her head spun. Loki was speaking to her, but she couldn't hear his words.

Every time she had lost her temper, every time she had answered back to Freya, arguing that her plan of action was better, every single snide remark made by Danae about Erika's heritage and all along she was a goddess. War was in her blood; it was in her makeup.

But that did not take away the fact that Tyr happened to be a stranger. As Erika looked up and saw lust in Loki's eyes, she couldn't help but wonder if he knew all along who and what she was.

His gaze narrowed as he read her thoughts, a small sigh escaping his lips. "That is not something I would have kept from you, Erika. Whatever you think of me, I have never lied to you."

Thor, oblivious to what was going on around him, clapped his hands before reaching down and swinging his hammer over his shoulder. "Come, let us return to Asgard and bring Tyr is daughter. I know he would come himself, but someone must stay behind to guard Asgard from Odin."

Erika backed away. "I'm not going to Asgard. I don't want to meet him. He would have known. Surely, he would have felt me when I ran through the halls as a child with Ever. We must have crossed paths, and he never once came looking for me. I never heard of anyone looking for the lost child of Livana."

Thor scratched his head with the handle of his hammer. "Tyr knew that assassins had killed Livana. He could not risk your life by announcing you to the world. Livana never told a soul who your father was. Their relationship was a secret one. If someone had captured you, think of what they could do with the god of war, if they controlled him. I assume that is what Odin wanted with you."

With the shake of her head, Erika mumbled, "It doesn't matter. This changes nothing. I'm still me."

Loki, a sad smile on his face, came forward. "Of course you are, Erika. You are still the brave, reckless, cunning, funny and sarcastic woman I know and who I..."

Holding up a finger, Erika growled. "Don't say it. Don't say it if you don't mean it. I am not her, this goddess of war that you proclaim me to be. I am Erika, daughter of no one, born of sand and blood. I am a Valkyrie and I am a general. I will not be someone's pawn, and I certainly will not be someone's plaything."

Gesturing between herself and Loki, she continued, "This thing between us, whatever it is, it's over. Do not come after me."

First, she flashed to the nearest place that sold alcohol, grabbed a bottle of Jack from behind the counter, tossed some notes to the cashier, and flashed to the shores of Valhalla.

As soon as her feet touched the sand, Erika screamed into the abyss and dropped to the sand. Unscrewing the bottle, she gulped down a fair amount, relishing the burn at the back of her throat before she paused for air. Beating a fist into the sand, she let the tears fall down, gulping down another shot of Jack, before she felt him on the sand behind her.

Of course, Loki would not have listened to her. Trying her best to ignore him, she felt the waves of anger seeping from him, and she lifted the half-empty bottle of Jack in salute. "Please, leave. Jack and I are having a party in the sand and you are not invited. Go find some other poor sap to warm your bed. I'm done."

She yelped as Loki yanked her off the ground, almost causing her to lose Jack, and pressed his lips hard against hers. When

Erika, who wanted nothing more than to drown herself in Loki, remained stiff and unyielding, he pulled back, his hands clasping her face.

"You do not just get to make that decision out of fear, Erika. You paint me to be this nefarious character and perhaps I am. But I have not, and will not, speak a word of untruth to you. I will gladly play this villain, if you really want to be painted as the hero."

She shoved at his chest, but the stubborn bastard refused to move. "I never claimed to be the hero. I feel like I'm sinking in quicksand. Everything I thought I was has changed with the click of fingers, and I don't know how to deal. I could stand by, thinking that I loved Ever and watch her with Derek because it was destined to be that way. But I can't let myself love you, and then later have to watch you be with someone else."

Loki leaned in, his lips mere inches from her own, his breath warm on her skin. "I do not like to share either. Thor was right when he said Tyr will likely strangle me for claiming you as my own. And I do claim you, Erika, daughter of no one. And I have claimed you long, long ago. Let me show you."

He pressed two fingers to her temple, and Erika's body jerked as the world tinged grey before she found herself looking at a late teen version of herself through Loki's eyes.

Oh, she is magnificent.

I stood watching her for far too long, hidden from eyesight, but every now and then, this girl who made me yearn for something more for the first time in an eon, glanced in my direction as if she knew I watched her. It was like I felt her every single time she accompanied Ever to the keep, using my sister's visit as a mask to see the Valkyrie whose smile lit up the room.

And pierced the wall encasing my heart.

The sky glistened with starlight, as she moved her body, eyes shut, her movements fluid and instinctive. Having watched her for hours, the other Valkyrie had retired for the evening, but not the general. She stayed long after day became dusk and dusk became night.

Her eyes snapped open. For a moment they appeared to hold mine, and I could almost believe she could see through my invisibility. See me. Opening a bottle of water, she gulped down the entire thing before smiling in my direction.

I stepped out of the shadows, her pulse racing as I became visible, and I hated how much it thrilled me.

"How long have you been standing there?"

I felt my lips tug up into a smile. "Longer than you'd like."

Folding her arms across her chest, she tossed her hair off her shoulders. "So you came to see Ever, right? She's back at her place with Freya."

I inched closer, wanting to get as near to her as possible, despite knowing it would be centuries before I could touch her. She may look like a grown woman, yet she was still a child. I would not stifle her growth with my possessiveness too soon.

"And if I said I'd come to see you?"

She laughed, and an iron fist gripped my chest. "I'd call you a liar. Anyways, I gotta get some sleep before the sun rises. See ya around, Loki."

I did not reply, simply watched her walk away from me, arguing with myself as I longed to follow her and hold her as we slept. I did not know what was becoming of me, but I knew this Valkyrie warrior would be my undoing.

Erika stumbled backward as Loki removed his fingers. She felt it, the intensity in which he loved her, how he kept his distance to allow her space to live and grow, and she managed to clutch a thought from his mind before he released her.

"You haven't been with anyone since you realized you might feel something more for me."

Loki inclined his head. "I tried, for a time, to rid myself of my obsession for you. But each bedfellow I had left me feeling hollow. When I thought on it, I realized that I could not be satisfied with anyone but you."

She put a hand to her mouth. "And you let me sleep around and said nothing."

"It was not my place to stop you. I had to believe that you would find me in the end."

He reached out and tilted her head up. "Turns out, we were both created in chaos, we were both born to destroy. You, Erika, were like war, and I was like death. And when we clashed, darling, I loved you."

Crushing his lips to hers, Erika kissed him back, her hand sliding up to tug at his hair, finally understanding what it was to be loved. Lost in each other's touch, Erika failed to sense the entity behind them. They were only alerted by the clearing of a throat.

Loki, bless him, shoved Erika behind him, trying to protect her, an action that had her lifting her brows. She stepped beside him and laced her fingers into his. He did not seem surprised by their visitor, the braided hair and chocolate of her skin reminding Erika of a forgotten people who lived in remote villages.

"What are you doing here?"

"I have come to see if you have changed."

The woman came closer and Erika could smell the magic on her skin. She reached for a blade, remembering with a groan that they were lying in the octagon covered in berserker blood.

"Fear not, little Valkyrie. I bear good tidings." She clapped her hands twice, clicked her fingers and muttered to herself before stamping her feet and tossing some dust in Loki's direction.

He coughed and hissed out a breath.

"Loki, forgotten son of Jutenhiem, put yourself in harm's way to protect this girl. You allowed her into your heart, abstained from having lovers because you knew she was the one you wanted forever."

"If you say so."

"The old you, the one who slept with my granddaughter and ruined her, spent a lifetime watching over Erika, putting your own feelings aside to make her happy. That is why I lifted the curse. She has made you better." The woman turned to Erika. "You did not want to love him, for you were terrified of being abandoned like your mother did to you. The future can be saved, but only if you stick together."

The woman disappeared in the blink of an eye. Erika peered up at Loki. "A curse?"

He leaned down to brush his lips over hers. "That is a story for another day. Let's go home. Shall we go to your place or mine?"

She smiled, her heart feeling like it might burst, while her thoughts raged inside her mind. What was it the strange woman had said? *The future can be saved, but only if you stick together.*

"You need to take me to Ever's right now!"

"Darling, I like your enthusiasm."

She smacked him gently on the shoulder. "Shush, I have an idea on how to stop Odin. We must go to Ever's."

He pulled her close, and she wrapped her arms around his neck. A second later, they were standing in Ever's living room, she shrieked and leapt up from the couch, book in hand poised to strike.

"Are you seriously gonna hit me with a book?"

"If I had something heavier, I'd fling it at your heads. At least knock before you flash in and scare me half to deat– what happened to your shoulder?"

Erika detangled herself from Loki. "Your dad thought I could do with a dose of lightning to the chest. Well, he aimed for Loki and like an idiot I pushed him out of the way."

"It was rather noble," he said with a grin and flopped down onto the couch, his legs dangling over the edge, a tumbler in his grasp.

"And then Thor appeared, Loki blasted Odin with ice, we kicked some berserker ass. I found out that I am the daughter of the god of war, oh and me and your brother have decided to give things a go. You cool with that?"

Ever's mouth dropped open, she tried to speak, and then shook her head. Walking over to take the tumbler from Loki, Ever said, "I need a drink."

When she had composed herself, she turned back to Erika and gave her a small smile. "So, Tyr is your father?"

Erika shrugged. "I guess so."

"Are you going back to Asgard?"

"Hell no. Midgard is too much fun."

Ever looked at Loki and then back at Erika. "Are you sure about this?"

Looking into the ocean coloured eyes of her best friend, Erika's heart did not flutter, it did not skip a beat or race while Ever held her gaze. "Yes, I'm in love with him."

"Then, that is all that matters."

Erika set a hand on Ever's arm. "Let me apologize."

Ever yanked Erika in for a hug. "There is no need for any apologises. I'm gorgeous, how could you not think you were in love with me?"

They both started to laugh as Erika said, "You are definitely spending too much time with me, that's totally something I'd say."

Tucking her legs under her butt, Ever sat down on the armchair. "So, Odin is awake and causing trouble."

"Thor has gone in search of him, but no doubt he will come visit soon. He is eager to see you." Loki said with a smile.

Ever smiled, but turned to look at Erika. "So why the late-night visit? What's got your eyes twinkling in mischief?"

Folding her arms across her chest, Erika smiled, because she was the goddess of war and if that was what Odin wanted, then who was she to deny him a glorified death. Because Loki was right, she was war and he was death, and together, they were unstoppable.

Loki lifted the new tumbler in his grasp in salute, and Erika turned and faced Ever.

"I need you to call Boyband and get the team here. It's time they all learned the truth."

Ever pulled her phone out of her jeans and hesitated before dialing the number. "What have you in mind, Erika?"

Erika grinned. "I am a general. I am the goddess of war. And I am putting together an army. Let's see who has the balls to volunteer."

CHAPTER
TWENTY-TWO

Ricky

"I knew we should have thought this through more."

"Donnie, how were we supposed to know he would go nuclear on us?"

"I know, Derek, but it's my mate that's bawling her eyes out thinking she killed the idiot."

Ricky heard the distorted voices of his friends as he woke up with the mother of all hangovers. It took a serious amount of effort for him to open his eyes, lifting his lids slowly, almost closing them again against the glare of the lights overhead. The floral wallpaper was not his cup of tea, so he knew he wasn't at his house, the memory of going to Caitlyn's house last night slowly coming back to him. He made to lift his arm and shield his eyes from the light, but found that his arm would not move.

Glancing down at his wrists, he saw that they were manacled to the bed in some way, preventing him from moving. A quick wiggle of his legs confirmed his suspicions. He was tied down.

"Kinky," he grumbled, snapping the attention of his two besties. He tried to get comfortable. The pressure in his head made him want to scream at the top of his lungs, but from the expressions on Donnie and Derek's faces, doing so might actually get him killed. What the hell had happened to put that terror in their eyes?

Memories came back in a wave that brought tears to his eyes. Ricky huddled in a corner begging them to not drain the drugs from his system, Melanie talking him down, Caitlyn drinking his blood and then the magic, all the pent-up magic in his system had exploded from him and tried to fucking kill him.

"Did I hurt anyone?" he managed to croak out, but his friends remained silent.

"Derek, who the hell did I hurt?"

Derek came over to crouch by the side of the bed. "When the drugs left your system, you sounded like you were being ripped apart. We tried to stop you, but you were on fire. Donnie managed to get you in a headlock and knock you unconscious. He's fine now after some blood."

Ricky closed his eyes so that his friends would not see the shame in them. "I'm sorry. I'm so fucking sorry."

"Don't sweat it, Ricky. I always said I was smoking hot. You just went literal with it."

Ricky barked out a laugh. "How can you joke when I could have killed you?"

Donnie shrugged. "I should have known better, as someone who drank your blood once. Since then, your magic has grown, and I saw what it was doing to you." Donnie tapped the side of his head. "I knew what was going on and said nothing, too caught up in drama with Cait and Melanie. I let you down, mate. I'm sorry."

Ricky shook his head, but Donnie went on. "I'm gonna go tell Cait that you're awake. She's been beside herself all day waiting for you to come around. Been muttering in French as she came down from the high. Under normal circumstances, Caitlyn stoned would be hilarious. Gimmie a sec."

The big man left the room with an ease that should not have been possible for a man of his size. Ricky watched Donnie leave, his shoulders slumped, and cursed himself for being such a burden.

Rattling the chains, Ricky angled his head to get a clearer view of Derek. "Fancy taking the handcuffs off now, D? I feel fine."

He shook his head. "That's because the chains are spelled to contain magic. We are waiting for something that will help you, in a safe way, to arrive and then I'll let you free."

So, that was why he couldn't feel the magic inside himself.

"Can you at least take the leg ones off so I can sit up?"

Derek rose, walked down to the end of the bed and unlocked the cuffs, and Ricky scooted to an upright position, arching his feet to remove the stiffness. Silence ensued for a minute or two before Ricky plucked up the courage to ask the question he was dreading.

"Melanie saw everything, didn't she? Did I hurt her?"

Derek pressed his lips together in a firm line, his expression grim before he spoke. "Ya, she saw everything, but you didn't hurt her. The moment she got near you, you turned the magic in on yourself somehow. While we were waiting for the chains to arrive, you woke up screaming. When Melanie reached out to grab you, the flames on your arms burned you, not her. Even when you were out of it, you wouldn't hurt her."

"I wouldn't be in this fucking mess if I hadn't of tapped into my magic to try and find you when you got yourself kidnapped."

Ricky cringed as his words came back to haunt him. "Until I open my mouth that is."

Derek leaned against the wall, folding his arms across his chest. "Good thing about truth seekers, they always can tell when you mean what you say. Doesn't mean the words don't hurt, so always try and mean what you say."

"Because you can't take them back."

With a smile, Derek nodded, remembering the words he had once spoken to Ricky. "Exactly."

Ricky heard footsteps come down the hall, and Caitlyn's tearstained face came into view, those onyx eyes filled with fear. Ricky hated that he had done that to her. He flashed a smile but Caitlyn did not return it. Surprise welled inside him, not because he and Caitlyn were not close, but he always felt that she tolerated him simply because he was a work colleague and friends with the other guys. While he considered her family, Ricky had never been sure that she thought of him in that way.

"And I am very sorry that I ever made you think that way."

Ricky wagged his finger at her. "Hey, no mind reading. One of you is bad enough. Plus, you drank my blood. I think in our weird ass little gang it makes us family."

Caitlyn began to tremble as if shock had suddenly hit her.

"Hey Caitlyn, I'm good. I'm still me. Although I'm not sure if that's a good thing."

The next thing Ricky knew, Caitlyn had her arms around him, the wetness of her tears trickling down his neck, and Ricky looked up at Donnie with eyes wide.

What do I do? He silently asked, and his friend helpfully just shrugged.

"Caitlyn, it's okay. I'm sorry I upset you. But it's me. It probably won't be the last time." Caitlyn said something in French, but Ricky had no clue what she said. Easing back, she sat down on the edge of the bed and looked him in the eyes. "I thought that I had killed you."

"Nah, I've got like nine lives or some shit. Can't get rid of me that easy."

She patted his cheek like he was a child, and he gave her a small smile. Looking back at Derek, Ricky said. "So what happens now?"

Derek pushed off the wall and came to sit on a chair to Ricky's right. He stretched out his long legs and folded his hands in his lap. "Draven is getting help from the coven to make something that will help supress your magic in a healthy way until you get the hang of things. There's no more self-medicating, Ricky. We can't go through this again. You will listen to what we have to say, got it?"

"Ya."

"Right now," Derek continued. "You are taking an official leave of absence from work to get to know your son. Paternal leave. Unofficially, Draven has arranged for you to go to a discrete clinic in Northern Ireland where you will spend at least 90 days working through your magic issues."

"Rehab?"

"Sort of. Your mom and Zach are going with you, and Draven will be going for the first month to help out. This isn't negotiable, Ricky."

"And if I don't go."

Caitlyn spoke next, her words chilling him down to the bone. "Then you lose everything. I have spoken with Fionn. While sympathetic, and also acknowledging that he may have added to your predicament by dropping a bombshell on you like that, he also states that he cannot have his nephew in danger."

"I would never hurt my son." Ricky growled.

"Then you will do as we ask of you. If you do not, then Fionn, as Sadie's next of kin, will sign over all parental rights to me. Sarge will not allow you to endanger the team, so you will no longer be an agent of P.I.T, and, as Melanie's sire, I will refuse to let a liability near her, so new into her second life."

Ricky squirmed under the intensity of her gaze. "Damn guys, way to bring a guy down even further. So basically, if I stay and try to kick it myself, you will take everything away from me?"

A chorus of agreements rang out and Ricky's heart dropped to his stomach. Panic welled in his veins and he felt the magic simmer, just a pulse. Closing his eyes, he counted to ten and then opened them again. Just as he was about to speak, he caught sight of a gorgeous redhead leaning in the doorway, her face stern.

"Caitlyn doesn't have to order me to stay away from you. If you don't go, if you don't do all you can to get better, then anything that might have happened between us is done."

This was a conversation they needed to have by themselves, but Ricky wasn't sure if the rest of the gang would leave them alone.

"Guys, can we have the room. Please."

All three supernaturals looked at Melanie who nodded, and then they walked out, leaving the door open. Ricky snorted at the illusion of privacy, knowing full well they could hear every single word spoken between them.

"Before you say anything," Ricky sighed, his path decided even before Melanie had come in the room. "I'm sorry that you had to see me like that."

"You saw me naked while I died from blood loss. I think this makes us even."

"Not until you've seen me naked," he said with a grin even as Melanie rolled her eyes. She was dressed in black skinny jeans, black boots and a t-shirt that read, 'Are you out of your Vulcan mind?' With her red hair pulled back into a ponytail, Ricky wondered why he couldn't be more like her, the human tech girl who became a vampire like it was nothing. As if this was who she had always been destined to become, when he felt like a stranger in his own skin.

"Why didn't you tell me about the drugs?"

"Because out of everyone, I couldn't bear the disappointment in your eyes."

Melanie frowned but didn't reply to that. Instead, she said, "You are going to that rehab."

"I know."

"And you'll do everything in your power to come back in control?"

"Ya, I will."

"Good."

They stared at each other for a few minutes before Ricky asked, "Do you have feelings for me, Lanie?"

"At the moment I feel the strongest urge to kill you, as if you haven't been doing a good enough job of that by yourself."

Ricky couldn't help but laugh. "Come here, Lanie."

Hesitating for just a second, Melanie strode over to the bed and sat down next to him. Ricky tried to reach out to touch her face, but the goddamn cuffs wouldn't let him. With a sigh, he lowered his voice and said, "I want to be a man that is worthy of being with you. I *need* to be that man. Right now, I have to get well, and be a dad to my son. I need to know that you can deal with the fact Zach is now in my life. I know you can, but I need to hear it."

"Zach isn't even the issue and you know it."

"Good. I will go to this rehab place and I will come back good as new. Then you and I have some things to sort out." Leaning forward, he captured Melanie's lips with his in a hard press of lips for a minute before he pulled away.

Melanie pressed two fingers to her mouth. "What the hell was that?"

The corner of Ricky's mouth tilted up. "A promise."

A knock sounded at the door, and Melanie jumped to her feet with a yelp.

"Sorry to interrupt," Derek mumbled. "But Draven is here."

His warlock friend Draven strode into the room, his dreads slapping against his shoulders as he moved. He glared at Ricky grimly and shook his head. "You have been causing much havoc, my friend."

Ricky shrugged his shoulders. "I call that Tuesday, Draven."

His friend chuckled. "Indeed, Ricky, indeed. Let's see if this trinket I brought works before we have to dig your grave."

"Always the optimist, Draven." Ricky cast a glance at Derek and motioned his head to Melanie. "Get her out of here."

She made to protest, but Ricky growled. "Please, Lanie. If I go nuclear again and they have to put me down for good, then I don't want you to see it. Just go."

Melanie spun and dashed from the room, passing Caitlyn and Donnie on their way in. Draven took a small square box from his pocket and pulled out a ring.

"I'm sorry, Draven, but I have to say no. You just ain't my type, sweetheart."

"Isn't it fortunate for me that I have a dislike of idiots."

Ricky grinned as Draven held up the ring for inspection. Ricky wasn't much for bling, and the ring certainly wasn't something he'd have gone out and bought, but the skull and crossbones design was something he could work with.

"This was spelled by me and by Samhain Chace, after your mother came to your defence. I would not like to cross your mother, Ricky."

Draven held the ring out to Ricky, then slid it onto the middle finger on his left hand. He could feel the magic in the ring, hoped it would be strong enough to withstand the fury of magic in him.

"This will dampen the magic in your blood, while still giving you access to it. It is only temporary, mind. I hope that after your stay at Havana, you will learn to control your magic and discover the full scope of it by yourself."

Derek came to stand beside him. "Now to test the ring," he said. As he began to uncuff Ricky's wrists, he tensed, waiting for the blowback of magic. Draven removed the other cuff, and Ricky hissed when magic flooded his system, the heat of the power burning him on the inside as if to chastise him for locking it away.

The magic within the ring came to life, washing over his power and dulling it to a hushed whisper rather than a roar. Ricky exhaled a breath, heard a gasp, and looked at the spirals of smoke that came out with his breath.

"Dude, I'm part dragon!" he exclaimed with a grin, hoping to elevate the tension in the room. His friends smiled, but as Ricky shuffled off the bed to stand, they didn't seem to believe that he could do this.

You can't do it without the drugs.

There's a stash inside your car.

Take off the ring and lose yourself in the high.

They are not your friends.

Ricky slapped the side of his head, as if that would dislodge the demons in his mind. He lifted his eyes to Donnie, who nodded. He would get rid of any drugs still lying around the place. Not that there were any.

Looking at Draven, Ricky asked. "So, when do we leave for rehab?"

"Right now. Your mother and son are waiting in my car for us. Donnie kindly went and got some clothes for you. I will wait outside while you say your goodbyes."

When Draven left, silence washed over the room, as if nobody knew what to say. Ricky went to Derek first, holding out his hand, but Derek engulfed him in a hug. Donnie did the same, and Caitlyn kissed him on both cheeks and told him to come back soon.

As Ricky made to walk from the room, he looked over his shoulder. "If this was a TV show or movie, it would totally be the time for Amy Winehouse to start singing about rehab. See ya on the flip side, folks."

Lump in his throat, Ricky ignored everyone and everything as he walked out of Caitlyn's house and opened the passenger door to Draven's car. Turning his head, he gave his mam a smile, and she patted his cheek.

"You okay, Ma?"

"I will be, son. I will be."

Looking at Zach, Ricky felt his heart swell for the little boy.

Derek's words played in his mind. *"They will take Zach from you and he will go into foster care. Do you want that?"*

No, that was not what he wanted. Had Sadie told him from day one that she was pregnant, that he might be the kid's dad, then he would have manned up and been there for Zach. Sadie had robbed him of five years; Ricky would be damned if he was the reason he lost another five.

Zach, nose in a comic book that Ricky recognized from his youth, lifted his head and pushed his glasses up the bridge of his nose.

"Hi, Ricky, grandma says we are going on an adventure. Is that true?"

Ricky winked. "Sure is kid. That okay with you?"

The little boy nodded and went back to reading the comic. Ricky blew out a breath and grinned at Draven. "Onward, Jeeves."

Draven chuckled. "Get some rest, Ricky. It's a long drive to Armagh. Then the real work starts."

Slumping down in the seat, Ricky happened to peer out the window as Draven put the car in reverse. Standing together were the people he called family, and the girl he longed to call his. His throat tightened. In that moment, Ricky understood how much he had to lose, should he fail in his quest to overcome an addition that should not have happened.

While Draven drove away from his family, Ricky closed his eyes, saying to himself: *90 days...90 days and things can go back to normal. I can do this.*

90 days...easy peasey...right?

CHAPTER
TWENTY-THREE

Ever

As the team made themselves comfortable in her living room, a nervousness took hold of Ever while they waited for Derek to arrive. As her eyes wandered around the room, she could almost laugh at the weirdness of having immortal gods and supernatural creatures all in one place. Not one human stood in the room. It made sense why Ever had never felt normal; she was far from it.

Erika stood off to the side, chatting to a young woman who was the image of Caitlyn and happened to be her niece. The woman laughed as Erika smiled, and Ever was happy to see Erika being so open with others. Ever knew how hard it was for Erika to be herself around others, and to think that had changed all because of Loki. Through the years, Ever had feared that Loki and Erika together might be the biggest disaster in the world, but since declaring that they were going to give things a go, a weight seemed to have lifted from Erika's shoulders.

And the way Loki watched her, Ever knew that her brother was as smitten as he claimed, a massive feat for a man who guarded his heart more than even Erika. He had opened up and made her best friend happier than Ever had seen in all her lifetimes.

Caitlyn perched elegantly on the edge of the couch, and Donnie lounged on the chair, his hand resting on her thigh. Ever felt an overwhelming happiness that they were finally together, and Caitlyn could grieve fully. What a terrible injustice to lose your entire family and be forced to live without them. And Donnie, what strength was contained within the vampire to stay by the woman he loved and not know whether he would ever be with her? Those two deserved nothing but happiness. Ever prayed to the gods that no more darkness would seep into their lives.

Next to Donnie, Melanie sat a little stiffly. The girl with so much spirit and light was engulfed in a wave of darkness. Perhaps it had something to do with Ricky's absence, since Caitlyn mentioned Derek would explain. Sarge had come when Ever called, and her godfather had pressed a kiss to her cheek before sinking down into one of the fireside chairs, his arms folded while they waited for Derek.

When the others had arrived without him, Ever feared that her mate had decided that she wasn't worth the trouble, despite the fact he had traipsed across the ocean to find her. During the last few days, she had time to consider her life without Derek, how her past selves had tried to go up against Odin alone and failed miserably. If she tried and failed this time, she wanted to know what it was like to be with Derek, not just remember some form of him.

Ever felt a presence next to her and glanced up to see Loki standing there, a tumbler of whiskey in his grasp.

"You have a drink problem, Loki."

"I prefer to look at it as stress intervention. Especially since my sister and my woman are about to embark on what might likely be a suicide mission." He sipped from the tumbler. "Besides, what fun would it be if I was sober? Then I might let the demons out to play."

"That is a very scary thought."

Her brother chuckled, his eyes once more wandering in Erika's direction. As if she sensed his gaze, she turned, winked at him, and then went back to her conversation with Kenzie, who was still sporting a bruise or two, courtesy of Erika. The two were arranging sparing sessions. No doubt, they would become firm friends.

Ever shook her head as a rap sounded at the front door. Hurrying over to answer it, she opened the door and her breath caught. Like the very first moment she had laid eyes on Derek Doyle, on the quad at the college where she had taught, Ever was captivated by him. Hazel eyes full of intelligence and strength, lush full lips that begged to be kissed, and chestnut hair that slightly dipped in front of his eyes. Handsome, but unaware of his own beauty, he reached out to cup her cheek.

They hadn't left things on the best of terms after she flashed them to Cork, with her slipping out of the room to leave him to deal with the team when she went in search of Erika. Ever had been so stupid, running away from her problems instead of depending on those around her. Thankfully, Erika had seen sense.

"Hey," Ever said softly.

"Hey," Derek replied, and when he removed his hand, Ever instantly missed his touch. "What's going on?"

She stepped back to let him in, closing the door as she said, "This is all Erika's show. Apparently, she thinks she can win a war."

"And can she?"

"Not alone she can't."

Derek's eyes widened as he seemed to come to a realization and nodded. "Ah, I see."

They walked in silence into the living room. Erika glanced over. "Took your sweet time, Boyband."

"Had to send a team to investigate a building used for underground fights that collapsed and has a few dead bodies. Know anything about that, Valkyrie?"

She grinned, leaving Derek to shake his head and flop down beside Donnie. Erika and Kenzie bumped fists, and Erika came to stand beside Ever. Loki pressed a kiss to Erika's cheek before he stepped to the side and left her to run the show.

She looked to Ever, who folded her arms across her chest and nodded, giving Erika free reign to try and convince the team to fight with them.

"First," she began, her tone crisp and clear, owning her status as the general of Ever's army. "I want to apologize for my deception, but in my defence, I was bound by the same curse as Ever, unable to say a damn word about what we are or what was going down. I never meant to lie to you all, but it was out of my hands. If you need someone to blame, you can blame him, because he devised the curse."

Loki lifted his tumbler, grinning like an idiot even as Caitlyn asked, "And who might he be?"

"I, Lady Caitlyn, am Loki. I am Ever's brother and Erika's lover. It is a pleasure to finally meet you. I have heard such amazing things about you."

"Christ Loki, please do not tell me that's the new way you're going to introduce yourself?"

"It might be," he replied with a grin, and Erika slapped a hand to her face.

"Stall the ball a second," Donnie said, sitting up straighter. "The Loki. Norse god of mischief? That's you?"

"In the flesh." Loki rolled his arm out in a bow, and both Ever and Erika rolled their eyes.

Donnie opened his mouth, closed it, then opened it again, and Ever chuckled. Loki had that effect on people. He clicked his fingers and a bottle of beer appeared so suddenly in Donnie's hand, he nearly spilled the bottle before he took a slug and said, "I've stepped into the twilight zone."

"Moving on before his head swells any bigger," Erika said with a smile, before she went back into General mode. "Odin is coming after Ever and will not stop until she is dead."

"Why would he want to kill his own daughter?" Melanie asked, her expression grim. Apparently, the team knew more than Ever thought. "I thought Odin was all about wisdom and poetry."

"He was all that once. I remember him telling me tales and reading poetry to me when I was a child, on days I would spend in the keep. He showed me art and literature. We laughed and had fun. And then Frigg died and every ounce of joy in him died," Ever told them, unable to hide the sadness in her voice for a man who once hugged her with such love.

"I never believed in a million years that the man I called papa could strike out at me, not until the first time he cut through flesh. The first time I died, and then got my memories back, I felt so empty because the person I loved was gone. I thought he would come to his senses, but the next time we met, he slit my throat."

This statement wrung a growl from Derek, but Erika cut him off. "I have spent eons trying to prevent the end of the world from happening with Ever's death. And I don't plan on letting her down. I am a Valkyrie, yes, as is Ever, but Ever is my queen. If she dies, the armies of Valhalla will once again belong to Odin, and he will usher in Ragnorok and end the world."

Erika paused, waiting for a response, but not a single supe said a word, Kenzie moving to standing behind Caitlyn and Donnie.

"I'm not going to bore you with a history lesson. We can rake over that later. But if I am going to keep Ever alive, then I will need your help."

"What do you want us to do?" Derek said, his tone rough and clipped.

"I'm getting to that, Boyband." Erika grinned. "Last night, I fought against Odin. Had it not been for Loki and Thor, I would have died. However, Odin made a fatal mistake; he told me who I am, and why he wants me dead."

Ever watched as Erika inhaled a breath and closed her eyes before reopening them. There was a slight waver in her voice as she spoke. "Many years ago, my mother, Livana, left me on the shores of Valhalla to train as a Valkyrie, I was five years old and until last night, I couldn't even remember my mother's name. As Odin tried to sway me to his side, he revealed that my mother had been involved with one of the Aesir, or gods in your terms, and I was the result of that relationship. My father is Tyr, the god of war, and I am very much his daughter."

A stunned silence greeted her words, and she shifted uncomfortably, before continuing, "For many years, I spent a lot of time unhappy with who I was, or maybe not knowing who I was. But, Odin said something to me that made me think that this time... this time, we have the power to shape the outcome.

"Odin wanted me separated from Ever because he knew that we were stronger together. Every single time that Ever lost was because she tried to go it alone. This time, that will not happen. This time we have something that Odin could not have predicted even with the strongest of seers."

She glanced around the room and stated, "This time, we have all of you."

Ever blinked in surprise as Erika's words sank in, this was what she wanted to avoid, involving the team in a fight that was not theirs. They looked at her, but Ever could not speak.

"I know what Ever is thinking and she is right, this battle is not yours. If this is not what you want, or if this is something you think you cannot face, then no one will think any less of you. My sisters and I cannot do this alone. We have lost many to this war, and we may lose more, but we cannot see the world ripped apart."

"Erika, we are not warriors...well, I'm certainly not. What can we do to stop a god?" Melanie wondered, and Ever echoed her thoughts.

Erika relaxed her stance. "When my mother left me on the sands of Valhalla, she told me that it was not the size of the girl in the fight, but rather the amount of fight in the girl. Each of you has your own unique qualities. Melanie, you survived a monster and have an inner strength that is enviable. Kenzie, having taken a punch from you, with a little Valkyrie boot camp, we will have you in warrior form. Caitlyn, you have faced evil once and prevailed, that is an inspiration to us all. Donnie, your brute strength and cunning will help me strategize."

Turning to face Derek, Erika nodded her head. "You and I, we haven't got on much in whatever century we've met, and that was all me. I was confused and even a little jealous. We need

you, Derek, as the queen's champion. Recently I met a medicine woman who said 'The future can be saved, but only if you
stick together.'"

She shoved her hands into the pockets of her combats. "Alone,
we are sitting ducks. Together, we could be a formidable force.
Odin has been beaten back for now, but he will come back
stronger and more cunning. Will you fight with us? Will you
help us save the world and Ever's life?"

Loki was the first to answer Erika, kissing the hell out of her,
before he pulled away. "For too long, I have skirted the side-
lines for fear of incurring Thor's wrath. No more. I adore my
little sister and detest the madman that Odin has become. I will
fight beside you, darling."

Sarge nodded, as Ever's chest tightened. Caitlyn gave Donnie a
look before turning to Ever and Erika. "If it had not been for
the help of others, the monster who stalked my nightmares
might still be alive. We will fight beside you."

"Me too. But Erika, you need to train me some more."

Erika grinned at Melanie. "Six AM starts for you then."

She groaned, muttered that she was so going to regret it, but
she was smiling.

Caitlyn glanced over her shoulder at Kenzie, whose grin was as
wide as the Cheshire cat. "Sounds like fun. Me and my scythe
can do so much damage. Man, this will do so much for my rep."

Donnie chuckled, as Caitlyn shook her head. Ever locked eyes
with Derek, who ignored everyone else as he growled. "I look
forward to ripping Odin's heart from his chest. No one touches
my family and lives."

Ever felt a tear trickle down her face as she said, "I can't stop any of you from doing this, but if it comes down to me or one of you, I will not watch any of you die for me. You did not sign up for this, and I dropped it in your lap."

Sarge stood, came over to her, and wrapped her in a hug. "I always knew you were special. I could not have imagined just how remarkable you would be. We are all grownups, and we make our own decisions. We will not allow you to sacrifice yourself for us."

With a kiss to her temple, Sarge walked out, with the rest of the team following suit, each bidding Ever goodbye in their own way. When only Ever and Derek, and Erika and Loki remained, Loki wrapped his arms around Erika and kissed her, before nibbling on her ear, to which she tried to smack him away.

"We do not have to fight gods tonight, my dear. Shall we leave the wolf and the queen to chat?"

She shook her head, and Ever saw happiness in her friend's eyes. "You just want to get me naked, Trickster."

"Naked Valkyrie is my favourite thing."

Erika glanced at Ever. "You gonna be okay?"

"Yes, be gone before I get sick at you two being all lovey dovey. I think I preferred when ye snipped at each other."

With a laugh, the pair disappeared, leaving Ever and Derek to themselves.

"I wasn't expecting those two together." Derek stated.

Ever shrugged. "They have centuries of pent up lust. I think it was written in the cosmos."

"Like us?"

"Derek," she sighed his name.

"I told you that we would all do this together."

"I guess I don't have any say in the matter," she remarked.

"You never did."

She shook her head as he rose, her heart thundering in her chest. "You never had a choice, Ever. From the very first moment we met, I knew you were mine. And I'm just gonna say this one more time. Fuck fate, screw destiny, screw angry gods, and everything in between. If you don't want me then just say it. Tell me that this isn't what you want and I will go. I'll fight beside you and keep you alive, but we won't be together."

Oh, she knew that he was serious, his tone told her that. When faced with the possibility that she might lose him, she had decided days ago to go with her heart and forget the nagging voice in her head.

Walking up to him, she inched up on her toes and pressed her lips to his. Her body ignited. Kissing her back slowly, he slid his hands into her hair, backing her up against the wall as he nipped on her lower lip. She opened her mouth and licked out, and he rumbled. She caressed the planes of his chest through his t-shirt, her brain fogging as he deepened the kiss, hungrily coveting her mouth.

Breathless, he pulled back, a wolfish grin on his face. Moving his hands down her face, he cupped her cheeks and pressed his lips softly to hers before kissing his way down her jaw to the nape of her neck until she could hardly breath at all.

He captured her hand and led her toward her bedroom, only letting go when they walked into the room. He sat down on the edge of her bed, and there was no more delicious sight then Derek Doyle with a smile only for her.

"So what do you think, Ever? Do we do this thing together?"

She faced away from him, closing the door before she turned back. Reaching down, she yanked her t-shirt over her head and dropped it to the floor, a rush coming over her as lust flared in his eyes.

Heart beating a tattoo in her chest, she came to stand before him and wrap her arms around his neck.

"Together, Derek. We do this together."

FREYA STOOD outside the door of Ever's home, watching as all of the people inside promised to lay down their lives for her daughter. Even the child of Tyr finally looked as if she had become who her mother wanted her to become, as she wrapped her arms around Loki and vanished.

When her daughter and the champion began to get intimate, Freya gathered her strength and left this mortal world for the shores of Valhalla, preparing to rally the remaining Valkyrie to make themselves known on Midgard.

It irked her that she felt sadness at not being included in her daughter's plans, that Ever had simply forgotten her. They dismissed her as a warrior, forgetting it was Freya's training that had prepared them for this day, for this fight.

The moment her feet touch the sand, she felt a presence and cursed herself for not being aware of her surroundings before she flashed to Valhalla. A hand clasped around her throat, a blade poised at the base of her spine.

"Come to finish me off, Odin. Took you long enough."

"I had forgotten about you, lover, much as Ever has forgotten about you." Odin whispered in her ear, his breath hitting against her skin. *There was nothing left of the man she had once bedded, the one who she might have once began to love.*

"I will leave you bleeding on these shores, and no one will come to look for you until they come to claim your soul."

Freya did not struggle, nor did she flinch. "Do your worst, lover," she spat out. *"I will smile down on my daughter from the skies above and watch as she sends you to Hel."*

"Goodbye, my lover," he began, then stopped. *"Maybe I will let you live, but render you useless in the fight that is to come. Unable to fight, unable to help. Maybe that is a fate worse than death."*

Odin licked the curve of her neck and slowly dug the blade into her spine. Pain ripped through Freya, yet she refused to cry out. He yanked out the blade, and Freya crumpled to the ground. He had severed her spinal cord, the pain a phantom in her mind as she no longer felt anything below her waist.

A scream built up inside her, but darkness came for her too soon. The last thing Freya saw before darkness came to claim her, was Odin striding away, leaving her broken in the sand.

EPILOGUE

Tadgh opened his front door and set his duffel down beside the coffee table. He was rather exhausted after attending the conference in Dublin with Anna, and could not wait until he washed the dirt off and crawled into his nice comfy bed. Flicking on the light, he was just about to kick off his shoes when the flick of a lighter startled him.

Almost leaping out of his skin, Tadgh cringed when he saw the man lounging in his grandmother's old armchair.

"Christ chief, you scared the holy hell out of me."

"The warlock's gone off to rehab."

Dammit! He should never have given the white rabbit to Ricky. Now he was totally in hot water.

"I'm sure he won't say a thing, chief. I'm almost certain."

The man known only as the Viking, named after the tattoo on his left arm, ran his fingers through the dark stubble on his chin and lifted a single eyebrow, a gesture that made grown men piss themselves. The Viking was the biggest dealer in Cork, and considering that he dealt specifically with supernatural drugs, his cliental had expanded two-fold.

"Almost isn't good enough, Tadgh. I took a chance on ya, bud, a big chance and it's about to blow up in my face. If the warlock spills his guts and connects the dots from me to you, then a six-foot-deep hole awaits ya."

Tadgh blanched, fear coursing through his veins. "I'll take care of it, sir, I promise."

"Even if it means killing a cop."

Tadgh froze, his legs suddenly feeling like cement. "You want me to kill Ricky?"

The Viking shrugged as if taking a life meant nothing to him. "Only if he becomes a problem. So, make sure he doesn't become a problem."

"And what about the rest of the team? I can't hold my own against all of them."

Standing to his full height, the Viking flicked his lighter on and then off again. "Vampires gotta sleep. Wolves gotta turn furry and howl at the moon. Set the house on fire and shoot the dog with silver. Problem solved."

The Viking strode past Tadgh, stopping with his hand on the door handle. "I hope it doesn't come to that. But, Tadgh, I mean it about the warlock. Shut him up before I have to shut you up. I don't want things to get messy."

Tadgh turned so that he faced the Viking, purely out of fear. The Viking grinned and Tadgh's blood turned icy.

"But Tadgh, I don't want to see a scratch on the body of Melanie Newton. If she is harmed in any way, I swear to God you will live to regret it."

Melanie had always been nice to Tadgh, and he didn't like the menace of the Viking's tone. Who was she to him?

"What do you have planned for Melanie?" Tadgh wondered, though he knew questioning his boss like that could incur the man's wrath.

A sardonic grin crept up the Viking's lips, his features darkening with a glare that had Tadgh shivering in terror. "You don't worry your handsome head about it. You leave Melanie to me. We go way back."

ALSO BY SUSAN HARRIS

The Ever Chace Chronicles

Skin & Bones, book 1

Collateral Damage, book 2

Smoke & Mirrors, book 3

Night of the Hunter, book 4

Never Back Down, book 5

Shortcut to the Grave, book 6

Arsonist's Lullaby, book 7

Of Gods And Monsters, book 8

Defy The Stars

A Tale of Two Houses, book 1

Until Death Do Us Part, book 2

In Defiance of the Stars, book 3

Shattered Memories

The Sanguine Crown

Chaos Theory, book 1

Butterfly Effect, book 2

Wicked Game, book 3

Burn Notice, book 4

Fight Song, book 5 (coming January 2022)

Character Playlist

ERIKA:

Headstrong—Trapt
You're Going Down—Sick Puppies
Lose Yourself - From "8 Mile" Soundtrack—Eminem
I Will Not Bow—Breaking Benjamin
Break Stuff—Limp Bizkit
I Want—Mantra Waking up (Acoustic)—Pvris
Belgrade—Battle Tapes
Exposed—A Day To Remember
Love Surrounds You—Ramsey
Scar—Foxes
Good Enough (feat. Jussie Smollett)—Empire Cast
Go To War—Nothing More
Legends—Sleeping With Sirens
Fuck With Myself—Banks
Elastic Heart (Rock Version)—Written by Wolves
My Favourite Game—The Cardigans
Just A Girl—No Doubt
Dream On—Aerosmith
Outro—NF
Anyone Else—Pvris
Blow Your Mind (Mwah)—Dua Lipa
IDGAF—Dua Lipa

LOKI:

Enemy—Fozzy
Thunder—Imagine Dragons
Cross My Mind—A R I Z O N A
Ritual Spirit—Massive Attack, Azekel
Double Darkness—Big Scary
How Could I Love You?—Little Hours
Waking Up The Giants—Grizfolk
Feel It Still—Portugal. The Man
Lullaby—Frank Carter & The Rattlesnakes
The Violence—Rise Against
Bottom Of The Deep Blue Sea—MISSIO
Someone Else to Blame—Evarose
When We Were Young—Andy Black, Juliet Simms
Sympathy For The Devil—The Rolling Stones
Made to Love You—Dan Owen
5—Cycle Of Pain
All In One Night—Stereophonics
Bear Claws—The Academic
Awoo—Sofi Tukker, Betta Lemme
The Devil You Know—X Ambassadors

DEREK:

One Step Closer—Linkin Park
Animal I Have Become—Three Days Grace
Fears—Twin Wild
Helix—Flume
Start A Riot—BANNERS
All My Friends—Dermot Kennedy
Golden Dandelions—Barns Courtney
Love Is Mystical—Cold War
Kids Suit And Jacket—Judah & the Lion

The Sky Is A Neighborhood—Foo Fighters
Look After You—Aron Wright
Dancing in the Moonlight (Its Caught Me in Its Spotlight)—
Recorded at Spotify Studios NYC—alt-J

EVER:

Periscope (feat. Skylar Grey)—Papa Roach
What's Wrong—Pvris
Six Billion—Nothing But Thieves
Half—Pvris
5AM—Amber Run
Holding Out for a Hero - From the Trailer for "Vikings" - Series
—Nothing But Thieves
Memory Lane (feat. Tom Grennan)—Bugzy Malone, Tom
Grennan
Love Me More—Chase & Status, Emeli Sandé
Brave—Riley Pearce
Need You Now - Acoustic—Dean Lewis
Worst In Me—Julia Michaels
Look What You Made Me Do—Taylor Swift
Hurricane—Fleurie
Silence—Grace Carter
Footprints—Molly Kate Kestner

KENZIE:

Last Young Renegade—All Time Low
Area—MagnusTheMagnus
Gloves Are Comin' Off—7kingZ
Don't Let Me Get Me—James Gillespie
No Apologies (feat. Jussie Smollett, Yazz)—Empire Cast
Drip Drop (feat. Yazz and Serayah McNeill)—Empire Cast
Nothing To Lose (feat. Jussie Smollett)—Empire Cast

Fake Love—Drake
Green Lights—NF
Im a Boss—Meek Mill
808—Eligh

MELANIE:

hate u love u—Olivia O'Brien
Back from the Fire—Gold Brother
Green Light—Lorde
Someone New (feat. Desi Valentine)—Unlike Pluto, Desi Valentine
Battle Cry—Empire Cast, Jussie Smollett
Nerve—DON BROCO
Sweat—The All-American Rejects
Young Lady, You're Scaring Me—Ron Gallo
White Lies—Dream State
Desire—Everything Everything
Sober - Stripped—RAYE
Love Me Again—Katelyn Tarver
Savage—Lights
Let Me Down Easy—Max Frost
New Rules—Dua Lipa

RICKY:

If I Get High - II—Nothing But Thieves
Bodies—Drowning Pool
Amsterdam—Nothing But Thieves
Drugs & Candy—All Time Low
Fire—Barns Courtney
Less Than—Nine Inch Nails
Feels Like Summer—Weezer
Song #3—Stone Sour

Itch—Nothing But Thieves
Sorry—Nothing But Thieves
In The Name Of Love—Too Close To Touch

DONNIE:

Run—Foo Fighters
Hook, Line & Sinker—Royal Blood
We Sink—Of Monsters and Men
Who Are You?—Spring King
Dead Man's Arms—Bishop Briggs
Freeze Me—Death From Above 1979
Saviour—Mallory Knox
LAIDBACK—RAT BOY
Siberian Nights—The Kills
Shape Of You—Eat Your Heart Out
Sugar—Mallory Knox
Pretty—DON BROCO
Never Let You Down—Barns Courtney
The Promise—Chris Cornell
Let You Down—NF

CAITLYN:

Long Night—With Confidence
Mind over Matter (Acoustic)—Pvris
The Other Side—Ruelle
Waves—Dean Lewis
Love and War—Fleurie
Forever Starts Today—Tim Halperin
Sign of the Times—Harry Styles
Praise You—Hannah Grace
Guilty Party—The National
Back When We Had Nothing—BANNERS

Walk Out On Me (feat. Courtney Love)—Empire Cast
Oblivion—Bastille
Coming Up Slowly—Nick Wilson
Where's My Love - Alternate Version—SYML
Mad Behaviour—Izzy Bizu
Bruises—Lewis Capaldi
Walk That Line—Lucinda Barry, James Graydon, Jan Cyrka
Good for Me—Aimee Mann

Acknowledgements

To the amazing ladies at
Crimson Tree Publishing,
Rebecca, Courtney and Marya for their continuous support
and belief in my books.
Thank you for allowing me to make my dream a reality.

Marya,
Thank you so much for the amazing cover for Never Back
Down and bringing Erika to life! And revamping the entire
Ever Chace covers with so much attention and vision!
I absolutely adore them!

Melanie,
There are not enough words to say how blessed I feel to call
you my friend. (I'm still blaming you for the pop doll addiction
though!)

Jaime,
My trusty Beta reader! You are the only person I would
consider sharing Tom Hardy with and that says a lot!

Kelly Risser,
I am eternally grateful to you for all the work you put in editing
Never Back Down. Not all heroes wear capes, but they do have
serious grammar skills!

Special thanks as well to Pam for proofing.

I feel extremely lucky to have such supportive parents. Thanks for the cups of tea and the snacks when I am off visiting fictional worlds!

I am blessed to have an amazing group of family and friends. I keep my circle small but those in it are more than I could have ever asked for. Sláinte.

And last but by no means least, the readers,
The series is only possible because you guys read my books.
Thank you for loving the characters as much as I do!

ABOUT THE AUTHOR

Susan Harris is a writer from Cork, Ireland and when she's not torturing her readers with heart-wrenching plot twists or killer cliffhangers, she's probably getting some new book related ink, binging her latest TV or music obsession, or with her nose in a book.

Susan LOVES connecting with her fans!
www.susanharrisauthor.com

Thank you for reading *Never Back Down*; I hope you enjoyed my book!

Want to be the first to know when I release new books? Here are some ways to stay updated:

- Sign up for my email list so you can find out about new releases.
- Like my Facebook page.
- Visit my website: www.SusanHarrisAuthor.com/
- Connect with me on Spotify

If you loved *Never Back Down*, please tell your friends about my book and consider leaving a review. Reviews are like potato chips; you can't ever have enough of them; thanks for reading my book!" ~Susan Harris

www.ingramcontent.com/pod-product-compliance
Lightning Source LLC
Chambersburg PA
CBHW022143170626
46807CB00005B/2057